MW01037450

FROM THE BELLY

BEING AN EPIC OF SEA-FARING ADVENTURE, INTRIGUE, & HORRORS FROM THE DEEP & BEYOND

EMMETT NAHIL

Cover Art by Chris Shehan
Interior Illustrations by Megan Llewellyn
Edited by Alex Woodroe

Content warnings are available at the end of this book. Please consult this list for any particular subject matter you may be sensitive to.

TENEBROUS

PRESS

Published by Tenebrous Press.
Visit our website at www.tenebrouspress.com.

First Printing, May 2024.

The characters and events portrayed in this work are fictitious. Any similarity to real persons, living or dead, is coincidental and not intended by the author.

Print ISBN: 978-1-959790-08-2
eBook ISBN: 978-1-959790-09-9

Cover art by Chris Shehan.

Interior illustrations by Megan Llewellyn.

Edited by Alex Woodroe.

Formatting by Lori Michelle.

All creators in this publication have signed an AI-free agreement. To the best of our knowledge, this publication is free from machine-generated content.

Selected Works from Tenebrous Press:

Mouth
a novella by Joshua Hull

Lumberjack
a novella by Anthony Engebretson

Posthaste Manor
a novel by Jolie Toomajan & Carson Winter

The Black Lord
a novella by Colin Hinckley

Dehiscent
a novella by Ashley Deng

House of Rot
a novella by Danger Slater

Agony's Lodestone
a novella by Laura Keating

Soft Targets
a novella by Carson Winter

Crom Cruach
a novella by Valkyrie Loughcrewe

Lure
a novella by Tim McGregor

One Hand to Hold, One Hand to Carve
a novella by M.Shaw

More titles at www.TenebrousPress.com

To all workers lost to the sea, and in the dust of history: may you rest peacefully, rocked in the cradle of the deep

CHAPTER ONE

WHEN THE MAN was cut from the belly of the whale, he was as soft and blood-mottled as a stillborn calf. Isaiah watched from the gunwales of the whaleship *Merciful* as Álvarez reached down with his pike and scored away at the flesh, and the body fell from the inner lining of the creature's muscled stomach and onto the water with nothing more than a muted splash, buoyed to float by the grease and viscera coating the wave caps.

"*Good gods above and below . . .* "Bellamy said, low under his breath.

It was as strange as anything Isaiah had ever seen in his already considerably strange dreams.

"How did he . . . " Fallon said, voice echoing up from where he sat in the skiff, alongside the other members of the crew who were responsible for the fresh carcass.

Isaiah flinched when the bony point of the man's cheek brushed against the whale's stomach lining. Unconscious, he floated on the surface, coated with a thin, iridescent layer of rusty blood mixed with fat.

"*Haul him up!*" Lice, the quartermaster, called down to the four in the hunting skiff. "Line over port side, NOW!"

Isaiah stared, transfixed by the planes of the man's face, before his arms, remembering their use, jolted into motion and threw down a loop of sturdy rope to them. Liu and Yesayan jumped to obey, and ran along the port-side railing to take up the wood and iron winches, hauling hand-over-hand to raise the skiff from water-level. The wind stung, sending up blood-mixed spray off the whale's great slaughtered body. It was common knowledge that you couldn't go very long onboard a whaleship without tasting blood. Isaiah spat it out, as the mineral taste soured in his mouth and made his stomach lurch.

1

Beside him, Bellamy had frozen, staring toward the spot inside the creature from where the man had fallen.

"You . . . you heard her," Álvarez said haltingly.

" . . . So we did," Bellamy said.

The man didn't slip below the water like he'd seen the freshly dead do before. Whenever someone passed into the next realm on board and was duly committed to the sea, their canvas-wrapped bodies would be weighed down so that they could sink in peace and quiet below the surf. The look of the man, bobbing naked and ashen in the scummy foam, made him shudder deep in his bones.

The two pulling the ropes up on the main deck pulled fast, but another order cracked out over their heads. "We haven't all day. Faster to it!"

Fallon snagged the line he had thrown down, and Hendricks roped the body in alongside the hunting boat. Álvarez returned to dutifully puncturing the whale flesh from his post, still-warm blubber giving way with a dense, wet, sawing sound. Isaiah wondered if the man's skin, dead as he looked, would still be warm, too.

"Let's get him over—Chase, Bellamy, c'mere," Hendricks said, hopping easily from the dripping skiff. Bellamy hauled up the weight of the head and torso while Isaiah took the feet and legs. As they laid him down on the deck with a moist-sounding thunk, the crew clambered around them to see.

The man's mid-copper skin was mostly intact, but he had the grayish pall of the grave on him. Although he was still slick with seawater and trails of the whale's bodily matter, Isaiah could tell that he must have known war, or some kind of torture; he had only seen such brutal wounds on a few of the other crewmembers who had been in horrible shipwrecks or seen battle in another life. A harsh gash spanned the width of his neck, long-healed. Puncture wounds sprouted over his chest and abdomen, muddled with raised scar tissue.

He had been preserved inside the body of the creature, somehow.

Isaiah brushed a tangle of the man's long, curly hair off of his face. He could have been sleeping.

Someone behind him began to mutter a quick prayer. "Gods above, take up this lost soul and preserve us against such a—"

First mate Sharpe elbowed his way past the crowd. "Pardon. Let me see him." He crouched gingerly above the man's head and floated a hand under his long nose. "No need to fetch the surgeon, then." He pressed two fingers to where the jugular should be, indenting the skin painfully. Isaiah's hand darted to his own neck instinctively.

"Wait. There's . . . there's a pulse."

A wary hum came from the crew. Bellamy gaped as Sharpe stepped back to let Lice through, deferent. She reached down to confirm the reading with her own be-freckled fingers, and frowned as she spoke. "Bloody *alive*. Somehow."

A louder and more surprised rumble rose from the crowd. Hendricks and a few others crossed themselves rapidly, Bellamy cussed once again. Álvarez and Yesayan both spat hard over their respective left shoulders in quick succession, and Demir muttered a frantic line of prayer under his breath.

Isaiah stood motionless before he remembered to cross himself, the motion not coming as automatically as it should. His stomach tugged in a way he couldn't place. From where he stood, he could see the slight, almost non-existent motion of the man's pulse, fluttering weakly like a bird trapped under the skin.

"Someone get Monteiro—" Fallon started.

"And not the Captain?" A voice said, rising up from the rear of the crowd. A number of the crew started and shrunk back from where the man lay. "You lot should know better."

As well-observed as Captain Erasmus Coffin was aboard the *Merciful*, he had an uncanny knack for walking silently about his ship. " . . . What in the cursed name is this?"

Sharpe sprung upright, falling into a natural attention stance that still put him a good half foot shorter than the Captain. "Pulled him up just now, sir," he replied.

Coffin elbowed through the last of the crowd, and as he came upon the still-unconscious man, his eyes widened and he stopped short.

"*Why did you bring him up?*" Coffin asked, wheeling to face his first mate.

"I only saw the body once it had been brought onboard, I—"

"Did he come from that damned whale?!"

"Aye, he was brought forth by the latest catch."

Coffin's eyes grew wider still, and he stared down at the body, eyes darting over the scars. After a long, tense moment, he set his jaw tight.

"And whose *damn idea* was it, to bring him aboard?"

"Fallon, Calder, Álvarez, and Hendricks were in the hunting party, sir," Sharpe said, with the air of someone who had just dodged a bullet. Coffin shook his head, as if trying to clear it of some thought, and stared back over the crowd, singling the four out with a brusque wave of his hand.

"Well. Step up!" Coffin called.

You could have heard a pin drop.

Suddenly, Isaiah was conscious of the fact that his hands were grimy and bloodied where he had touched the man, and shoved them in his thin linen jacket pockets.

"Can any one of you lot explain yourselves?" He said, turning on Álvarez.

"The body was just *there*, Sir." Álvarez looked down, not meeting Coffin's eyes.

"And you decided to take it upon yourselves to—"

"Bad luck to abandon a man lost at sea, Captain," Fallon said, piping up. In a whirl of motion, Coffin turned from Álvarez and laid a heavy, resounding slap square across Fallon's face. Those closest to him flinched, but nobody moved from their spot.

"And *worse* luck for all the rest of you when there's another mouth to feed!" Coffin said, breathing heavily. Isaiah could feel his palms start to itch. "If I wanted to hear an old wives' tale, I'd have asked for one."

Fallon blinked rapidly but stood stock still, a patch of red already blooming on his cheek. "Yessir. Captain, sir."

Coffin didn't acknowledge Fallon's words and turned on the others instead. "Calder? Hendricks? Any further superstitions you'd like to inform me of?"

"*No.* No sir," Calder said.

"Me as well, sir," Hendricks intoned, eyes staying on Coffin's well-polished boots.

"I thought not."

The wind had grown as still as the man on the deck, and Isaiah watched carefully as his chest rose and fell by only the smallest of degrees. The Captain's eyes searched the body once again, lip curled in something like disgust.

"Butcher and try out that whale, before the gutshawks bother it." Even though Coffin had schooled his expression into one of cool authority, something in his eyes seemed wild. Loosed from its proper seat. "Back to stations! I'll not have a drop of whale oil lost aboard my ship."

"*You heard him,*" Lice yelled, and the assembled whalers scrambled, scattering along the main deck, returning to the rigging and to their posts bearing knives and pikes and hammers to carve up the rest of the whale flesh, to take the creature apart piece by piece.

Isaiah shrugged off his jacket, not quite thinking as he did. The man must have been cold. If he was still alive, if he still breathed, then he could catch cold and get sick—

The Captain had turned to Sharpe, drawing close to speak under his breath. "So long as he still lives, he'll be kept locked below."

"The brig, sir?"

"The brig," he said, matter of fact. "Monteiro's not to be called down. I won't have this written up."

Isaiah darted down and tucked the garment around the man, too small for his broad shoulders. A hand seized the back of his shirt before he could finish. Coffin hauled him upwards, and Isaiah was tossed stumbling back to the deck.

"If you're so damn concerned, you can feed him from your rations, Chase," Coffin said, as Isaiah scrambled to recover. "And if he dies, you can dispose of him yourself." He barked a toneless laugh.

Isaiah ducked his head, righting himself. "Aye sir." The Captain turned heel, stalking back to his quarters below without another word.

"Well," Sharpe said. "You'll get no relief from me. Back to it, Chase."

"Hey! What's that?" Someone called from high up in the rigging as they continued work through to the afternoon.

"Enough! You lot have jobs to do!" Lice shouted. From just beyond the rail, the wind had picked up once more, the waves had grown choppy again, and in the whale dregs left behind there floated up a broken piece of intricately carved wood.

The sea carried it closer to the bow of the *Merciful* and it trailed a strange line of debris behind it from the barren, open ocean.

Calder was bold enough to stop his work for a moment to investigate. "It's a *railing*."

"Don't be stupid," Hendricks said as she peered overboard at the carved chunk of oak. "How long has it been since we've seen another ship?" As if in response, a frayed corner of mildewy canvas, long since covered with streaks of mossenweed and limpets, ghosted after the wooden railing. " . . . Back since we left the last supply post in Auld Taggart in the spring, at least," she finished.

"Him that was in the whale had to come from somewhere," Bellamy supplied. "Could be that he's the last one alive, on whatever ship he came from."

Calder squinted toward the horizon. "Last of who? Or what?"

The debris floated unhindered off into the open ocean, and no other remains appeared. Fresh wind couldn't blow away the smell of decay from the deck as the workers dissected the whale with speed and precision. Isaiah rushed to catch up as the crew returned to their work, and the man was brought down to the brig below.

"I don't like that he's just lying down there."

Hendricks was in a foul mood. She still smelled of oil and soot, along with the rest of them. Isaiah had changed out of his work shirt immediately, but he was certain he still stank of whale remains just as badly as she did.

Down the aft-end of the deck, the tryworks were still burning, and the second shift was well in swing. Above them, gutshawks and black-tipped gulls had started picking at the corpse while the Captain had been busy settling the man's fate. The sharks and flesh-loving fish had already scooped up a good amount of the creature by the time third mate Flores ordered shots to be fired. Warding them off was more important than it seemed, and the greener deckhands were kept busy beating back some exceptionally tenacious hawks until eventually Sulaimi took initiative. Sling-shot plucked them out of the air, one by one.

"Hasn't woken up yet or anything," Calder said. "Oh, you

starting a new one?" He leaned over to where Hendricks was squaring off a fresh block of pale wood with a stubby knife.

"Yeah, Morrow wanted to trade for it," she replied.

"Weren't they already owing coin for last month's supplies?"

"Not my business if they were or not."

" . . . Shoulda left him down there with the rest of that whale's guts, for all the good it's going to do us," Bellamy said. He sat scrubbing at the front of his top, mostly soiled still from work. His brow crinkled deeply, and the rough scrubbing didn't seem to be doing him or the shirt any good.

"Let me at that," Isaiah interjected, pulling the linen from his hands with a sigh. "Your mum wouldn't want you to wear a hole in it, after all the work she did patching it up for you."

Bellamy huffed, slouching back against the mast, but relinquishing the once bright green tunic. He'd worn tears in it long ago, and he'd had Isaiah help stitch up the spots his mother hadn't gotten around to fixing back on land.

"You think it's better, then," Isaiah asked, not looking up at him directly. "To let a man die." He could tell he was testing the group's already sour mood. Deciding to prod at Bellamy was usually the safer choice; he was the more thoughtful of the lot. One wouldn't know it by looking at him, with his prickly black hair and arms twice the size of Isaiah's own.

"You're too soft-hearted, Chase. But Fallon was right. It's nothing but bad luck to throw a still-live man over, now that he's been brought aboard," Bellamy amended. Isaiah applied a careful directional hand to the rough weave of his shirt and the grime loosened. "Besides. Cap'n wasn't anywhere near fond of keeping him. Gods know why."

"Seemed damn well close to suggesting he go back from whence he came," Hendricks said, as she paused her carving to shake loose her locs from the bundle in which they were normally neatly arranged. "Not certain I'd blame him either," she said quietly, folding the red and blue patterned scarf neatly and tucking it in her shirt.

"Nor I," Calder said. He scratched at his jaw, a daub of grease caught in the patchy, light brown stubble.

"He's still a *person*, though," Isaiah said, and it felt like a risk. By the time he'd had his small altercation with Coffin, the rest had already been set to their tasks. Nobody had seen him, and they didn't need to know that his soft heart had earned him the punishment of half rations and duty owing.

"And what then, if he stays . . . like that?" Bellamy asked, nose wrinkling. Isaiah could feel him peering over his shoulder at his handiwork. "If having a human body inside that whale means the oil's gone *off* somehow, and we're already behind quota—"

"Then there's nothing we can do about it now," Hendricks replied, wood chips falling between her feet.

"Nothing we can do until we're behind on charter and run up *more signing* debts over our take," Bellamy said.

"Don't even begin to talk about such things," Demir interjected as he strolled by, still in his work slops and looking haggard. "And don't let nobody hear you even *talk* about running behind on charter." He rubbed a hand across his grey-flecked beard. "You're forgetting the 'Coffin' part of Pyle, Thacket, and Coffin Trading Company."

"Can't go disappointing daddy dearest," Bellamy quipped.

"*Stop* it. Someone'll hear," Isaiah said.

"Monteiro'll judge if the man'll survive, if she hasn't done so already," Hendricks replied. "Like I said, what's done is done. Can't very well get rid of him now."

Isaiah finally made a break in the layer of encrusted blood and grease, the green linen of the shirt poking through. "There. I'll not be your washerwoman." He held it out for the group's approval and Hendricks nodded appreciatively. "Not so bad now, huh."

Bellamy brightened, snatching the shirt back. "A real blessing y'are, Chase." Inspecting it against the lantern light, he grinned widely and bundled it up in his lap. "How'd you learn that anyway?"

"It's nothing," Isaiah said, rolling his eyes and grabbing the shirt back to re-fold it neatly. "My mum would have to fix up me and my pa's clothes herself and eventually got tired of not having any help. Not like you city folk, just sending it off to a tailor down the street whenever you like." In the handful of months he'd been concealing himself within the crew of the *Merciful*, he'd found that staying casual, light, in his mention of his father was better than avoiding the subject entirely as he wanted to. It was good to give the others the sense that they knew what you were about; could get the size of you. Being seen as someone who kept secrets was suspect at best and dangerous at worst. "You just have to know what you're doing."

"And now we're *all* stuck in the same great stinking tub in the middle of the ocean, that man along with us," Calder said with no small amount of bitterness.

"Better than doing my mum's washing . . . " Bellamy said, glancing sidelong at Isaiah. He nailed the bigger man in his side with an elbow.

"Hey!"

Isaiah forced a laugh and returned to picking bits of grime and meat off his own work shirt, and the four of them fell into companionable silence. The cutting spray that had pricked at Isaiah's face earlier that day changed to an unceasing wind that wound around them, buffeting the crowded deck jammed with people working on the second shift, around crates and supplies, stacked high with rope and empty barrels waiting to be filled with whale oil, racks of harpoon heads, axes, scrub brushes and heavy wooden wash buckets clustered in between it all. Isaiah was used to being out in the open air—six months at sea was more than enough time to grow accustomed to the way the sun beat down even on cold days, and the manner with which the clouds above their sun-bleached canvas sails changed shape before the wind did.

Calder stared out at the rapidly darkening horizon, while Hendricks continued to chip away at the indistinguishable wooden form in her palm. Isaiah breathed deep, but the freshly-burnt fatty scent of the tryworks hit the back of his nose harshly.

The brig where the man from the belly was being kept didn't even have that. No wind, barely any air to breathe.

"What happens if he wakes?" He asked, against his better judgement.

"I dunno," Hendricks said, the carving knife sitting idle in her hand for the first time since they'd sat down. "Fetch the Captain, I suppose. See that he gets a place and duties."

"You saw his face. Putting him to work is the last thing he'd give two hard shits about," Bellamy said.

"Nobody's doing a damn thing without his go-ahead now. Especially seeing how Fallon got it," Calder said, voice low.

Bellamy's mouth tightened. "I don't like it much."

"Nor I," Calder said. "Another mouth to feed. And bad luck to boot." He spit over his shoulder with an air of finality.

That was the trouble with sailors, Isaiah mused. They were more than content to pinion the mechanism of their lives on something as shifty and nebulous as superstition, but when faced with something truly out of the ordinary, they didn't know how to place it. Anyone or anything beyond the order of things was a liability.

"Good fortune for him though," he said, careful not to look up from a particularly wretched grease mark on his vest.

"To be half-alive like that, and under *Coffin's* mercy? I'd rather just sink like a stone. Have done with it," Calder said.

Isaiah plucked at the stain intently. "Perhaps."

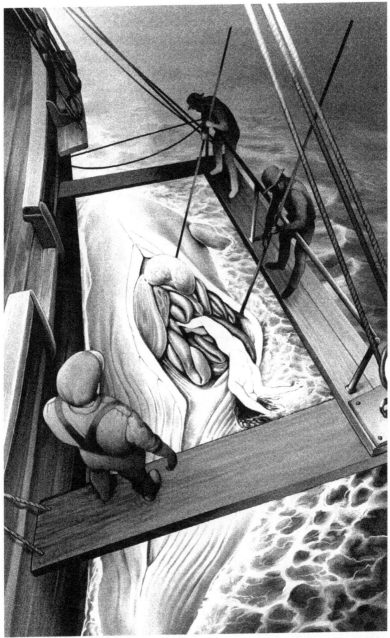

When the man was cut from the belly of the whale, he was as soft and blood-mottled as a stillborn calf.

CHAPTER TWO

THE FIRST BRUSH of evening deepened into a velvety darkness that wasted no time falling over the *Merciful*. Clouds had moved in sometime after third shift took over, and Isaiah had spotted Sharpe fretting over the look of them, spyglass in hand.

The rest of the evening was occupied by eating dinner, drying his shirt, playing a game of gin-jack and losing a not-insignificant amount of tobacco in the final hand with Bellamy, who claimed it was pure justice for Isaiah elbowing him so hard earlier. He gathered up his things only a little bit peeved, re-shuffling his cards twice after to ensure they were all present and accounted for. His mother had always taught him to keep careful hold of a full deck, no matter if you won or lost with them. With a tilt of her head, she'd remind him that the cards would know if you cared for them well. *Things always remember*, she'd say.

Isaiah laid down for the evening and the usual anxious feeling curled up tight in his gut more prominently than usual. It had been a good long time since he'd had any eerie dreams, and as he cinched his eyes shut, he hoped that none would come that evening. Mention of his father usually made him nervous about the possibility, regardless, but something about the presence of the strange dead-undead man from the whale's stomach unsettled him.

It was only as he was attempting to empty his mind that the thought of *food* floated up from gods knew where. Dinner had come and gone and he'd polished off his own meal without a second thought. The man in the brig might not have woken yet, but guilt pealed through him. He should at least try to find something to bring to him. Just in case the man *did* wake up, in a strange place, chilled to the bone, and alone in the dark. It was only decent.

The kitchens weren't forbidden ground to regular crew like Isaiah, but they weren't necessarily a place to loiter either. He eased out of his bunk and crept to the opposite end of the middle deck, where small brick-closed stoves and one hulking iron oven stood at the far end of the space, partially walled off from the area between the bunks where they ate their meals. With the cook long since retired for the evening, her assistant, Tania, was occupied swabbing down the floor. Isaiah coughed tentatively.

"Um, 'scuse me."

"What is it?" he said, barely looking up.

"I . . . was wondering if you had anything? Leftover, I mean."

"You've got some nerve. Get gone, rations are set until we restock."

"I was charged with feeding the man who got brought aboard—"

"Heard about *that*. Should've thought twice before finishing off your own portion," Tania said with a snort. "Not my problem."

"I know, but I'll be sure to remember next time—" Isaiah started.

"Of *course* you will."

There was only one surefire way to get what you wanted aboard the *Merciful*, but it was by no means ideal.

"I'll owe you," he said, edging in front of Tania. "Log it down in the ledger, whatever you think an extra portion is worth, it'll be official money owed once we account for debts accrued back in Shaliston Port."

"Cook said, *specifically*, that he wasn't to get fed anything extra." He appraised Isaiah, squinting. "So it's worth a good bit."

"Four?"

"Ten."

"*Ten?*" Isaiah balked. "You're not serious."

"As the grave." Tania smirked. "It's my skin on the line, after all."

Isaiah groaned internally. "I'm not made of money. I'm sending wages back home."

"You and everyone else," he scoffed. "Nine, then. Because I'm in an agreeable mood and I don't need to hear a sad story tonight."

"Eight and a half."

"Fine."

"*Fine.*"

Tania reached behind him and produced a packet of what was—if the sheen on the paper was to be trusted—a few slices of salt pork from dinner. He took down Isaiah's initials and the ridiculous price, and Isaiah made his way below, just beyond the kitchen, down a dismally rickety set of stairs that descended precipitously into the dark of the lower deck.

The brig had been left unlatched, only because the inner wrought-iron cell was kept barred at all times. Despite the constant motion of crew and rigging moving about on the two decks above his head, it was nearly silent below, save for the creak of timber shifting against timber, and the slow drip of water leaking in somewhere. Dark, and speckled with mildew in the corners, the inner chamber was composed of metal bars, semi-rusted, and a small rectangular gap at the base to slide through a tray.

Someone had papered the floor with straw some time ago, but not much else. The man was out cold, lying on the lone item of furniture within, a limp-looking mattress.

It wasn't that he didn't *look* like a man. He seemed to be one, and a reasonably hale and well-built one at that. Besides the jacket he'd left wrapped around his shoulders, whoever had brought him below had left him with an overlarge pair of grubby grey pants.

Apprehension burbled up in him, and Isaiah crouched to slide the food through the slot.

He was doing his duty. He was supposed to be doing this.

As his hand crossed the iron bars, it crackled as if with static, pins and needles shooting through it. He gasped aloud, scooting back and retracting it quickly. When he shook it out, the sensation dissipated as quickly as it came. His hand *looked* normal. Back and front, all the bones and muscle were in place, each fingernail where it should be, a few moles still dotting the olive-brown skin. When he looked up, there was a single, gleaming brown eye stared back at him.

When he blinked, the man's eye was closed, curtained behind through his long, bedraggled hair. For a moment, Isaiah stared, dumbfounded.

" . . . Hello?"

The man didn't answer him. He didn't even so much as move. Isaiah backed through the door the way he'd came, hands still shaky.

By the time he returned to the middle deck to settle into his bunk, there was an anemic scattering of moonlight bleeding down through the deck above. Bellamy always shifted around more than was comfortable, which would have been neither here nor there in any other circumstance, but as Isaiah's bunkmate it was a less than ideal quality. After the first couple of months of the *Merciful*'s whaling voyage, he'd learned to wait it out by counting what streaks of light he could see through the timbers. His usual count faltered, and the shape of the man's body on the floor of the brig bloomed as he closed his eyes. It soon dissipated into the darkness of sleep.

He immediately retched upon waking that morning. His hands still felt and looked normal, but for some unknowable reason, the mineral tang of saltwater laid heavy on his tongue.

No sooner had he gathered himself than the bell for the early shift rang, familiar and rowdy in the morning light. He could feel Bellamy stretch and roll like a dog in the bunk beneath his, and Isaiah's feet hit the floor before he could stir further.

"Alright, today's the day we're finishing trying out that whale! I want it done, *finished,* by supper bell. We're to keep on our present course and get all we can from 'er," Lice said. Their quartermaster stood, arms akimbo at the head of the mess benches, all gingery five feet of her strident and unruffled by the strangeness of the previous day. "Morning crew to relief, as soon as you get your food in!"

Lice's command was punctuated by a chorus of strident 'ayes'. The daytime and nighttime shifts traded places with the practiced, mechanical nature of a crew that had been long at sea with one another. Before the previous day, there had been precious few surprises on the voyage from Shaliston Port down the Netherside Coast.

Not long after, Captain Coffin made an appearance on the raised quarterdeck, heavy bags under his eyes, dark hair looking vaguely unkempt.

"We're going to be passing through the Southerly Reaches within a fortnight. I want to make damn sure that if we see even a whisper of a whale between here and the Fell Coast, we get after it. Merciful I will *not be* if I catch a single soul slacking about on my ship." He rapped his knuckles sharply against the rail, eyes scanning the assembled. "Am I understood?"

A stronger rash of ayes rang out again. Isaiah returned to his spot beside Demir and for the second day in a row, they flayed out the meat, measuring and cutting strips of fat off of larger chunks of muscle, partitioned out from the now bare ribcage, elevated by a series of hooks and pulleys. They would move the leaves of fleshy, greasy muscle to the tryworks, where it would be processed and cooked down to extract the oil. The company's lifeblood, and theirs too.

Others had already done the job of splitting the spine, piecing off the flippers and removing half of the titanic organs that filled its main cavity. Some of the crew had claimed bits of bone, from the skull and joints, eager to scrimshaw them into something that could be sold. Anything that could be spirited away to pay down their signing debts would be taken quicker than you could blink. Isaiah had tried it, at first, but hadn't been able to shake the gruesome element of it. Holding onto the bones of a once-living thing that they'd killed for the company's gratification felt wrong.

He and Demir, not prone to small talk, stacked the leaves up for boiling in silence. Pinpricks of not-yet-drained blood bloomed from the ends, seeping down to the floorboards to be scrubbed away later, as if nothing had ever bled on the deck of the *Merciful*.

Isaiah had pushed himself to get accustomed to the foul work; he hadn't had much of a choice. Demir, however, moved with an enthusiastic kind of economy, eyes trained on the gross matter.

Someone beyond Isaiah's field of vision whistled something tuneless. The whistling reminded him of his father, and Isaiah unsuccessfully tried to shake the thought loose from his head. Pretending to avoid the thought of him entirely tended to have the opposite effect.

He would sit at his workbench, arms steady as he worked, ready to correct Isaiah if he sheared a sheep spottily or faltered when tying up ducks for transport to market. His father, with no sense of tune at all, would whistle or hum until he saw fit to tap Isaiah on his shoulder. It was a gentle, wordless correction that required no translation.

His mother had always been talkative before they'd moved to the outskirts of Shaliston Village proper, the town had turned on them, and the farm had been lost in the aftermath. The reality of his father's absence didn't so much hit them all at once as crawl in on its hands and knees, a feverish infant crying for attention day in and day out. It was an injury that festered. Nothing he could do would bandage it.

In his own hurt and cowardice, he'd given up. He'd escaped out to sea under the premise of finding fortune and freedom where he and his mother both knew there was none, could never be any. Of the two of their family left behind, neither of them were foolish; no whaler who wasn't the son of someone important came back from the sea rich in anything but calluses and wind-lashed skin, if they came back at all.

It was best to cauterize a wound to prevent it from spreading.

As his mind wandered, his grip on the curved flaying knife grew loose, and it slid up the whale fat and sliced the inside of his hand. His hiss of pain drew Demir's eye. "Ah, pay attention, Chase."

"I'm fine."

He huffed, taking the knife from him, and nodded down the deck. "Take care of that before you foul the oil. Lice'll be after you if you do."

Besides weathered wood boards and crewmembers, the deck was a long, crowded assortment of ropes, cargo, sail, barreled oil, and racks of tools for sparkling and healing the *Merciful* that lived comfortably nestled next to tools for hunting and butchery. Tools, both human and inanimate, had their *place* aboard a whaleship. Coffin, a legacy captain of a long line of merchants and whale-hunters, knew that order and enforced it severely.

"Quartermaster?"

Lice whipped around from where she was winding a large pile of rope almost half her size, and spotted his bloody hand immediately.

"Clumsiness will get you nowhere, Chase."

"Sorry, Miss."

"Very well, it'll be added into the ledger tally." She plunged a hand into her jacket, handing him a strip of clean cloth and a battered flask from her hip. "That's six for these. Soak it well. I'll not have another finger lost in this crew so soon after Goddard's."

He cringed at the idea of more fees added on so soon after his prior mistake, but ducked his head in gratitude and traveled below with the supplies. The cool dark enveloped him, and he shivered at the change; they were somewhere deep off the hilly coast of Ballingreve and had been relying on the persistent mid-autumn sunshine for most things, not the least of which was keeping warm above-decks.

Squatting next to the row of bunks, he uncorked the bottle and drenched a spot on the cloth, clamping the dressing to the cut and clenching it tight until the stinging sensation dulled. His father would have been proud. He had been trying to get him used to pain, to the small injuries and bitter disappointments that came along with a normal working life. A life that was to be unmarred by strange visions or unusual dreams. Isaiah had never told him that the dreams had already become regular visitors. If anything, they'd made themselves at home, popping up to ask for further hospitality at the most inconvenient moments.

He closed his eyes and let his head fall back against the edge of the bunk with a soft thunk. By the time he opened his eyes again, they'd grown unadjusted to the dim light. And so it took a moment for him to realize that the man from the belly was sitting on the bed opposite him.

The man flickered in, then out of existence, staring straight ahead with eyes unseeing. The man's eyes focused, darting around wildly, but before Isaiah had a second to try to speak, the mirage flickered again, in and out.

He gaped at the space where the vision of the man had been, heart pounding.

Isaiah was halfway down the stairs to the brig before he could think better of it. Just as before, the man was out cold, this time curled away from the steel bars. Isaiah studied the slow rise and fall of his shoulders.

"Hey. You there."

He tapped a bar of the cell with a finger. Nothing.

"If you're awake . . . stop that." There was none of that tingling shock that had sparked up on his hand as before. "Whatever it is."

A shout rang down the steps from the upper deck, and he startled for the second time that afternoon.

"CHASE, if I find that my flask is empty by the time you return, I'll make you regret it—"

He scrambled, heart hammering in his chest, and bolted back upstairs as quickly as his legs could carry him. He didn't dare glance back over his shoulder to see if the man from the belly had woken up.

When he resumed his post next to Demir, the old man had already finished his own as well as five more leaves of whale-flesh. He shot him a look that was just shy of withering.

"All better?"

It hadn't occurred to him to tie the bandage tightly around the place where the cut had been. He lifted the cloth. The cut was no longer the same as it had been before. The flow of blood had stemmed, but it looked like it had been healed for days, not minutes.

His hand shook, and he clamped the fabric back down into place. "I . . . yes," he said, voice rough.

Demir huffed in his general direction and gestured toward the remaining pile, along with the clean blade he'd taken from him. "Better be."

Isaiah barely remembered the remainder of the workday. He descended the middle deck stairs for supper with his whole body hurting, only for Morrow to corner him as he entered the mess hall.

"Quartermaster told Monteiro that *you* were the one charged with keeping the man alive," they said. "She wanted me to tell you that if she finds you tampering with him in any kind of way, you'll be up for punishment."

Isaiah cringed. "I'm sorry, I just forgot to bring him dinner—"

"And she's not happy about it, mind you," Morrow said, frowning. "She's interested in studying him. And if you slack off it'll be my job next. And I'm *certainly* not giving up rations because you're shirking."

Isaiah could only nod and stare down at his still-empty tin dinner plate as Morrow stalked off, back to Monteiro's offices. Apparently, the Captain's charge to keep the man's presence from the ship's surgeon had already failed. Word moved quickly onboard the *Merciful*.

He sat in his regular spot between Bellamy and Hendricks and quietly portioned off half of his food. Hendricks looked at him askance.

"What'd Morrow want?"

"Now both Coffin and Monteiro want to keep him fed . . . *hey—*" he started. Bellamy plucked Isaiah's spoon from his hand, portioning off a quarter of what Isaiah had set aside. "They asked me to do it." Not telling them why exactly he'd been the one charged with the job seemed wise.

"Don't be stupid," Bellamy said.

"Bold words, coming from you," Isaiah said, reaching for the utensil. "*Asshole.*"

"Contrary-wise," he said, waggling it just out of reach. "I may be dumb, but I'm not stupid." Isaiah hopped to snatch it back. "You're listening to the letter of what Monteiro and Coffin tell you to do but missing the *spirit*. That's stupid."

Isaiah snorted, and re-portioned a full half of his food, edging it out of Bellamy's reach. "So what am I to do then? Let him starve?"

"No. Make sure *you* don't starve." Bellamy shot him a significant look, and continued to lay into his own serving with gusto.

"He's right," Hendricks supplied. "What do you care about him?"

Isaiah studiously arranged the rest of his meal on his own plate, and when he glanced up, Hendricks was studying him, eyes squinted.

When he went below to deliver the food to the man, heart pounding high in his chest, the man was still and quiet, barely breathing. As if Isaiah had never seen him move at all.

CHAPTER THREE

THAT NIGHT, he fell into a dream faster than he'd known possible. He was drowning, encompassed entirely by the weight of the salt sea. Isaiah had no recollection of how he'd been pulled below in the first place, he only felt the brittle matter of his bones crush and compact beneath the pressure of the waves. No wind reached him under the surface, and when he opened his eyes to spot some distant shadow of either coast or ship, he could discern neither through the warping green-blue of the world around him. That tension, the dire absence of breath, bound his lungs taut to his ribcage, straining to get something out of whatever oxygen was left, until bit by bit, the force of the sea shriveled them up.

Isaiah felt the life pass out of his body.

It was only when he was certain that he was dead that Isaiah became conscious of a hand wrapped around his ankle, long fingered, its clean white nails gripping him and holding him under the water. He knew immediately that it was no use struggling, as he was already drowned. And so, he let himself be dragged down without any resistance, all trace of sunlight faded to pure dark.

It was strange that he was dead, specifically because he could still see through the inky water. Not far enough to tell who or what was pulling his body deeper down, but enough to see shapes pass him as he went. The outline of a porthole, the rough surface of the outer shell of a boat's hull, the spear-like point of a mast tilted sideways at a precipitous angle. Shapes moved around him at a distance, fish of massive size with terrifying hinged jaws and silvery, needle-thin teeth passing dangerously close to him as he sunk lower and lower, a wall of smooth, impossibly quick shark-flesh darting after them. If he still had a heartbeat, it would have

EMMETT NAHIL

spiked high and fearful—instead, he simply watched the creature glide through the piles of shipwreck, safe in knowing that there was nothing they could do to him anymore.

In his long, midnight-black drop through the depths, he felt the essence of what made him, him, slipping. Instead of allowing it to fall through his fingers, he scrambled, trying to hold tight onto his place within his husk of a body. He was still barely conscious of who he was when he reached the bottom floor of the ocean, and the hand around his ankle that had pulled him down had disappeared.

Isaiah. Isaiah. I—

There was the corpse of a whale, drifted down to the murky bottom. It had settled on its side, massive mouth open. Isaiah tore his eyes from the impossibly huge maw, and the pointed teeth embedded within. A wide, rippling cut split its stomach where the meat of the creature had frayed and parted some time ago. Through the darkness below, a roiling mass of crab and shrimp the likes of which he'd never seen scuttled, already well on their way to picking the whale's bones clean.

Something about it pulled him, beckoned him forward toward the hollowed-out space in the whale. *Isaiah.*

The voice that he'd thought that was his own, repeating his own name, suddenly wasn't. He couldn't make out what, exactly, lay within the creature, but he wanted to see what it felt like, to take rest within it. It felt like the safest place in the world. It was what had called out his name through the water.

IsaiahISAIAHisaiahisaIah—

His soul drifted outside his body, and he followed the voice calling him inside.

He woke gasping for air, choking on his blanket, which had somehow wrapped itself around one leg and snaked around his middle. Isaiah kicked himself free and gulped in the musty cabin air. It was thick, and still felt like he was choking.

Quickly swinging a leg down from his top bunk, he hopped down and tucked his bedding into a shape that might resemble his approximate size. He had to hope that nobody would be passing

22

by to tell the difference. Avoiding the step in the middle that he *knew* creaked terribly, Isaiah darted up the stairs to the main deck. There was nobody standing in the fore. The evening watch shift paced about at the opposite end of the *Merciful,* the periodic metallic creak of the oil lantern all watches carried echolocating back to him. Isaiah didn't want to try to explain why he was up and about at such an hour, or worse, be cornered into small talk.

The smooth chill in the air was a balm to his lungs and he drank it in like he had *actually* been drowned. Rubbing sleep away from his eyes, he tucked himself atop a heavy crate near the bow, resting his chin on his knees. It wasn't unbearably cold, yet. They had a long way to travel before they reached the frigid Southerly Reaches that made up the whale's sanctuary ground. There were all manner of things that could go wrong before then.

Like bringing aboard a man from the stomach of a whale. Like his dreams regaining a vividness they hadn't had since his father died. He didn't know what true madness felt like, but he had to imagine it was something close to this.

From beyond the oak ridge of the deck's handrail, the water stretched out into infinity. No light glowed on the horizon, no shadow of land rose up in the distance. No other ships.

A clenching sadness, almost as dire and crushing as the dreamed sensation of drowning, buried him up to his neck. If he could keep his head above it, and his feet kicking furiously below, he would be able to draw breath, as he'd been doing for the past six months onboard the *Merciful.* He'd been sleeping wrapped up in blankets, curled in on himself, hoping against hope that he wouldn't talk in his sleep, or that the doorway in his mind wouldn't crack open and let in visions from another world.

Hendricks had been on a ship two years before whose captain, known as Bullet Briggs, had put a pistol to her own head and pulled the trigger. It hadn't taken much more explanation on her part to elucidate how the captain had received her current nickname. He found himself wondering what had led her to it.

"Chase?"

Álvarez happened to be the watchman that evening.

"Oh, sorry. Didn't mean to surprise you," Isaiah said, squinting into the bright lantern light. Álvarez tsk'ed gruffly in return, but didn't move the light.

"You should get back to bed while you're still able." He looked out to the waves, following Isaiah's gaze. "It's an odd hour to be up and about."

"I'm cursed with light sleep," he replied, forcing out a congenial laugh that sounded unnatural even to him. "But there are worse things in the world."

"S'pose so." He meandered over to the edge, testing out the rigging with a free hand, sending the boats creaking in their berths off the starboard side of the ship, and the lantern light flickered.

"You went down to that man today. Earlier." Álvarez gave him a look a few shades away from suspicious. He set the lamp down between them, and leaned back on the rail, cast light setting his face in shadow. "How come?"

"I . . . I didn't." A lump immediately rose in Isaiah's throat.

"Neither the Captain nor the gods truck with liars," he said, not moving. "I was trying to get some sleep this afternoon and you ran off below."

"I just—"

"I don't care what you think about the unnatural thing, I won't watch you shirk duties in order to keep some castaway company."

"The Captain *asked* me to check in on him."

"I heard, idiot." Álvarez leaned in to pull a face at him. "Just let it be, and don't do anything stupid."

Isaiah swallowed as quietly as he could, what with his esophagus tying itself in knots. "I don't mean anything by it, but he doesn't seem well. I just . . . don't see any harm in checking in on him."

"You may have decided you're well and finished being the green hand on board, but if you keep acting like a damn fool you'll make us all come to regret it." Álvarez loomed, picking up the lantern. "I'm no great lover of the Captain's methods, but take it up with the surgeon if you're so concerned."

He strode off down the deck in long strides, the pillar of lantern light sending a shuddering, yellowy beam into the cool night.

Isaiah slid back into bed with a swiftness that would have been astonishing by the light of day. He hunkered back under his blankets, rolling over to the side to peek out into the sleeping berth. Assorted snores and sleepy grunts aside, there wasn't any other indication that anyone else stirred that night. The thin sliver of moonlight coming in through the porthole window was weak, and he was too tense to fall back asleep. He tried not to think of the idea that if he moved, if he dreamed again, the man from the belly would be awake and staring back at him, eyes wide and dark.

Morning dawned and breakfast was just as crowded and raucous as normal, but Isaiah's appetite had abandoned him. Out of habit, he picked at some of the reconstituted fish and pan bread served, and, committing to the necessity of the venture, shoveled down the meal as fast as he could.

If Bellamy or Hendricks or Calder noted any change in him, they didn't mention it. Álvarez was loitering and yawning at the end of the line for morning rations, and Isaiah filled his plate and emptied it before he noticed he was there.

The end of the meal blended into more work, which blended into a long, still, afternoon. There wasn't a whiff of a breeze to speak of, and without clouds to give cover, the cooler air didn't do much to fight off the autumn sun. Isaiah was either sweating or shivering by turns.

After the whale was finished being tried out, the Captain charged those of them not barreling up the processed oil with swabbing the deck nails holding the ship together until they shone, and disappeared to his cabin. Rope was untangled and re-coiled, the *Merciful* was cleaned to a spit-shine, and Sharpe flitted about the deck, watching over them in the Captain's stead like some kind of anxious schoolteacher.

"Bet you Bellamy won't notice I've moved both his shoes."

The cleaning tasks were supposedly designed to stave off the boredom and troublemaking that came after a fresh kill. Everyone felt flush with rigor, and no place to put it.

"His shoes? For what?"

She rolled her eyes. "You're no fun. Both left, no right. You'll see."

He and Hendricks sat in wait, theoretically oiling down harpoon handles to keep the wood solid. They took turns flicking off the occasional wood beetle, and waited. Success came in the form of Bellamy thundering up from belowdecks, barefoot, clutching two suspiciously identical shoes.

"Well Fallon's asleep, so which of you whoresons—" He was cut off by a distant crackle. A massive, charcoal black storm cloud moved in fast on the eastern horizon. It prickled with electricity, and the hairs on the back of Isaiah's neck stood on end.

"*Shit,*" Hendricks said, going from cross-legged to up and running in an instant. "BATTEN DOWN—STORM ON THE EAST AND RISING QUICK!"

Isaiah was running before he'd even had the thought to do so. Harpoon handle tossed back into the lockbox, he lashed rope to sail, slung boxes over one atop the other, and tried to avoid the frantic activity spanning the deck. Coffin emerged from his quarters in the far aft, looking pale and dissipated. He cracked his spy-glass toward the horizon.

"*Damned spirits . . .* Easterly gale! SHARPE, ensure that sail is tied down fully!"

"Aye, sir. Shutter the tryworks, ALL HANDS—" Sharpe was cut short by Coffin's hand coming down hard on his upper arm.

"I *did not* say to *shutter them.* I want every last drop of that blasted oil barreled up and sealed before the storm catches up."

Sharpe stared for a beat too long, slack jawed. "But the storm is *coming*, they'll be—"

Coffin gripped him. "Do I make myself CLEAR, Master Sharpe?"

" . . . Aye. *Aye sir.*"

He gave Sharpe a stiff shake before loosing him. Stricken, Sharpe ducked his head and scuttled off to push back some of the mates who had already begun to shut up half-full barrels of oil.

For a mad, unconscionable moment, Isaiah felt the urge to stay on the main deck. Just to see what might happen to the men Coffin had been willing to sacrifice for a few more barrels of oil. Beating back the thought into the furthest corner of his brain, he took up a pallet of rope and leather cording, and ducked out of the way as Bellamy sped past him with a gruff "'Scuse!", disappearing from view in the blink of an eye.

"You have that lashing in hand, Chase?" Lice barked.

"Yes miss—"

"Well, *use it!*"

Isaiah jumped into motion, darting back down the deck and trying to put the cruelty in Coffin's snarl behind him. He pulled the lashing tight over some boxes, covered the pallets with canvas and tied everything down to the boards, the rope winch creaking in his hands and straining against the rising wind. The clouds moved infernally fast, the charcoal shapes turning nearly green the closer they came toward the ship. When he'd been on land, Isaiah had loved the rain and wind, despite how much trouble it gave his parents on the farm, but now—

"Chase, you've done enough!" Hendricks shook him, and he realized the cords had gone over-tight under his hands. "Let's *go*!"

Within scant minutes, the rain blew sideways and so did the *Merciful*. The crew, most at least halfway drenched, took stock, and already starting to bicker in close quarters.

"Easy now, hand me that pipe there—"

"Oy, careful! You'll ash on my leg."

"—Don't you take someone's eye out with that."

"Oh *shut* it, you—"

Cramped and crowded as it was, Isaiah couldn't tell if they were as on-edge as he felt, or if it was just annoyance at the interruption of the hunt. Fallon, the unlucky soul, was ordered to take a lantern and to retrieve the men who had been left above to finish packing away the oil. He came back drenched to the bone, cap gone, eyes bleary with brackish rainwater, and tracking in whale grease. He shook his head like a dog and the two nearest to him moaned in mock disgust. The others weren't with him.

"The gall of them," Bellamy said, firmly ensconced between Chase and Hendricks. "Fretting over a little water."

Hendricks snorted and pulled her carving from its hiding place somewhere within her tunic. It was nearing some kind of curved form, but Isaiah couldn't discern the shape. Sudden waves rocked them, hitting the vessel's port side. There was a loud creak that sounded almost like an aching roar, or a scream, that came from the deepest part of the *Merciful*. From where the man from the belly was being kept.

"SHIT—" The quartermaster's cussing rang out above the rest, as Lice fell off the barrel where she'd perched, scrambling to right herself. "*Fallon*! Where's the others up top?!"

EMMETT NAHIL

Rainwater formed scattered rivulets from Fallon's mousy brown hair and ran down his face unimpeded. "All gone," he said, eyes hollow.

CHAPTER FOUR

ISAIAH DID NOT dream that evening, because he did not sleep. By the time the crew had worried themselves into exhaustion and moved to their beds, Sharpe and Lice had decided that group watch shifts were to be the order, regardless of any missing crew. Checking for cracked beams, loose sails . . . those were the things that mattered. The *Merciful*'s capacity to continue the hunt was paramount.

It was simpler to think about the storm hammering a perpetual drum beat on the deck above than to imagine the condition of the man who was now locked in the furthest depths of the ship. Who had gone from one stinking, rotten carcass to another.

The brig was the lowest place on the ship, used for storage for extra supplies and sometimes people, when crewmembers sick with liquor from some port city mid-voyage would roll back on board. It would no doubt be sodden by now, and the thought of the man stowed way down below, likely doused with fetid seawater, pricked at Isaiah.

His guilty conscience stirred him from his bunk by the time Bellamy was out cold and snoring below him. He gingerly picked his way around the sleeping crewmembers, the shifting creak of the boards below his bare feet covered by the howling wind.

The hold stunk even worse than it had when he'd first delivered the man's food, like a mixture of mildew, whale flesh, and wet metal. The dregs of the storm were sloshing up against the walls of the lower hull as the deck pitched up and down. Isaiah supposed that explained the smell of whale drippings. He edged against the wall, grabbing handholds in the low ceiling supports along the way.

Isaiah had barely closed the entrance to the brig when he

gasped, and landed hard on his tailbone. The man was awake, and sitting on the cot.

"You, you're—" Isaiah managed to say.

The man blinked like a house cat. "You look well," he said, in a voice that sounded like wood scraping rocks. As if it was raw with disuse.

"I mean, you're—" Isaiah stuttered, looking over him carefully. "You're awake."

The man's sturdy chest rose and fell evenly underneath the jacket he'd covered him with. His skin was now more of a regular brown shade, only slightly cast with a chalky pall. If Isaiah didn't know better, he'd have thought it was the fine dust of salt left behind after seawater evaporated off a stone. The man exhaled pointedly, as if irritated by the comment.

"And you can talk."

"I can do more than that." The man blinked again, pressing his lips together in a firm line.

Isaiah righted himself, and desperately tried to hold back his expression. "Apologies, I just thought—"

" . . . That just because you haven't heard something, it isn't so?"

"No! No." Isaiah's tongue was suddenly leaden in his mouth. "Are . . . are you ill? Do you remember anything at all?"

"I'm awake now." He tapped a long index finger on his knee. "That's all."

"You don't recall anything useful? Where you came from? A name?"

"Useful." The wind howled and clawed at the side of the ship. " . . . And what would be *useful*, to you?"

Isaiah balked. "Anything. How you came to be inside a whale, for one. But I'm not important to you on this ship."

"How would you know what's important to me?" he said, plucking at a pant leg with two fingers, almost daintily. "These are yours, are they?" He really did have quite long fingers. The nails were as clean and smooth as the inside of a conch shell.

"No, actually," Isaiah said, trying not to stare. "Do you remember being brought aboard?" The ship swayed hard, and Isaiah stumbled, just barely getting his legs back under him. The man stayed perfectly stationary, shifting with the motion of the deck easily. He could see the tense set of his jaw from beyond the cell bars.

"Suppose that I do."

Isaiah gave up on subtlety and let himself linger on the man's face. "Do you remember the captain speaking? Or the first mate?" It appeared slightly healthier than it had been when he'd first been brought up from the whale, unconscious and cast all over with pale death. It was a handsome face, even.

"Captain Coffin." The man stood, taller than Isaiah by a head even in his bare feet. The waves clapped the opposite side of the hull.

The ship tilted on its axis once more, and the man stood as still and upright as a driven stake, even as Isaiah had to lean hard, and brace himself against the cage. What must've been a massive wave rushed up to wail down on the side of the ship like a dozen hammers, and the man's eyes were as hard as two flecks of frozen amber.

"Is he what's important to me?" the man hissed. "As a *valued* guest onboard Captain Coffin's ship?"

Isaiah breathed hard as the *Merciful* recovered creakingly, and he extracted himself from the bars, moving back as far away as he could. The man seemed to lose grip on something he'd been holding tightly, and he shook his head, chest-length curls curtaining his face. The gale continued to howl fiercely beyond the ship's walls.

"You're Chase, aren't you?" The man said, sinking back down to the cot.

"How do you know—"

"It's on the jacket," he said drily, flapping open one side of Isaiah's coat to reveal the small, tidy label his mother had made him stitch inside. "Are you worried you'll lose it? Or that you'll forget your own name?"

A bitterly embarrassed flush rose in his cheeks. "You've got to keep track of your own things, onboard." The man had seemed full of rage not a minute ago, and yet here he was, prodding at him.

"Giving away your things seems a poor way of doing so," the man said, cocking his head. "Or is this how Isaiah Chase treats a guest?"

The use of his full name caught him off guard. "I guess so. You can keep ahold of it," Isaiah said, face still hot. "For now, at least."

As he moved to go, the man piped up over his shoulder. He leaned chest-first, hands dangling loose through the bars. "I would much appreciate if you didn't relay our conversation to the others, Isaiah."

To make matters worse, he shot him a crooked grin, teeth pricking white against the darkness. Isaiah nodded curtly, and his heart hammered in his chest as he bolted the door behind him.

The following day, nobody dared to venture back above to search for the crew that had been casking the last of the whale oil. Coffin had remained stowed away in his quarters, and as such wasn't there to order anyone else to the task.

Instead, they waited for the storm to break, huddling amongst themselves, some taking turns praying or cursing Coffin's temper in turn. At first, the storm and the disappearance of the two crewmen had thrown things into a kind of frantic disarray, and everyone seemed to be privately bracing themselves for something worse to happen, for more to die, or for the men's bodies to turn up in the cleft of a new wave. It was close to tidal season after all, and high winds and heavy rain were by no means a rare thing. Every soul on board knew that it was a time of celebration for the gods, who were prone to fits of joy and anger that kicked up winds and storms aplenty. The crew made their offerings and tied their protective knot-charms with the fixedness of children in school. It would have to do, for now.

Eventually, the hellacious gale faltered for a few hours. The crew of the *Merciful* emerged back onto the deck in one long, continuous stream. They took stock of the shattered containers, frayed bits of rope, and splinters of rail and mast that sprinkled the deck like so much confetti. Two long, dragging scrapes in the planks above were found, leading from the tipped-over casks and zig-zagged along the deck and over the side.

Just as Fallon had said, the crew that had been left up top was gone. What oil that hadn't been washed away by the storm pooled on the interior of the wooden barrels and dribbled out onto the wreckage, where it leaked between the floorboards down into the body of the vessel.

"Did you go walking about last night, or did I dream that?" Bellamy asked, ambling up to him and punctuating the sentence with a wide, unselfconscious yawn. Isaiah was picking palm-sized chips of wood from the pile of oilcloth sail patching.

"You must've dreamed it," he said, staring intently at fabric passing through his hands and trying to breathe normally.

"Chase, it's a good thing you're not a play-actor."

"Why?"

"Because you're a *terrible* liar," he said, unusually peeved.

Isaiah fixed his expression into one of pure and total innocence and looked up.

"Why would I—"

"I don't *know*, Chase. I was trying to give you a shot to tell me straight, but I suppose you don't want to." Bellamy tsk-ed, leaning back against the railing. "The last thing you should be doing is get caught sneaking about. Not with the captain in such a foul way."

"I was just restless. That's all." If Bellamy had heard him get up *last* night, through the gale . . .

"Could have *sworn* I heard you wandering down to the lower deck, is all." The bigger man leveled an apprehensive look, and Isaiah felt a chill roll over him.

"Well, you heard wrong."

"I sleep heavy, I'm not deaf. I heard you get down from over me," he said. "What were you up to?"

"Good Gods and all, I don't know how you could have heard a *damn thing* with that wind going," Isaiah said, rolling his eyes.

What else had Bellamy heard while he'd thought he was asleep? Isaiah took stock of the six long months they'd been aboard the *Merciful*. He could count the dreams he'd had on one hand, but if he'd started talking in his sleep again, who else would have heard? His stomach winched tightly around itself.

"Fine! Be a liar then."

He stormed off, round shoulders pulled up tight around his ears. A tonic of guilt and paranoia slid down his throat.

Bellamy reminded Isaiah of the dependably cheerful young men you'd run into on an errand going into town, more than happy to make small talk about their work, their impending trips into the standing conscript army and how they were happy to be shipping off soon enough. It was all well and good, so long as you didn't do anything too odd around them. He never could relax around the type. Not really, not so long as he knew what he was; what his family was. The threat of what would happen if they sniffed something off about you loomed large and violent, even before his father's death.

The billowing storm clouds lingered and as the morning edged into afternoon, the air fell humid and thick. Whether from the weight of the lie or from the weather, Isaiah found himself exhausted, his thoughts circling back to the man below as he picked away at the tarps. Splintered wood hid in the waxy canvas like strange prizes among the cloth. The pile grew and the mates gave up hunting for the two men's bodies among the sea foam when the downpour returned.

The heavy wind and rain that pummeled the *Merciful* in the days after the initial gale was brutal, but claimed no more lives. Daily work was raw hell for two days straight. Nobody wanted to head up into the rigging for too long, let alone venture alone to the upper lookout nest to spy for whales, and the argument between Coffin and Lice that ensued over the matter was nearly as bad as the ongoing rain itself.

"If you can't convince them to do their *jobs* I'm not certain you're *worth your keep*—" Ramsdell, Hendricks, and Isaiah wolfed down breakfast and eavesdropped heartily while the two had it out behind closed doors in the officer's quarters.

"*Sir*," Lice's tone toed a careful line. "The fact of it is that they can't look out for catch if they can't *see*—" There was the sound of shattered glass, and a thud.

"*I am not your Captain Briggs*, Stowe, don't make me relieve you of your post."

They couldn't hear if Lice said anything in response; or if she did, it was so quiet as to be inaudible.

"No, I don't think you have anything more to say on the matter."

The thud of Coffin slamming the cabin door open echoed down the passageway. Lice slunk out as though kicked, and Coffin disappeared once again back to his offices in the far rear of the ship, a hand propping him up against the passage wall.

"Drunk as a hellion," Ramsdell said with a snort. Lice stalked past them with a blunt scowl on her thin features and a fresh gust rocked them something fierce.

"Crew, trouble in the mainmast! Deck hands to Calder!" Yesayan shouted. Sure enough, the towering pillar of oaken wood had suffered a sizable crack down the center, the battering taken during the storm. He darted along with the rest to attend to the break; the mast wasn't broken off entirely, but it was on its way. One of them was already up in the ropes, affixing a wide strip of canvas to a tarred-over section of the splinter. The crew muttered and fretted as one—such a break spelled disaster if the wind decided to turn on them again.

Below them, the ocean churned, the refracted echoes of the storm rolling the ship. The deck heaved and with a cry, Jerry Calder fell, putting the full force of his arm against the splintered edge of the mast. The cry turned into a raw, mangled scream. Blood colored the canvas, and the crew below cried out.

"Jerry! Don't move—"

Quicker than Isaiah could blink, Fallon was up the rigging and edging closer to him. Yanking a blade from between his teeth, he sawed the offending spear of mast from the rest. Calder's face roiled in pain and his shouting carried to the deck.

"Get him down fast! Someone lighter up to finish the job!" Yesayan yelled.

The wood broke off with a resounding snap, and Fallon wrapped Calder's arm with a long strip of cloth, holding the spar through his arm in place.

"Someone bring Monteiro!" Fallon called, and Isaiah held his breath as he helped Calder back down to the deck. The two picked their way through the crowd, Calder shaking and moaning, his arm hanging limply by his side. The make-shift bandage couldn't hold back the blood that oozed from the speared limb.

Hendricks darted to the mast and was up the rigging in a flash of moving limbs and accurate hand-holds. Isaiah ran forward, suddenly assured of what needed to be done, and joined her, straddling the opposite side of the mast. They affixed the rest silently, sanding down the sharp edges and offending pieces and handing back and forth the canvas wrapping until the wide bandage circled the mast, sealing it with pitch and tar, until the spray of Calder's blood was covered entirely. Tying it shut to cure, they carefully descended, and only the loose shifting of the breeze could be heard above the murmurs of the rest of the crew, scattering back to their work.

That evening, Jerry Calder's cries from the surgeon's quarters echoed throughout the lower levels of the ship, until Monteiro plied him with enough liquor to let the noise fade into quiet, languid moans. Hendricks didn't bother to speak further about the matter, and disappeared to see to her duties. Bellamy in particular hadn't tried to speak with Isaiah since their conversation up on the main deck. And yet, the sea still looked angry to Isaiah, and the clouds hung low overhead. The day passed them by, grey and sour, and Captain Coffin didn't bother to make an appearance.

"Calder'll sleep a while yet, I'd think," Sulaimi said. "Was he alright when you left him?"

Fallon jutted a chin out, shaking his head brusquely. He'd only just washed the blood off of his shirt, when someone pointed out that it was putting people off their supper.

"Reckon that means no."

"I mean, he's still out cold isn't he?" Bellamy interjected.

"Sure, but that doesn't *mean* anything," Sulaimi added.

Fallon nodded by way of response, staring down the mess hall bench, away from where their group sat. He picked at a stub of rope he'd been fiddling with and didn't meet anyone's eye.

The waves had calmed by late evening, and the night crew pushed past their table, heading out to take watch.

"It'll be a while yet before he's in any fit shape to do much," Fallon said, finally. "If he gets back the use of that arm."

"If he keeps the arm at all," Sulaimi said, with a blunt finality that didn't invite much further comment. Bellamy shifted awkwardly in his seat, running a hand through an inky tuft of hair. Isaiah held out a hand to collect the rest of the group's tins and dishes for the wash and departed, leaving them to marinate in their discomfort.

In the two days following the storms, Isaiah hadn't really given much further thought to the man belowdecks, or so he repeated to himself. If he looped the phrase over and over again in his mind, it might start to feel more true.

In actuality, he had taken to thinking about him in bursts and starts, when he'd least expected it. As he sharpened the heads of harpoons, or as he was charged with scrubbing down the quarterdeck. The smell of wood soaked in seawater and the abrasive wetness called up the image of him, enmeshed in the briny dark below their feet. He would think immediately, intentionally of something else, anything else. Trying to picture a map of his father's land, of the exact lay of the hills that had made up their home, only worked for so long. The dearth of grass, soil, richly black mud and stone about him made this easier said than done. The cool, continuous swell of water didn't do much to calm his imagination.

Each night Isaiah dared to venture below with the man's food, he'd been fast asleep. The remains of the scant half-meals he brought were there when he came to deposit the next, and he didn't dare rouse him to speak again.

The mainmast was cured solid, the sails were patched and turned out, and the *Merciful* gradually corrected course under Coffin's invisible hand.

They moved at a hasty clip toward better hunting grounds, and Demir regaled them with grandiose stories of the massive groups of whales and fish a thousand-head strong that were just a few scant weeks away from where they were headed, *if* they could navigate through the trickier part of the lower Southerly Reaches. He leaned back easily into his seat at one of the heads of the mess hall tables, arms akimbo, and told them of the crisp air that made whaling as easy as waking up in the morning, about the currents that corralled the beasts into massive herds, as if the gods of the deep tides were serving them up on a platter for the crew to take. He'd seen it many times before, he said. It was their privilege—no, their *right*.

They'd fill their contract with Pyle, Thacket, and Coffin twice over, and every soul would have fish aplenty to tide them over back home to Shaliston Port. He didn't promise it in so many words, but everyone leaned in to soak up his assuredness of an unceasing plenty. Debts paid, stomachs full.

But the man was still belowdecks. Presumably mired in darkness, with no indication of what would come or how long he'd be a 'guest' aboard. No amount of mental backflips Isaiah could pull would erase that fact. The vitriol on his tongue when he'd spoken of Coffin hung in the back of his head. Hendricks had said that she'd seen Coffin going below to the brig. For what purposes, nobody could be certain, and when it was brought up Isaiah felt a dull ache of jealousy twisting his insides. He tried hard not to dwell on what Coffin could possibly want with the man.

He gave in to the itching, niggling feeling of curiosity sitting in his brain after three full days of waiting.

CHAPTER FIVE

O N THE THIRD DAY after Calder's injury, the wind drew down to a tentative breeze. They were settling back into their regular motions, standard rotations resumed, and so it was the usual early morning watch that was the first to notice that there were hundreds of fish lying on the deck without anyone having cast a line or dropped a net. Better still, that a good amount of them were still *alive*.

"Oy! First mate!" Phelan called, grabbing a sizable rockjaw by its spiny tail and holding it aloft, a massively toothy grin splitting his rain-splattered face. Its glassy marble of an eye rolled and its body fought its death throes.

Sharpe raised an eyebrow archly, but hustled over. "Damn," he said, eyeing the size of it. "Nets and barrels then. Collect what's still alive."

Every kind of fish that could be found, from nippers to melon-fish had come up on the deck, drawn from the sea.

"It's like someone picked them up for us." Fallon gaped as he emerged from the mid deck.

"What, the gods making good all of a sudden?" Hendricks responded. The metallic, still-moist bodies wriggled in staccato time, tapping out an irregular, fleshy drum beat on the wooden planks. Collecting them as fast as they could, no small part of the crew metered brief prayers of thanks as they hacked the heads off right then and there and tossed the bodies into a barrel to sit ready for the cook to salt. As Isaiah plucked fish after fish from the deck, the creatures' glassy eyes followed his. Yesayan jostled close to his side, poking a still-moving whitefish into his face.

"If I didn't know better, I'd say that man from the whale was intent on blessing us." He barked a laugh and darted off down the water-slick deck. The thought didn't bring Isaiah any kind of comfort. It struck him as just as strange and ominous as the miraculously healed cut on his palm.

The sun sank toward the horizon, and dinnertime came and went. Isaiah's meal of rice mash and sausage sat like a stone in his stomach, and the image of the fish's staring eyes lingered at the surface of his mind like an air bubble.

By the time he brought a warm bundle of freshly cooked fish to the man, package still leaking cooking grease, night had fallen thick over the *Merciful*. The crew was, by and large, sleeping soundly, well-sedated by the scale of their fortune. He had double-checked, and Bellamy seemed to be asleep. The anxious voice in the back of his head prodded at him that he might not be. And then what?

"No lamp, hm?" The man's voice emerged from . . . someplace in front of him, enveloped within the darkness. After a long moment's wait, his patience paid off, and Isaiah's eyes adjusted enough to pick out the man's form, a silhouette against the shadows.

"No, sorry."

"Don't apologize."

"Oh, sorry, I . . . " He cringed. He could hear the man sigh somewhere in front of him, and there was a shuffle of movement on the other side of the room. The dark shadow of the man's form rippled, over-long.

"They left me with matches, but nothing to burn. I can't seem to get them to work."

"Probably soaked. They like to do that." Isaiah frowned, despite himself. "Thinking the dark makes people penitent, suppose."

"Do I have something to do penance for?" For the second time, Isaiah got the inexplicable feeling that he was being mocked. The shadow moved closer, taunting.

" . . . I suppose not."

"*Suppose* not. What crime have I committed?" The man's voice turned plaintive, but there was a cold edge of mockery. "You lot could have just let me be."

Let you be where? Below the sea? The question teased at him, but he swallowed it down.

"So." Isaiah stepped a touch closer to the bars. "Why can't I tell anyone that you're awake and talking? I know the Captain's been down to . . . visit."

"Ah. Sharp of you." He wrinkled his nose. "He was awfully swift in clapping irons on me, and is far less interesting than you."

Isaiah flushed. "Interesting?" He couldn't tell if it was a compliment.

"He doesn't know we've been speaking. Not to worry."

"But you did speak to him."

"Certainly."

"About what?"

"He was extremely curious about the recent storm, and those fish on the deck. I asked him nicely if I could be released," he said, matter-of-fact. "He didn't seem quite interested in the idea." That sarcastic bite was back in his voice again. "I'm sure you'll see his character soon enough."

What the hell did that mean?

"He's not *kind,* but with everyone onboard under his care . . . "

"And I'm to assume you feel . . . cared for? Awfully easy for excuses to be made when you're safely employed with your hunting, and I sit in here." He huffed. "Besides, I'm not certain that you can effectively judge blame from all the way out there."

Isaiah felt the blood rush to his face, and he instinctively stepped backwards.

Even through the thick darkness, he could see the iron bars soldered floor to ceiling in the hold. The man's long fingers held them tight.

" . . . Unless you'd like to step in here with me," the man said, voice tinged with an emotion Isaiah couldn't name.

He froze still as a hunted deer. "I . . . I can't."

"Speaking of." The man leaned against the bars, body language slack and easy as if they'd just been having a casual conversation anywhere else than in the most dingy, uninhabitable place on the ship. "I'm sure a resourceful soul such as yourself *would* be able to find some way to release me."

Something in Isaiah shrunk back at the words. The timbre of them seemed wrong, unnatural. The request seemed almost too easy to acquiesce to.

"I *can't.*" He swallowed, hard. "The captain most likely keeps the keys in his cabin, if not on his person, and the Quartermaster keeps them on her." He didn't know why he was telling the man this. The words simply fell out of his mouth, unbidden.

"But surely you'd know how to get them, or find some way to change Coffin's mind about it. Wouldn't you?" The man's cajoling tone turned sweeter. The edge of mockery was well cloaked, like a piece of rotten fruit covered in honey. Isaiah's mouth watered.

He wanted to do it, desperately. It would have been easy to wait until Coffin was well and drunk and—

Isaiah's stomach churned hard at the thought. His gut tugged at him, bringing him back to himself.

"I'm sorry. I just can't." He straightened up and steeled himself. "He's given orders."

The man's hands slid off the bars with a dull scrape, and he slumped back, more exasperated than relaxed. The blade of light from above skittered off his arms as he let them fall.

"Fair enough, Isaiah," the man said. His tone was curbed. Careful. Not quite angry, not quite sad. He settled back onto the cot in the corner of the cell, crossing his arms and kicking out his legs, dismissing him.

Isaiah resigned himself to no further sleep that night as he clambered gingerly back into his own bunk, the salt and metal, near-animal stench of the hold still clogging his nose. As soon as the man had mentioned the key, he'd wanted to take it for him. *Needed* to, as if he wasn't already deathly afraid of being found out as some kind of seer by the rest of the crew.

He didn't know what kind of man could have the gall to suggest such a thing, and what kind of man could get him to actually, really consider it, even for a moment. He tried very, very hard not to mull over it too deeply, and waited impatiently for daylight to come.

The call for assembly on the main deck came just as the sun began to nose over the horizon. All thirty-odd of them had arranged themselves in more or less regular lines, shambling forward, half still mostly asleep, with the few who'd been on night-watch looking haggard and ready to drop. The light cast coral-pink and shone brightly in Isaiah's sleep-clogged eyes. He rubbed them open, just in time to see the captain already striding out from his cabins, half-dressed.

"We happened upon a boon yesterday." Coffin stalked before them, like the head of a cavalry rallying the troops in anticipation of a hard battle. Fine spray off the port side of the gunwales blew up into their eyes, and Isaiah could only blink it out of his face as quickly as possible. He didn't dare to actually wipe the water away with a hand, lest the motion draw undue attention.

"Can anyone tell me, exactly, what that boon was?"

"Fish?" Someone called out, tentative.

"Correct. Fish." Coffin replied, spitting out the word like a curse. "And what was supposed to happen, with said fish?"

"Divide it amongst the crew—" Another voice called out.

"Just so." the Captain said. "It was decided, in interest of fairness, that the aforementioned catch would specifically be collected and split in accord with rank." He halted his striding back and forth abruptly. "So why, might I ask, are we utilizing storage *meant for oil* to stow this fish?"

Silence reigned. Isaiah dared not breathe, eyes locked on his feet.

I'm sure you'll see his character soon enough.

"No? Nary a single one of you dogs has a single blasted idea *why* such a thing was done without express permission? When we're down nearly a week of hunting because of some blasted storm?" His stillness was even worse than his incessant pacing. Coffin's eyes were bloodshot, and it looked as if he had gotten even less sleep than the night watch had.

Isaiah drew a single, shallow breath inwards, and held it for as long as he could. He was not the type to pray, but he did, silently.

"Since none of you seem to be able to comprehend the gravity of our charter onboard . . . Master Sharpe. Would you do the honors?" The First Mate gestured toward the crowd, and a few crewmembers helped to roll the sizable fish barrels out from the mess hall. They still leaked a mix of seawater and fresh blood.

"Dump the lot."

A collective intake of breath rose from the assembled.

"And Yesayan, since you seemed so enthusiastic yesterday, assist him." Coffin beckoned him over with a loose gesture, leaning back on one hip and watching as the First Mate struggled to bring the first barrel lid over to the rail. Yesayan took a hold of the opposite side, a deep resentment in his eyes.

"Every man must earn their keep aboard my vessel." The first of the fish hit the water with a limp, wet splash. Then another, and another, until the impact mimicked the endless rainfall that had plagued them for three sodden days and nights. "He that does not work, does *not profit.*" Another barrel was lifted, and dumped. "*Nothing* comes for free without my say so." Then, another. "Not from the gods, not from lucky chance." The last of the rich catch flopped over the side and disappeared. "—And *certainly not* at the expense of the company's resources."

He clapped Yesayan on the shoulder, more of a shove than a friendly gesture. Not for the first time, Isaiah blinked spray out of his eyes and breathed in, out. Measured, calm.

He could nearly taste the fresh, delicious fried fish from the previous night's dinner on his tongue.

I'm sure you'll see his character soon enough.

When the crew dissipated from the deck to tend to their duties, Bellamy cornered him almost immediately.

"So?"

"So what?" Isaiah replied.

"So, I imagine you owe me."

"What could I possibly owe you?"

"An apology, for one. An explanation as to why you were walking about again in the dead of night last night, for two. Give it up."

Isaiah groaned, turning to the rat's nest of rope he was supposed to be coiling. "I wasn't doing *anything.*"

"What did I tell you? That you're a dog-shit liar." He eyed him, squinting. "You're not going to see that man from the whale, are you?"

Isaiah fumbled the rope badly. "I'm not *going to see him,*" he spat back, gut curling. "I brought him some of the fish from yesterday, that's all."

"If the captain wanted to punish us, he would have found some way to do it anyway." Bellamy said, pondering it carefully. "But he wasn't this bad before that man was pulled up."

"I'm not sure if that's true."

"You know it's true, and don't deny it."

"Come on. He loves a bottle," Isaiah said, collecting the dropped line. "And he's been put off by that man since the beginning, and angry at the lack of whales besides. We could have detoured to Port Bel Yarin and got enough barrels for the oil before now but we didn't."

Bellamy exhaled heavily through his nose, rolling his eyes. "You're still not telling me what's going on."

Isaiah rolled his eyes. This act was getting old. "So? Tell me what *is* going on then."

"GENTLEMEN," Lice's clanging voice rang out over the deck, cutting between them with more efficiency than any knife. "*Move.* Social hour this isn't."

Bellamy huffed and stalked off to his post by the lookout tower, with no further argument to give. Isaiah coiled up the once-tangled rope, and considered.

This was now the second time that Bellamy had tried to pick a fight in nearly as many weeks. He'd been so easy to talk to, before, when Isaiah had been better at pretending that he was just another regular member the crew. The man from the belly had made everything about it that much more difficult. His irregularity had sparked up something strange in Isaiah, and it set him on edge.

If there was any chance of Bellamy speaking up about his hunch, he certainly wouldn't know about it until the captain decided to punish him for it. And why was the captain visiting the man's cell, at any rate? The idea of Coffin stumbling drunkenly down into the hold struck him as wrong. He let the loose, warm feeling of anger settle in his chest, and went about his work with a vengeance.

As he turned back to the patched-over fissure in the mast where the crack had once been, the image of an iron-wrought key sprung to mind. It shone dully in his thoughts, glinting and sparking against some intangible illumination.

The workday wavered in and out. Wind turgid with humid air blew across the deck, the dull and heat-stricken remnants of the storm passed over the crew like a sour memory. Isaiah waited and worked and sweated. He mopped a handful of curls off of his forehead and settled into a crouch to give his aching knees relief for a brief moment before returning to his deck-scrub brush.

Night came soon enough, and with it came dinnertime, when food and a cathartic wash of drunkenness reigned belowdecks. Most avoided touching on the topic of the lost barrels of food, and if anyone spoke of it, they were quickly hushed into silence by their friends.

The latter part of Isaiah's evening was occupied by an extended game of knucklebones, as the crew settled in for the long stretch of evening dark to come. As the perennial loser, Isaiah had taken the penalty of ensuring Bellamy got to his bunk in one intoxicated piece. He swayed, and leaned heavy on Isaiah's shoulder, less than conscious of their difference in scale or the fact that they had been arguing. Hendricks had just laughed at the sight of them and meandered somewhere up to the main deck.

"Y'reckon . . . y'reckon you'll go wandering off later?" Bellamy slurred.

Isaiah tensed. "Bellamy, *drop it.*"

"*You* drop it—ah, shit!" Bellamy tripped over a poorly-affixed piece of decking and Isaiah very nearly went down with him.

"Easy on, you big—"

"Easy on yourself! *Oof.*" He punctuated the retort with an admirably muffled belch.

"Foul." Isaiah tried not to laugh and deposited him against a pillar holding the near end of their set of bunks up. He scrubbed his hair out of his eyes, sinking to the support opposite him.

Bellamy considered, only wavering slightly. He evidently decided that sitting down was the lesser of two evils.

"M'sorry, alright," he said, palms heavenwards.

"Sorry for calling me a liar?"

"Well. No. 'Cause you *are*." He let his head tilt slack against the beam. "For telling y'so in the manner . . . the manner that I did."

Isaiah blinked. "You really are drunk."

"You lost and I won. *Earned* it." He chuckled. "Besides, I wasn't distracted. Unlike *some* of us."

"Well, you've got an extra eye handy. It's basically cheating." Isaiah tapped below his own hairline, at the back of his neck. Bellamy had, some nebulous time before their current voyage, acquired quite a few tokens. Most who made sea voyages did eventually, but his was an impressive collection already, and his prize acquisition was an exceptionally large, black lined tattoo of a wide holy eye, keeping perpetual watch behind him.

Bellamy nodded, hand drifting back to the place where the ink had been carefully laid under the skin. "Uh-huh. Just to keep a weather eye out."

"For what?"

His expression darkened. "To watch out for whatever's on your tail. Following you. Be it strangers or angry gods or death."

"What makes you worry about gods and death?" Isaiah was content to pursue this line of questioning if it let Bellamy talk about himself rather than him. "Strangers, I understand."

"The first hunt I went out on as a harpooner, there were thieves who were chasing the ship. Got on our aft-side with a trim little clipper as soon as we started hitting a streak of good luck out in the Strait o' Jade." He rubbed the back of his neck, but continued. "They corralled the hunting boat as soon as we were sent out after a grey whale, and boarded us as quick as I'd ever seen. It was just myself and the five others who were onboard along with." Isaiah let out a low whistle. "The stripped us dry as a bone, took half our provisions and the half-dead creature we'd been towing. The lot of us nearly starved."

"What did you do?"

"Nothing to do. We stayed hungry and prayed to every god above and below." He let out a minute, child-like shudder. It seemed at odds with his big frame. For a moment, Isaiah almost felt bad for thinking poorly of him earlier. Almost.

"We were far and away from the main ship, had been out waiting for the whale to die and tire itself out from pulling us. The greedy bastards were waiting too, I suppose. Eventually we laid into tattooing tokens with soot and grease, instead of ink. Blood for blood, and the like."

"It worked."

"That it did." He sighed. "Mighta been dumb luck that let us make it back to the main ship in time. But who can say who gives and takes chance?" Something in him still seemed fearful, in a way. Even drunk, he had the carefully measured tone of one not looking to tempt the skies to prove him wrong.

"Besides, leaves those two eyes up front to keep a steady hand on the harpoon, if the time comes." Isaiah supplied.

"When," he replied. As if it'd never been brought up in the first place, Bellamy grinned once more, running a hand over his hair, eyes crinkling in a smile that Isaiah desperately wanted to believe was as good-natured as it seemed. "A little faith, Chase. *When* the time comes."

CHAPTER SIX

"**P**OOR NEWS ABOUT Calder, I heard." A voice came from behind him, soon revealed to be Senna Morrow. They plucked a leg over the mess hall bench and leaned in to where he and Yesayan were seated. Their plate and fork clattered to the hall tabletop with a tinny clatter.

"Poorer than he already is?" Yesayan said.

"Just overheard Lice and Monteiro talking about it. Asking to keep extra stores of cleaning alcohol."

"How's that?" Isaiah asked, turning to them. Yesayan eyed him, but answered.

"You weren't on the voyage with Briggs. Sulaimi lost toes on that trip, all from infection. Monteiro was onboard too, and the only way she was able to salvage the rest of the foot was by having the whole thing swabbed down constantly, before, during, and after the toes were long gone."

Isaiah brushed the point on his palm where the cut had rapidly healed over, feeling a kind of twinge run through him. Yesayan shuddered, fingers curling.

"Point stands." Morrow had already started tearing into their food. "If she's needing more cleaning alcohol, it's infected. Badly." They gulped down a mouthful of bread, and fell silent.

"He's losing the arm, you mean." Isaiah amended.

"Gods keep him." Yesayan spat hard over his shoulder. "If it's his time."

Morrow scoffed. "I should hope not. Monteiro's not letting anyone in to see him yet."

"Why not?" Isaiah asked.

"Couldn't tell you." They scraped up the last bit of stew, the fork dragging metallic over the tin surface. "Must be foul as all hell."

As he and Yesayan beat a retreat out of the mess hall and back to the main deck, Isaiah was stopped in his tracks by an arm, which, as it turned out, belonged to Álvarez. The arm was carrying a bucket of clothing, smelling none too fresh.

"Chase. I wonder if you could do me a favor." Álvarez's tone was loose, easy, but something in his eyes seemed pointed.

"Depends what the favor is."

"When you go to clean out your things, bring these with you, won't you?" He blinked slowly, not breaking eye contact. "Bellamy mentioned that you'd be *more* than willing to help."

Isaiah nearly swore aloud. He should have known it was too good to be true, to have Bellamy simply let their argument go because of one good conversation that he probably didn't even remember. He took a deep breath.

"Sure." Snatching the clothes out of Álvarez' hand, he walked off as coolly as possible. He scrubbed them until his knuckles were raw, letting the water rinse over them and trying not to think what else Bellamy might have told him.

That night, the man below was sound asleep, and Isaiah dreamed of toes detached from limbs and fishbones and arms falling from shoulders and woke with the healed-over cut on his hand aching fiercely.

As he'd suspected, Bellamy continued to ask 'favors' of him. One of them, as it turned out, was to assist in counting out the barrels of bread and flour meal in the hold. Look for pillbugs and water damage for the Quartermaster's ledgers. "In case the storm got to it", he'd said. Needless to say, the lower hold was cold, musty, and just as miserable as Isaiah had expected. Somehow, the atmosphere matched his mood perfectly.

The barrels and crates were, when they'd first set out from Shaliston Port, stacked up in orderly lines. Not a sack or case out of place. However, by this point in the journey, with nearly a third of the food stores within them consumed long ago, there was space for the casks to shift about with the roll of the ship. As if to prove the futility of the task, a swell brewed beneath the boat and sent a small barrel of something liquid tumbling across Isaiah's path.

There was a sizable splash as it hit the bottom of the floor. General damp and a small amount water in the hold was normal, but the small pool in which the barrel had fallen was easily a few inches above Isaiah's admittedly bony ankles. He groaned.

Lice would have a fit at the idea of food supplies being ruined, and she wasn't the type to discern between message and messenger.

It'd have to wait, however—stores came first, as well as finding the source of the leak. He marked hashmarks on the palm-size slate Lice had thrust into his hand, double checking the numbers and quantities as he zig-zagged through the maze of stores, righting containers as he went.

It wasn't until he reached the far end of the hold that he found the full extent of the damage. A dark, wet, mildewy stain had crept up a barrel of salted meat, and was climbing further and further up the pillar upon which it leaned. It crawled toward the ceiling of the deck above, and split off from the very wood in living, mossy stalactites. The water had somehow rotted the wood where it had seeped upwards. Isaiah pressed a finger to wood and it gave way beneath his touch, softly spongy and weeping seawater. He retracted his hand, skin crawling.

"How . . . "

There were supposed to be regular checks of the stores, it was one of millions of checks and logs and lists kept on board any ship. The endless pieces of paper that ensured their survival as much as tied them to their debts to the company. They were supposed to find these things quickly, efficiently, and let the upper command tell them how to fix them. The water in the hold looked as if it had been accumulating and rotting their food for *weeks*, not days.

He tilted one end of the barrel, and was greeted with tufts of emerald green seaweed, slick with moisture, growing straight from the rotted wood beneath. Where there should have been dry wood, there was briny mush, almost mid-calf high. It took the better part of an hour for him to scour through the pools of water, dipping a hand in periodically and feeling along the base of the hold for cracks. He was rewarded with no leak, no source at all of the collected salt water and accompanying freshly-grown seaweed.

As he counted the remaining undamaged stores, the knot in his gut cinched tighter and tighter.

He went back to deliver the paltry, half-moldered store quantities and received his tongue-lashing from the Quartermaster in silence.

Hendricks reached over to shake his shoulder, and Isaiah felt himself startle. He felt himself pluck at the hem of his vest before he could stop the nervous tic.

"What's wrong with you?" She asked.

"Nothing," he stammered, and tucked his fingers under his leg.

"Never mind. Where's Morrow?"

"Down aft. Don't sneak up on me," he replied. Hendricks snorted, jauntily edging him out of her way.

"Dunno why you're always so nervous, Chase," she called over her shoulder. "C'mon, you look dour." She reached back to grab him by his arm, dragging him down the hall.

He followed. "Why Morrow?"

"Because if they're off assisting Monteiro, it means something bad's happened with Jerry's arm. And because you look like you need something to do," she said, with no small amount of relish.

The two of them crept aft, toward the surgeon's offices. It wasn't so much offices as it was a solitary cabin, adjoined by a larger room. The second space was both an operating theatre and examination room, as well as a store-room for the surgeon's supplies. Monteiro was not one to truck with just anyone peering into the theatre. No performance, no unnecessary movements. Everything about her was as strict and scalpel-spare.

"Easy, Master Calder." They were close enough to hear the surgeon's clipped tones bleeding out of the second room.

"Will—Will I—"

"Enough of that. Morrow, the wrapping please."

"Yes'm."

Hendricks turned and raised one eyebrow in his direction, tugging on Isaiah's arm to slow their brisk walk down the hallway.

"Tonic. No, the other one if you please."

"Smaller dose or larger?" he heard them ask.

"Larger, I should think," she replied, impatience lightly dusting her voice. Isaiah inched closer to the doorway, nearly pressing his nose to the linen fabric that divided the interior from the passageway. He could see a glimmer of reflected light coming through a porthole window, glancing off an enameled tray of tools. Pinchers, knives, a saw. The large bottle of rubbing alcohol sat next to it, nearly a third empty already. The golden-brown liquid glimmered like amber, briefly interrupted as Morrow passed a long dosing spoon in front of it to deliver to Monteiro.

Calder's legs were limp on the flat of the operating table.

"Has it . . . has it gone bad?" Calder's voice faltered and trailed off, and the words barely made it out of his mouth.

"It is badly infected, Mr. Calder," she said, with a kind of immutable seriousness that left little to the imagination. She addressed Morrow brusquely. "We will need to let the skin fall away from where the infection has started. The tonic will do so, and will sterilize it as it dissolves. It will make operating easier for you and for me, once it becomes necessary."

She set down the rag she'd been holding, now stained with a putrid-looking rust-brown splotch. "Luckily, you will not have to do anything but leave it be for the coming few days. That means staying off it, Mr. Calder, no work using it. I expect that you will find a way to do that."

There was a long, heavy pause. " . . . Aye."

Hendricks shot him a significant look. Anyone shy of knocking at death's door was expected to work through injury and sickness alike. They were supposedly blessed with the chance to labor for Captain Coffin's generosity.

"Good," Monteiro said. "The wrapping has been infused, and I'd advise you avoid getting water or oil on it. I'll have Quartermaster Stowe inform Captain Coffin of your condition."

"Aye, Doctor."

"Now, up you get." From her eavesdropping spot next to him, Hendricks tapped him, nodding back down the hall. Isaiah tore himself away, and followed along after her, taking care to step lightly. They emerged in the far end of the bunks, where half the previous watch members were still at rest.

"No good," he said in low tones.

"Don't think so."

"I don't much like the thought of having to sit calmly and feel my skin slough off from under me." Hendricks pulled a grotesque face, shuddering. He felt a tug at the pit of his stomach. Calder had been sitting in there alone. Liu and Fallon had been on duty, otherwise he would surely have wanted someone to sit with him while his arm was being tended to.

"Do you think we should have looked in on him?" He said, trying to ease the idea in gently. "He would have wanted us to."

"What for? We can't do much to get him better."

"I just thought . . . "

"Lords *above*, you are soft," she said, punctuating with a snort. "Isaiah, listen. We cannot do more by him." She fixed him with a steady look, wide brown eyes on his. "Pretending we can is nothing but foolishness."

She sighed, tugging on a strand of his hair and letting it bounce back into his eyes.

"Hey—"

"Hey yourself. If the Lords Below want to take his arm, that's a small price to pay for a fixed and steady mast."

Isaiah mimicked Coffin's dour tones. "Sweat now or blood later."

"You may not like it, but he's right."

"You're right . . . "

"Of course I'm—"

" . . . I *don't* like it." He replied drily.

"*Chase.*"

"You sound like Demir, now."

"You're a foolish piece of work, y'know that?" She said. "How many hunts've you been on, hmn?"

"This one."

"Sure. This one," she replied, squaring up to face him. "And how many do y'reckon Coffin's been on?"

"Enough," he said, with what he could tell was a childish twinge to his voice.

"More than you. That's for damn sure."

"No more than Lice's been on."

"And do you know why he's captain and not Lice? Because she's got an impulsive streak a mile wide—"

"And no rich shipping family to buy her a hunting commission. Hendricks, something's not *right* about this hun—"

"Isaiah." Hendricks' voice turned dark. "*Stop.*" She turned from him, as if by looking straight at him she'd be made susceptible to whatever lack of faith he'd acquired. He took a small, conciliatory step back.

"I'm sorry."

"Sure you are," she replied with a heavy breath. "I've got to get back to it. Fallon'll be waiting. I'll tell the rest of them myself if you're going to be such a bleeding heart about it."

A reply died in Isaiah's chest before he could get the words out. He wondered if she had ever given her doubts full voice at all.

That night, the man was awake. Isaiah brought a light, and half a dozen matches he'd pilfered from the stores.

"There you are." The man perked up visibly. "Have you given any consideration to my request?"

Isaiah frowned, firming up his shoulders. "The answer is no."

"I'm disappointed."

"No, *no*, we're not discussing this." He took a deep breath. "What did you mean when you said we'd see the Captain's character soon enough?"

"I only meant that any man's character is best told by his actions, not by his rank." He raised an eyebrow.

"No, the timing of the storm, and then so many fish just placed on the deck . . . I've never seen the like before! Not ever."

"Well, there *is* a first time for everything."

"No, no, *no*, not like this there isn't!" Isaiah could tell he was raising his voice and clamped down on it quickly.

"And what happened?" The man asked, with a wide, wide grin. Isaiah gaped. *He knows.*

"He dumped out the stores to make room for more oil," Isaiah said. "And besides that there's . . . things growing in storage too."

"Are there?"

"Yes! Plants, and water weed, and there's seawater leaking in from who knows where and it *wasn't* there yesterday." Isaiah couldn't look at him, all mock-surprise, any longer. His head was beginning to hurt.

"Isaiah," the man said, his voice almost kind. Almost. "Men don't change. Only grow to be more so who they always were, under the skin."

When Isaiah was able to look at him again, he looked thoughtful. Like he was pondering him.

"Who *are* you?"

"Someone who's always been the same," the man said. "And, if you get me out from behind this blasted iron, you might come to find out."

Isaiah set the food down, the tin plate clattering against the floor. He still left the matches next to the food, and stalked off to go to sleep. He could feel the man's eyes tracking him as he went.

The next morning, Lice called him over to her corner of the deck. Most times, a summons from her meant sure punishment, or at the very least, extra duties to take care of, or fixing of what you had already done to bring it up to ship-shape standard. This time, however, Lice Stowe's expression was more one of apprehension rather than anger. Isaiah still tread carefully.

"Chase."

"Yes'm."

"When you were taking stock of the hold t'other day, you said there was a leak but knew not where."

"Yes'm."

"Show me where you already looked."

"Aye, Miss," he said, ducking a cautious nod, and led the way back down, through the mess hall, past the cabins and down through to the still-rank and cold store room. The barrels and crates had shifted again since he'd executed Bellamy's little chore, despite the seas being no more rocky than was normal. Left, right, then left again . . . .or was it right again . . .

"Raw bleeding hell—" The quartermaster swore behind him. Assuming the comment wasn't for him, exactly, he turned and peered under a few crates, following the deepening ocean water until he'd reached the portion of the hold where it was now solidly at calf-height.

It had gained depth since he'd last gone down.

"There. This is where I'd looked, but it wasn't this bad yesterday . . . "

"All the fucking lords and ladies. Chase, this is no good at all." Lice cussed, rolling up a linen pant leg. It was well on its way to her knees. "I'm going to fetch the carpenter after this, we need to dredge immediately."

"Hold on a moment—" Isaiah started shifting boxes. She had to see the rot. To understand what dire straits they were truly in.

"Sorry. There was a part of the wood that was soft . . . here." He pointed to the track the water had left behind. Where once the water had climbed a slender trail up the pillar supporting the hold's roof, the trail had widened to a broad pathway.

"Water doesn't soak up that hard . . . "

"It does here. If you'll pardon me saying," he said, and she shot him a look of unfiltered irritation.

"Fuck." Lice rubbed at her temple, putting out her other hand to press a tentative finger to the spot. It sponged away at the lightest pressure, and the water ran down her arm. "*Fuck.*"

She paused to rub her hand dry on her shirt, before half-mumbling, half chanting under her breath. "*Lord of the long-low bless us and keep us.*"

Isaiah tore himself away from the pillar, pulling up the very barrel he'd inspected last time. The seaweed had spread, wide and dense as a thicket. Green tendrils of growth now covered the entire underside of the wood, snaking in and out of the boards themselves, wrapping around the iron band holding the planks together like hands grasping for tools. The fingers of it radiated, barnacles dotting the surface like irregular pockmarks on the face of the wood.

Something about the growth seemed impossible. Water-weeds didn't just grow from nothing. They certainly didn't spring up dense and verdant overnight.

As he ran a hand over it, the growth cleaved to his hand. The strands were delicate and soft as a rabbit's fur, and they wrapped in between his fingers for an instant before he dropped the barrel, sharpish.

Shaking his hand off, his skin crawled. The weed had *moved* toward him.

Lice stood upright, shaking the water off her free hand and rubbing along her pointy jaw. "I'm sending the carpenter down below. You assist her as she needs, until night watch."

She gazed into the deepening pool, eyes scanning—for what Isaiah could not tell. "We'll find the leak, so help me."

"Aye."

"And Chase," she said, "I don't need to tell you: keep this to your damn self, or I'll have you bloody keelhauled."

Isaiah swallowed. "Aye, miss."

CHAPTER SEVEN

NO LEAK FOUND, and no reprieve from water either. The carpenter, Moirah, had strode in with sharp eyes and a brow like thunder, but despite the amount of time Isaiah spent on his hands and knees under her watchful gaze, neither of them could find the source of the flooding. He'd gone to his bunk with fingers crinkled and pruned and back aching, and Moirah still cussing a blue streak into the ever-pooling water. When he'd left, the carpentry tools were still scattered around her like an iron-wrought halo.

He clambered up into his bunk with an apprehension that belied his exhaustion. The net cause of the leaking and the bizarrely responsive plant growth that followed was a mystery that somehow had been applied to him, against his will. Just like the man below had been applied to him like some kind of horrible, persistent riddle he'd been tasked with solving. And who seemed just as interested in solving him, too.

His bed was stiff and none too luxurious, and he could not tell if he or the blankets smelled of rank sweat and seawater. Somehow, as he laid on his back and stared at the blackness of the ceiling, the dark around him faded and shifted into sleep.

This time, his mind didn't conjure up endless depths or dark swelling waves of seawater. He opened his eyes in the dream and he was home. The rolling arcs of grass sprawled away from his mother's house and he soundlessly walked up them, to the elm-shingled building that crowned the hilltop. He could feel the soft tamping of the generous earth beneath his feet, making the way to the front door easy. Clouds dusted the skyline, and he looked up, eyes not quite catching the exact shape of them. His chest ached and ached and ached with the look of it.

His father had always taught him to watch how clouds moved, to be able to predict when there was a heavy storm coming in off the coast, or to tell exactly when would be a good time to begin harvest. The sky had told his father some things less earthly, too. Isaiah had only occasionally caught him telling his mother of his dreams once they'd thought he was sound asleep in his bed. His father spoke of visions, or ill portents that the sky whispered in his ear, or scenes in his sleep that played out like a drama on a stage, in which the players would show him puppet shadows of things yet to come, of urges the gods above and below wanted to make manifest. His mother would listen silently, closing windows to shut out any curious ears and ingesting her husband's visions in grim silence.

Even when he was small, Isaiah had learned to make a habit of crouching quietly in the shadows outside the kitchen past his bedtime. There were almost always stories to hear.

Without knowing how, exactly, he'd spanned the hill, Isaiah reached the dream-door to their old house, rough panels of whitewashed wood lined and cracked with age and battered by coastal winds. A small glass windowpane cut a square into the wood. He could see through the warped and rippling glass; figures were moving inside. Their swooping walk and irregular gaits sparked fear in him, and he could hear voices speaking within. He could make out some language he couldn't recognize, in various voices. Before he could open the door it swung open of its own accord. Things, after all, usually moved on their own in dreams. When his father had described how easy it was for the gods to send messages in sleep, he had immediately understood.

Sometimes things just happened in Isaiah's dreams, and it was as if he had been dragged before them to bear witness.

Despite the uncanny shapes through the window, there was nobody else in their old kitchen. Instead, there was only his father, hunched over their dining room table. He looked haggard. His shoulders and back were lean, almost hollow, draped with a linen shroud over his burial clothes. It was the one they had left in his grave with him. The minute swirls of embroidery thread glinted red in the candlelight.

"Isaiah." His father's voice was hoarse. Motes of grave-dirt dusted his nostrils, his mouth. It was caked along the crow's feet by his hazel eyes.

Isaiah opened his mouth to respond, but no sound came out. He could feel himself gulp and strain to speak, to say something, anything at all. Instead, his throat was dry and dusty, and his tongue gained no purchase behind his teeth.

His father reached to the corners of the shroud, fingers thin and bony, as if he'd been deprived. The nails had dense half-moons of dirt caked underneath them, as though he had clawed his way out of the loamy hill where they'd buried his body.

"My boy . . . " The shroud fell to his father's elbows. The noose that the court had decreed he must be buried with to ensure the seer's body stay dead was still slung about his neck. The horrible piece of jewelry looked as fresh and clean as the day it had been tied.

"Are you listening, Isaiah?" Isaiah opened his mouth again, and still, no words passed his lips. He felt the raw force of a scream grow in his belly and chest. The sound simply came out as a choking, rattling exhale. He nodded instead.

"You shouldn't lie. You haven't been hearing at all." His father dipped a finger into his mouth and drew out the tip black with tarry mud. "You've hidden yourself away from our gift." He dragged it along the boards of his childhood table. The ragged fingernail scraped against the wood and left a trail behind. He drew out a pattern.

A child's drawing of a whale, mouth to tail over and over again. One horizontal line of whales, beginning on another. When Isaiah blinked, there was a new line.

"You have two good eyes to see, so use them. You'll need them soon enough, when the blood comes." His father's hand moved unerringly as he spoke. " . . . And love not the sea."

Isaiah finally was able to cough up a question. "Why?"

His father lifted his face to look at him. He had not noticed that his eyes had rotted out of his head. "Oh, my son. Because it will not love you back."

Tears pricked at Isaiah's eyes, and when he went to wipe them, he only felt the metallic stinging sensation of dirt. Looking down at his fingernails, he saw that they were covered in fresh, dark, earth.

In an instant, he was back outside, feet drowning ankle-deep in soil. As he was sucked below the cold surface of the ground, he woke, gasping, eyes wet.

Isaiah blinked into the dark, willing himself into consciousness and biting the inside of his cheek hard enough to draw blood, for good measure. He made his way out of bed before the rusty taste dissipated, his father's desiccated face a slender shadow in his head.

There was, as always, the likelihood that he was going completely insane. The thought lingered as a strong possibility, that his mind had simply gone sour, what with the eternal swaying of the ship, the bizarre manner of the man from the belly and the never-ending stretch of water slowly seeping into the hold.

There was also the somewhat less likely chance that he was not losing his mind. That his father's gift ('*our gift*' he'd said) had come back to him all the way out here, thousands of miles from home and after a long hibernation. If it was true, if there was something to it . . .

You'll need them soon enough, when the blood comes.

He ran over his father's words like a whetstone over a dull steel blade, unable to stop himself as his thoughts came to a sharp point.

The straining sound of the bunk creaking against itself seemed thunderous as he passed Bellamy, who, as far as he could see, was sleeping like the dead below him. If he heard him rising, Isaiah would just have to confront that issue in the morning.

On the main deck, he drew up a bucket of salt water from the side of the ship. Taking it in his hands, careful not to spill a drop, Isaiah tip-toed toward the rear of the *Merciful*, where the moon shone down unimpeded by sail or clouds. The moon wasn't as full as it should be for something like this, and pinprick stars speckled his portion of sea. The moonlight was drawn into the reflective surface in his hands, as if pulled by a magnet.

He dipped his hands into the bucket shakily. He'd seen his father do this all of once before he'd died—no, been executed. Killed, without mercy, for doing things just like this. For playing

EMMETT NAHIL

in ritual that showed that he could pull secrets from the lips of the gods above and below. That he needn't employ the services of a pastor or shrinehold with a coin or a promise of services rendered.

They never had found out who it was that had turned him in to the town authorities. They simply appeared with a jailer's summons and iron cuffs one day. The next time he and his mother had been allowed to see him, he was kneeling in the penitent's station before the council, both wrists akimbo, linked to the ground with another pair of iron cuffs. To dissuade him from doing any witchery, they'd said, before condemning him to hang by the neck until dead.

The day he had first seen his father scrying into a bowl of water, he had happened to peek out from behind the root cellar door where he'd been sorting a pile of turnips for the winter. His father hadn't heard Isiah go downstairs, and doubtless thought he was in the barn or elsewhere. He had set a basin on the table, under an open window. The night breeze rippled it and then, a sliver of a waxing moon had shone down into the kitchen. It turned the dark water reflective and shining, and his father had stared into his cupped hands, speaking into them as if whispering a secret into someone's ear.

Isaiah lifted the cupped water close to his mouth, whispering low and cunning into it.

"What you let me see in sleep, Gods Deep and Gods Above, let me see in waking. As we sail the line between your worlds, show me what blood is coming to the whaleship *Merciful . . .* " He paused. "Please."

His father had pressed the water to his eyes and tilted his face back. He had seen the water run from parted fingers down to his mouth. He had breathed out in a strange, stuttering pattern, droplets of water spluttering out from his lips.

Isaiah pressed his own palms, the salt stinging his eyes and crossing his cheeks. He took three rough breaths out, and opened his eyes to stare down into the bucket.

For a long, long moment, there was nothing. Only the wind off the deck rippling the bucket in tiny waves. His eyes prickled and stung but he dared not blink.

Useless. It was useless to do this. It was just another thing that his father had left him—a strange memory to haunt him and no answers, no way forward.

He blinked, and the waxing moon's reflection warped, tugging against the direction of the ripples in the bucket.

Dappling shadows formed a shape—Isaiah squinted hard. Even if his eyes watered salt, he didn't dare close them again.

The shape was an eye. An unblinking, harsh-lined eye. A small voice inside him said that it was Bellamy's tattoo. The eye seemed to crack. A long dark bolt of lightning cut it in half, and the pupil in the center turned black entirely. The eye had been parsed into two. The ripples themselves formed the deep shadows and harsh crags of a human skull, the moonlight highlighting the bare surfaces and planes of bone, as the skull tilted sideways like a man cocking his head to the side. It grew and stretched until it became an outline of a man just standing, features fuzzy, but Isaiah could *feel* him staring out behind long hair and he slammed his eyes shut, holding his palms to them, and pressed until he saw stars. He stood as quickly as he could, tossing the water overboard, only hearing the light splash as it rejoined the sea. Setting the bucket back on its hook, he dried his face with the hem of his shirt, waiting until the stinging of the salt water abated.

A shape in the far periphery of his vision *moved*. Isaiah instinctively darted into the cast shadow from a mass of crates nearby, and held his breath until the shadow, human shaped, was gone and Isaiah *had* to breathe or else he would scream. Someone had seen him. Had seen him doing *something*. Even as he took a few rattling breaths, his pulse hammered somewhere up in his neck.

Isaiah sat up on the deck, afraid to move an inch until the faintest glow of sunlight began to haze its way over the horizon, and he crawled back to sit in bed, his father's warning ringing in his ears.

"There she blows! Spout on starboard!"

It was late afternoon by the next day when the deck exploded in a flurry of motion, and all hands rushed to stations. The crew darted to loose sail and chase after the newly-spotted whale, and the boats were filled with tools and supplies at a rapid clip. Isaiah moved along with the quickest of them, rushing to the starboard side of the *Merciful*. In the distance, he could barely spy the far-off spout of water piercing the cloudless sky, like an ethereal geyser from the earth's crust. Lice's raucous shouting followed soon behind.

"*All hands,* heave to and loose the topsail. Bellamy, take your away crew to boats, now!"

"Yesayan's not well, miss—" Hendricks yelled over from where she'd already scampered over to the side of the smaller boat.

"Take Chase, it's time he live up to his name—I said HEAVE TO, YOU DOGS!"

Isaiah's heart leapt, and he darted to gather up some spare rope and a boat axe into his arms at top speed, the sharpened edge of the axehead pressing dangerously near to his chest, the cold of the metal almost shocking him. Bellamy caught his eye, and stared with something unreadable coloring his expression. Isaiah froze dead.

"*Chase, move.*"

The lower half of the boat was quickly filled with the remaining tools he and Hendricks had carried, and Sulaimi and the rest had begun to pile in, faces lit with a kind of feral glee that looked foreign and childlike in their features. Some were serious, but most were in high spirits.

Before he could settle, the whaleboat was speedily lowered on creaking lines to the surface of the water, landing with a splash. Immediately, a wave arced above the side and splattered them. Shaking it off, he, Morrow, Sulaimi, and Toole heaved oars, and pushed off from the side of the *Merciful* with Bellamy at the prow. The eye on the back of his broad neck stared down at him, almost accusatory.

"Catch it, lads!"

"Get after the beast!"

A few crewmembers cheered rowdily above it all, and Bellamy laughed heartily, yelling over his shoulder from the fore. "She's in our sights! You won't have no time to worry!" Isaiah could hardly breathe right and focused on the wood in his hands.

Sulaimi and Toole jeered and called back, and they all pulled hard on the oars. Spray pulsed up from the waves and onto their backs as they got in time with one another, shoulders straining and breathing as one many-limbed animal. Hendricks held the rudder and steered behind them and made no sound at all, but Isaiah could feel her cool gaze above his head, eyes trained on the place where the whale had been spotted. Bellamy was easily the loudest of them, and was used to taking lead harpooner position.

"Heave, crew! Let's away!"

"Aye—"

"Aye sir!"

"Aye." Isaiah was nearly breathless from the unexpected rush of being hustled into the whaleboat, but he eased his shoulders, putting his back into it. The ship strained against the waves, bumping below them with sudden chops and gutters. Isaiah dared a glimpse back at the *Merciful*, sitting heavily off their aft, with the crew made minuscule on the deck by the distance, and growing smaller by the minute. The ship was a child's toy bobbing in a wash bin far too big for it.

"Spout sighted to the south-east!" Hendricks shouted toward the fore. "Make hard for starboard, we've got to cut her off before she gets too far!"

Isaiah couldn't draw his attention away from the *Merciful*. There was an odd, cloudy-looking splotch of inky shadow steadily growing underneath the ship itself, sprawling larger than any natural-cast shadow could have done in broad daylight. He swallowed hard and tore his gaze away from the murk under the waves, and tried, *tried* not to think of the Bellamy-shaped shadow that had watched him on the deck.

The crew pounded the oars against the waves, hauling hard. Isaiah's back strained, and the rest of the crew grunted and some let out yells of strain. Hendricks scrambled to the small topsail attached to the boat, and a billowing gust of wind loosed it in the right direction. The wind was with them and the small ship surged forward faster than they ever could have rowed, toward the creature, gust after sudden gust.

"*There!* Another spout, careful!" Bellamy hollered from the bow and as soon as he'd said it a burbling tower of spray emerged from the depths not twenty yards from the boat, running high above their head and blowing away off their starboard side and glistening in the sun. "Hendricks, angle to port, I won't be caught by her head again!"

"Aye! Angle fore and to port, crew—" Toole called back.

"Clear away the track then, boom's heading 'round!" Sulaimi shouted.

"Loosing sail—watch out!" Hendricks yelled. The crew responded with a chorus of 'ayes' and Isaiah ducked out of way of the boom in time for it to swing over his head. Morrow grabbed a rope to gather it up again and they advanced close, with Hendricks holding them about the upper part of the creature's body. Sure enough, ten yards away from the whaleboat, a massive, shuddering shape shifted below the surface and swiped impossibly wide fins, about to propel itself away from them. With a grace belying his stature and faster than lighting, Bellamy hefted the wood-and-iron harpoon in one hand, muttering words below his breath as his eyes trained on the whale.

"BRACE, men!" He shouted.

One arm tensed back, taut as a bowstring. Isaiah blinked, and the harpoon was gone. With a precise splash, Bellamy had buried it deeply into the creature's head.

The sea churned hard. The whale thrashed and the mechanism holding the rope end of the harpoon to the boat went taut and strained. They all rocked heavily starboard.

The cable that was set to unspool did, with a rapidity that took Isaiah aback. The line hissed and whizzed as the whale ran and rolled away from the impact. Out and away from the boat it pulled, faster than any wind.

"*Morrow, after that sail!*" Hendricks shouted. The canvas was taking a hard battering and was strung taut as a drum, the force of the whale's attempted escape yanking them further and further from the ship.

"Let 'er run herself out!"

"How long *for*?!"

"As long as it takes!" Bellamy set his jaw hard as the creature pulled.

The rope strained, and the waves whizzed by faster than Isaiah had ever seen them. His skin prickled. Sulaimi's eyes were wild and excited, even as they worked to bring in the oars and batten down all of the stores. Hendricks had pulled in the rudder and was hard at work lashing the sail to itself.

"Eyes up, lads—Bellamy let that line *be*!" She shouted over the sound of the rushing water.

The whale boat flew at an astonishing rate, skipping over wave caps and zig-zagging left and right. Bellamy kept a hand on the rope, the taut line straining against the creature. The whale would slow, then pull hard to port, then hard to starboard, would slow and suddenly speed up until, finally, the boat reached an almost dead stop.

"To pikes! She's rolling!" Bellamy called out from his point of observation on the bow, while Toole let loose a continual stream of curses.

Bellamy grabbed a heavy hold on the suddenly-slack line once more, and hauled, back straining until the line retracted quickly. The whale surfaced, jaws open, and a tidal wave of water sent the boat crashing sideways.

"PIKES, at her side—"

No sooner had Morrow and Sulaimi moved to spear the creature than its massive mouth emerged once more. With a thunderous SNAP that echoed in Isaiah's gut, the whale made to bite at the boat with ivory teeth, missing the whaleboat by mere inches, the resulting wave of water drenching them all. One stab, then another, and the whale was bleeding thick red, blood from where the pikes had speared her blubber.

She breached, rolling to her far side, thrashing like a bug being burnt in the sun, and her roll rocked the boat to the other side and Isaiah saw the churn of the depths rising up almost to meet him and this is how he would die—

"LEAN, ALL!"

—And with a yell from Hendricks his body took over where his mind had absolutely failed him, and he threw himself over to the near-vertical side of the boat and the sea receded before his eyes and the whale was dying this time, surely—

"Let spirit leave you!" Sulaimi yelled with a desperate ferocity, stabbing into the whale once again with the full weight of their body into it.

The whale shuddered, falling into a desperate, shallow rocking motion.

It was a ghostly reflection of their prior fight, and the creature slowly, deliberately, grew still. It kept breathing, a hollow, shuddering, whistle coming from the hole at the top of its head where it took air. The skin of the beast was slick with near-purple blood and half submerged in the water.

"You speared 'er first," Toole intoned. "Send 'er to death."

Bellamy, unhooking the harpoon head from where it was attached to the rope itself, took up a spear, and deliberately, assuredly, plunged it into the side of the creature's skull. The whale's bloodied eye rolled to fix Bellamy with a cold, hard stare of raw, unfiltered hatred.

He gasped and, with the rope still in his hands, the whale dove down, down, dragging him with it.

Bellamy disappeared below the waves without so much as a scream.

CHAPTER EIGHT

THE SUDDEN LOSS of weight and the ripples from the place where the whale had dived set them swaying. The rocking slap of the waves against the sides of the boat was the only sound.

"Gods above . . . " Sulaimi said hoarsely, frozen in place.

"He—he's . . . " Morrow stuttered, as their pike dropped to the deck with a clatter.

" . . . Gone," Isaiah said, close to a whisper. The sun was setting beyond them, nearly touching the horizon.

"Get a weighted line down there! NOW!" Hendricks commanded with no small amount of panic in her, and Toole scrambled to knot a net weight to the end of a length of rope.

Isaiah could hear him praying under his breath as he heaved the weighted line, and peered over the side of the whaleboat. It disappeared with a splash, just as Bellamy's had.

"We pray to Lord of the Deep Tides return our brother to us— ferry back the soul of one Simon Bellamy from where he's been taken, let the gods below and above bring him safe from the water . . . " His words blended together to Isaiah's ear. All he could hear was the rushing of his own heartbeat in his head, as if someone had wadded up his ears with cotton. The water rippled as the line continued down, reaching no bottom.

"Belay that," Hendricks said. They halted the rope and waited at the spot where Bellamy had been pulled below, all five sets of eyes trained on the surface of the water. The sun crossed over choppy horizon and below the waves, to the underworld, and they dared not move as the light fast dimmed over the edge of the sea.

The shadow of the tattooed eye split in two that he'd scried the night previous was painted in bold, dark stripes in his mind and

Isaiah wanted nothing more than to scream and rave as if he truly *was* going mad. The reality of it was much, much worse.

"We . . . We'll be needing lamps soon," Sulaimi said, tentative to break the silence.

After a long beat, Hendricks sighed quietly, and nodded. "Right," she said. "Fetch up the line."

"No, *wait*." Isaiah said. "It's only been a bit and what if—"

"Chase, don't," Morrow interjected.

"Did you see him surface anywhere?" Hendricks asked. Isaiah couldn't summon up a response, and shook his head.

" . . . We head back," she said with a grim finality. She ducked her face away from his, and set about lighting one of the few lamps they had. He could have sworn he saw her scrubbing away tears.

It was too dark to see whether the shadow below the boat was still there, but as they rowed the whaleboat back to the ship, Isaiah felt sure that it hadn't been a trick of his imagination. He felt observed, watched.

Instead, the very tangible shadow of Captain Coffin loomed above them, stretching long and terrifying above the crewmembers. He rested an elbow on one of the lights before him and he scanned the boat, eyes immediately widening at the absence of Bellamy and a whale carcass in tow.

Lanterns had been lit on the deck beyond, enough for Isaiah to tell that the crew was still milling about in wait. They had watched them tear off toward the infernal whale but had not seen Bellamy towed into oblivion.

"Miss Hendricks." Coffin turned to address her as she slunk from the boat. "Let the crew stow the whaleboat. Then I'll need a full report on what in *all infernal hell happened*."

"Aye Captain," she said grimly. Sharpe eyed her from his position at Coffin's side.

"Hands, stow aft!" Sharpe called out, eyes trained on Coffin. "Morrow, Chase, Toole, Sulaimi—be sure to eat something before next watch. There should be rations still below at the mess."

Coffin gave a curt nod toward the first mate, and stalked back far to the quarterdeck, with Hendricks trailing miserably in his wake.

Isaiah clambered onto the deck and quickly made his way below, past the mess hall, hands and arms weak. He nearly tripped down the stairs to the bunks, eyes of sundry other crewmembers following him as he went.

"Chase?"

" . . . Where's Bellamy?"

"Chase what's—"

He caught himself ducking his head to avoid them as he went. The image of Bellamy falling head-first into the waves was playing over and over behind his eyes. Again and again, his body disappeared, towed by the half-killed whale. The shadow of the man trailing down, until the green-blue depths gulped him down whole, like some sick actor re-enacting a grotesque stage play into infinity.

Toole's prayer to the god that held the deep tides and all the creatures that resided there had done nothing. Less than nothing, even. Isaiah's head throbbed as he sank down to the floor. Bellamy had sat there not two days ago and rambled onto him about death being always on their heels, about how he was surely protected because of the inked eye staring unblinkingly out from the back of his neck. He'd been so certain, and it was as though Isaiah's vision had taken his certainty to twist into some kind of perverse joke.

He pressed the heels of his hands up to his eyes until fuzzy bright dots appeared behind his eyelids. They fluttered for a moment, before adhering together, forming the shape of Bellamy's corpse descending. The way he went head first, tugged thoughtlessly by the dead, not-dead creature.

Isaiah had seen the dark cloud-like shape below the *Merciful*, but he had just put it out of his mind. He hadn't said a thing to Bellamy, nor to Hendricks. It was a bad omen he'd kept to himself. But something within him whispered that even if he'd alerted the others, they might not have seen it either. Or believed him. And then what?

But Bellamy was still dead, leagues below the surface and Hendricks was likely taking the blame even though it hadn't been her doing, even though Bellamy should have *known* better than to detach the line before the creature was stone dead—

Isaiah's eyes burned where he'd pressed his grimy hands to his face. Tears had wet them, and he hadn't taken notice as to when they'd began. Slowly, the other deckhands filtered in after they'd eaten, but he couldn't think to rouse an appetite for his own rations. The sounds of the crew faded from rowdy post-dinner conversation to second-hand recountings of what had happened on the hunting boat. He tried to keep out of sight.

Toole and Morrow made their way past his bunk, talking in hushed voices. When things fell to silence, he wiped his face, righted himself, and crept down to the brig with his untouched dinner.

The man was sitting up this time. Fully awake, black-brown eyes shining like wet obsidian in the dark and trained on Isaiah.

"I thought you'd forgotten all about me."

Isaiah hadn't noticed before just how widely the man's irises extended. They seemed to chew the light hungrily.

"Why would I have forgotten, exactly?" Isaiah replied, placing the tray in the slot under the bars.

"Well, you've been kept busy, haven't you? Doing all sorts of things."

Isaiah paused, taking stock of him. He seemed . . . focused. More so than before.

"Yes. Another man died today." The shadow from the scrying bucket flashed across his memory.

"Oh?" He spoke with the matter-of-fact tone of somebody who'd already been told some piece of perfectly mundane news, but was making the polite pretense of ignorance, so as to not offend. As if Isaiah had told him that they were due for rain, and he'd already read about the weather.

The thought made him see red. "Oh? That's all you have to say, is *oh*?"

"My apologies. For your loss," he said, not a trace of distress in his voice. The man wasn't being shy about taking stock of Isaiah, either, and was looking him over with what might've been called curiosity.

Isaiah felt his pulse quicken. "He was the one who helped cut you out from that whale where we found you."

"How did he die?"

"He was drowned. By a whale, on a hunt."

"Is this not a whaleship?"

"Yes, but that's—"

"These things are known to happen, are they not?"

"He was *experienced*. A good, solid harpooner, one of our best."

"I'm sure he was," the man replied, cocking his head to one side. He eyed Isaiah through a gap in his curls. "The only thing that seems to be certain is that such creatures *are* unpredictable."

Isaiah leaned back against the wall opposite the bars in stunned silence. "You're a bastard."

"Well, look at it this way. Now nobody will bother you about where you go at night, or what sorts of things you happen to do."

Isaiah's blood ran like ice. " . . . How did you know that?"

The man gestured skyward, up through the wooden boards which composed both the brig's ceiling as well as the floor of the orlop deck. "I heard."

"That's *not possible*."

"Isaiah." The man fixed him with a stern look. "A whale ship is a noisy, weak little charnel house, much more so than you might like to think."

Isaiah exhaled hard, scrambling to get a hold of himself. "You *can't* have heard that conversation. Not from all the way down here." The image of the man standing uncannily still against the rolling waves of that first, brutal storm flashed across his mind.

"I would greatly appreciate it if you would stop pretending that you're just a humble, stupid sailor, yourself," the man said, exasperated.

In that moment he wanted nothing more than to reach through the bars and move a long curl out of his eyes. He just wanted to see him plain, to really get a look at him. The next moment, however, something shifted in the man's face, his eyes narrowed and he leaned close to the bars.

" . . . That'll be your Captain."

Isaiah sprung up, his already-churning stomach working itself into instantaneous knots. His eyes darted from the end of the narrow, bare hall to the equally bare brig and back again. "I was just bringing you your rations. That's all."

"Yes, because you're *such* an excellent liar." The uncannily pointed barb did not have time to land, because the sound of irregular, booted footsteps had begun to creak toward the hold door.

He was turning to the door handle, when it swung open, slamming to the opposite wall. Coffin swayed where he stood, on the other side of it.

"Chase?" The fermented, rank scent of liquor emanated from him, and his regular brass-buttoned coat had been sloppily thrown over a nightshirt and pants. He blinked slowly. "What's . . . get gone!"

"Sir, I was just bringing his rations like you said—"

"I don't give a bleeding fuck. He doesn't eat food." Even knock-down drunk and middle-aged, Coffin was tall and wiry-strong. And when he grabbed Isaiah by the front of his shirt and threw him back to the doorframe, it was enough to rattle him. When he looked up, the man from the belly was holding on to the bars nearest to him, an expression of raw disgust on his face.

"*Get out* and don't speak of this, b'fore I charge Stowe to flog you for it."

Coffin slammed shut the door to the brig just as loudly as he had opened it, leaving Isaiah on the opposite side. The door was solid wood, but sound-proof it wasn't. Catching his breath, he heard a loud clang of something hitting the iron bars. Heart staccato sharp against his ribs, he pressed his ear to the crack in the door.

" . . . What'd . . . what'd you *do*?" Coffin half-slurred.

There was a beat of silence before the cage bars were rattled. Presumably for emphasis.

"You damn well did *something*! It's already begun and you won't say a *thing* about it?!" The Captain bellowed as the cage bars shook again. A fallow stretch of silence followed.

"*Curse you*. Curse you all the way to hell and back again." Coffin's voice leaked defeat. "I'll have them toss you back, we . . . we'll turn back as soon as the tide allows—"

"You know that's not how this ends." A sudden draft of frigid air pushed through the crack in the door and a shiver ran through him. The rough, echoing voice that emitted from the other side was not Coffin's. "*Let me out of this cell, and you will know exactly what a curse can feel like.*"

The words snaked into his ear and curdled something deep, deep within his brain and an ice-spike of terror plunged through him. Isaiah lunged back, only thinking to get *away* from the thing on the other side of the door.

He did not remember falling asleep, but morning came again seemingly as soon as his eyes closed, with the sun beating down relentless and unceasing on the *Merciful*. He crawled out of bed, and breakfast was had; the news of Bellamy's death finally reached those who hadn't been awake to see the hunting party's return. Hendricks and Morrow had, apparently, taken it upon themselves to sort through the majority of his belongings in the early hours of the morning, and pulled Isaiah aside to assist them. He obliged, silently, and flat-out refused to think on the man listening from all the way below, or the bizarre voice answering Coffin last night.

They separated out a packet of letters to his mother and younger siblings (to be dropped off at next port, along with a notice of his death and their inheritance of his debt accrued on the journey), a finely detailed cut-away diagram of a whale's head, well worn and well observed, and a few spare tools which were less worn than usual and might fetch some coin back home. A battered ring with some initials engraved inside, which none of them could discern the origin of, and a small logbook with a jumble of half-finished entries. The clothes not on his back when he'd been taken, and the small altar-coins he kept in his pack were to be sent down to join his body. It was commonly understood that anyone who passed at sea would need them in the next kingdom below.

It seemed so stupid, and superstitious, and downright foolish. And yet, he couldn't help but think that there was now no one who knew of his nighttime trips to the brig.

"Crew! Assembly, at three bells," Lice yelled with a mite less of her usual vitriol. "We're to have service." It was well past an acceptable hour by the time that Sharpe went to rouse the Captain. Morning duties were, for the most part, finished entirely and it was just odd to have a burial at midday—dawn or dusk were commonly known to be better times to send off someone's spirit.

Everyone scrubbed themselves as well as they could, given the circumstances, and gathered at midships. Coffin finally rolled out, barely dressed. He wore the same stained linen nightshirt as he'd worn the night previous, along with his same rumpled coat. Notably, he had deigned to add fresh pants, this time.

He cleared his throat, clasping his hands before him in prayer. He wavered slightly with the roll of the ship, and Isaiah had a feeling that if he were downwind, he'd be able to smell the liquor-soaked odor he'd caught last night. He looked frenetic.

"*Ahem.* Today we assemble to honor the life and sacrifice of one Master Simon Bellamy, Able seaman. A true whaler to the bone. May his spirit be commended to the Lords that Rule the Deep."

With a wave of his hand, he beckoned a crewmember forward, who presented the small bundle containing Bellamy's remaining possessions. The outside cloth wrapper had been inscribed with the curling sigils that signified the proper care of They That Takes Souls. He doubted that the captain had been the one to take the time to write them on the fabric.

"We commit this mortal soul to the endless, boundless depths, to travel far through . . . through the underworld and back to the ends of the earth," Coffin said. Isaiah glanced at Hendricks, who looked as if she was actively biting her tongue.

Coffin took up the bundle from the crewmember and held it aloft above the rail overboard. He held it overlong, staring at the meager remnants of Bellamy's life.

" . . . Let his soul find his body where it lies."

The crew repeated the line of prayer after him, seemingly in one voice, but Isaiah could feel his waver. The bundle hit the water with a splash that seemed too light to be carrying a soul with it.

CHAPTER NINE

DINNER PASSED SOBERLY. Isaiah's body felt as if he'd been strapped to the prow and run ragged by the waves, but his head was still buzzing with symbols and the dank smell of the rotting hold beneath their feet, and the way that the man from the belly had looked at him when he'd gone to speak to him and *gods* knew what else. He shoveled down his rations as quickly as was decent, as he didn't trust himself to make small talk with the others. Luckily, Hendricks hadn't said a word before the meal, and had barely opened her mouth during, except to rebuff a few of Fallon's less sensitive questions about the expedition. He'd left them in a huff, Morrow had wished them a good evening, and Isaiah hadn't known what to say to her in the meantime.

Neither of them were particularly skilled at addressing the finer nuances of grief, and even if Isaiah had been able to think of something skillful and conciliatory to say, he had a feeling that Coffin's odd, stunted eulogy had shot down any chance of comfort.

The idea of going off to sleep, and to another potential dream, was not entirely appetizing. Isaiah decided it was better to take precautions.

"I'm off to watch."

"But I'm supposed to be on," Hendricks protested.

"Not if I go instead," he said, picking up a plate and utensils as he went.

Something in her expression shifted away from solemnity, and she shot him a brief, tight-lipped smile that was nearly grateful. "Keep a weather eye out then."

She lingered at the dinner table, alone. He hadn't even thought to ask what she'd told Coffin about Bellamy's death. Or what she could have said that had driven him to the bottle so hard, and to interrogate the man from the belly besides. *No, to plead with him. But over what?*

There was a thread, real or imagined, that tied the man in the brig with Bellamy's death, and the Captain had caught the frayed end of it. He had drunkenly tried to pull it loose, and failed.

So why had the man nearly admitted it so *easily* to Isaiah? Then again, hadn't Isaiah been fed knowledge from the other realms?

Didn't Isaiah know things he shouldn't?

His head spun as he crossed up topside from the orlop. Álvarez and Morrow were chatting amongst themselves on the other side of the mainsail. He grabbed his watch-light and held it still and quiet on its hook, the hot metal nearly singeing his fingertips.

"Calder's passed out cold," Morrow said, from just out of view.

"Is he?" Álvarez said. "How long?"

"Oh, I dunno. Few hours at least." Isaiah slowed his footfalls, walking carefully. Quietly.

"The real question is, how's he going to look when he's woken up?"

"How d'you mean?"

"Monteiro had mentioned that the end of the arm was really badly infected. Because of how it had to come off, they had to split a joint and—"

"Eugh. I don't need to know."

"They're just bones. You've got 'em too, y'know."

"Yeah, inside my skin. Not outside. Or detached from one another," he said, distaste clear. Morrow guffawed, and Isaiah could hear them slap some part of him in jest.

"Bones aside, the end of it got *black*. Like, tar-black, and had these . . . I dunno. Bumps on it."

"What, like infection?"

"Look, give me some credit." Morrow said, affronted. "I may not be fully fledged like Monteiro but I damn well know what a bad wound looks like. This ain't it."

Isaiah realized that he'd been frozen in place. Demir was eyeing him strangely from the far side of the deck, and he quickly bent down to pick at an imaginary splinter in his foot.

"What is it then?"

"That's just the question."

A beat of silence, and Isaiah found the end of his imagined splinter, creeping sideways to peer off the *Merciful*'s port side. The voices were more distant, but he could still make them out.

"What was that?"

"Never you mind. Sure it's the next watch coming soon, but I didn't see anyone." Álvarez replied. "The arm . . . can't come off further, can it?"

"Certainly not. Not unless they want to saw through the long bone, which Monteiro doesn't much like to do. And if she won't do it I certainly won't either," they replied.

"Ugh. Can't much blame you."

"Point is, the bumps aren't part of the muscle. They shift around a bit," Morrow said. "Not much, mind you, but you can wiggle them around."

"Souls above." There was a wet thwap as Álvarez spat over his shoulder.

"Aye. Monteiro won't let me touch it. Not that I much want to."

Isaiah felt his arm prickle, and he instinctively grabbed at the place where his elbow joined his upper and lower arms. He let his watch-light creak a little and cleared his throat. Heavy-footed, he walked back down the deck as if for the first time, and came upon the two. They separated, and Álvarez glared at him.

"Where's Hendricks? It's her watch," he said.

"Can't get to sleep. I took her shift instead," Isaiah replied. He let Morrow cross down the deck past him, and Álvarez leaned back on his elbows on the railing. Isaiah couldn't tell where his gaze landed—his eyes were distant, staring at some invisible point off the opposite rail. What he was looking for, Isaiah couldn't say.

"I'm sorry."

"For what?"

"About Bellamy. Captain didn't give much of a tribute." His mouth twisted into a grimace.

"Aye. That he didn't." Isaiah stiffened his shoulders, beginning to make a round. It hadn't been two days past that Álvarez had been more than happy to take advantage of the argument between him and Bellamy, and the idea of making nice curdled his stomach. He couldn't quite tell what had made the two friendly when

Bellamy was alive, and he wasn't keen to find out now that he was dead. " . . . If you'll 'scuse me."

He gripped the lamp tightly and moved down-ships from Álvarez, who faded backwards into the shadows of the mainsail until he couldn't see him any longer.

Isaiah didn't loosen his grip until Álvarez's shadowy form disappeared from the corner of his vision. The waves lapped at the side of the ship, scraping their way against the wood, no doubt leaving trails and rivulets of salt water on the *Merciful*. He wondered if the water could tell that it was slowly breaking down the ship. Rotting timber and hull alike with mold, reaching through with insistent fingers to scrape away at the food necessary for their survival. The stores, diminished as they were, could only last so long. Likewise, Coffin seemed to be breaking down just as badly as the stores, in the grip of something far stronger than him.

The man, where he sat at nobody's mercy, deep inside the iron-clad brig, doubtless couldn't see a thing. He would only be able to hear the beating of the tide. Perhaps he would press his ear against the curved wooden wall that made up one side of his cell, hoping to be reunited with it once more. Perhaps he slept the sleep of the dead.

Instead of mulling further, Isaiah tore his eyes away from the endless water, and did another round, and hoped nothing would follow him through the night.

Besides his brief brush past Morrow and Álvarez, not a single other soul entered his line of sight on the watch. The moon tracked its incremental arc overhead, and time slid over itself as slippery as freshly peeled fish skin.

He had made a critical error. Minutes, hours spent just *standing* on deck, waiting, watching for something to creep out of the darkness, was worse than just going to sleep.

Blinked into the endless, velvety blue-blackness, he felt helpless against the centripetal motion of his own thoughts. Had Coffin been willing to turn around, to go home, every single one of them would have been fully burdened by their contracted debt to the shipping company, and less than half a hold of whale oil to boot to ameliorate the damage. The *Merciful*'s reputation would be ruined. Coffin's family would no doubt cloister him away somewhere until he could be shunted out on a different ship, take the financial losses and sink the company's money into some other hunting voyage. Speculate with people's lives as they were prone to do.

But crewmembers' livelihoods would be left in shambles if they *all* came back with money owing to the company, the Captain's failure writ permanent in an inky contract that they had all signed, that *all* whalers signed: Should collection of goods fail to meet projected numbers, debt of speculated funds lost on the voyage were to be distributed equally amongst those at fault for said losses.

Isaiah pictured walking through the door to his mother's house, empty-handed at 25, poorer than when he'd left and seeing his dead father in his dreams, half on his way to losing his mind entirely. The thought was too sharp-edged to linger on.

That was if they would even make it back home. If there was enough food to last them all through the long, uncertain return trip.

Isaiah hadn't realized that he'd been just standing stock-still, until a gust of cold ocean spray hit him across the side of the face. Shaking himself out of the cycle of worry as best he could, he walked a round on the still, quiet deck, the creaking of the rigging his only accompaniment to his footsteps.

There was another option, of course.

He had to know something of the situation that had taken hold of the ship. *Not* knowing, waiting for things to fall apart at the root when he could be using the gifts his father had accidentally given him, felt unconscionable.

He did say that I would need to pay attention, Isaiah thought as he hunted down a wide bucket and a length of rope, and drew up a serviceable amount of seawater. The knocking of the pail against the side of the ship seemed like gunshots in the night, and he cringed, grabbing it up as soon as he could reach. He tried not to consider the idea that the man below might somehow, against all logic, be listening.

He scooped up a handful of seawater in his cupped hands, breathing in the brine, and breathing out a quick, whispered plea into the scrying water.

"What you let me see in sleep, Gods Deep and Gods Above, let me see in waking. As we sail the line between your worlds, show me . . . show me . . . " He paused. "Show me something. *Anything of how this will end.*"

The salt water ran down his face, and Isaiah hissed as it stung his eyes. He faced the water, eyes slipping in and out of focus, the shapes made by the ripples thrumming before him.

The images were not loose shadows, this time. They were painted in crystalline black and white and yellow strokes, as lamplight and moonlight cut into the dark water. He tried to let his eyes relax and take them in, but the ripples cohered into a body with a line rising from it—

It was a man, hanging. The outline of his head had rolled to one side, his profile silhouetted clearly. The body dropped, and the ripples warped, became unnaturally angular. The body wasn't a body, but a casket.

A coffin.

Isaiah gasped and overturned the bucket. He felt sick to his stomach, as if he'd been pulled suddenly upwards from a great height. The cold water ran down the deck in rivulets, and he grabbed hold of the railing closest to him.

"I didn't mean how . . . how . . . " *How the Captain will end.* The thought popped into his head, in a quiet voice not quite his own. *You did say anything.* It seemed as true and as obvious as the sun rising in the morning and setting at night. *A red sky at morning signals storms, you have ten fingers, and Captain Erasmus Coffin of the whaleship Merciful is set to die. And who will believe you?*

Sitting in the vision felt soporific, like if he'd wanted to remain there, he could have easily seen more. As if he could have sat staring into another realm for hours, days. It was profoundly unsettling.

Hendricks had only spoken occasionally of the aftermath of Bullet Briggs' suicide onboard the *Dolphin*. They had been run aground on a sparse spit of island some thousand-odd miles from the nearest merchant port in Steer-Jaw Bay, and there was a struggle. Some of the crew had stayed on the island. They had been content with waiting for another vessel to pick them up rather than submit to the new captain, who was, apparently, ready to send them through a trial by fire and extend their hunt out by another two years to bolster his new captaincy, so that he could return to the whaling company like a conquering emperor.

Some stayed with the *Dolphin* and its new captain, and those that did disappeared into the waves along with the *Dolphin* itself, and whatever take she'd been carrying. Lice and Hendricks had been among those that took a third option—Isaiah had heard Sulaimi gossiping that they'd stolen a hunting boat and made for the nearest port. It was rumored that Lice would have to spend the entirety of her career making up for the debt incurred and trust lost by the theft, and by their survival. Hendricks hadn't spoken about it at all.

The death of a Captain, even one as severe as Coffin, was nothing to laugh at.

As quietly as he could, Isaiah neatly replaced the bucket and rope. He curled up next to the lantern, scrubbed the last of the salt water from his face, and tried not to let a tidal wave of panic overtake him.

By the time his watch ended, Isaiah's body was giving up, unable to hold out on sleep any longer. He left things off for the next watch and staggered down below decks just as the bell was being rung for the early shift. In a daze, he clambered into his bunk, rolling over like a dog to get comfortable as many times as felt right. His body gave up on him and fell to dreaming quicker than seemed possible.

His father did not appear this time. Instead, he found himself back on a boat and alone, far from the *Merciful*. Nearly alone, that was.

A woman was at the tiller of the tiny boat, decked out in wealthy captain's garb. A red, high-necked jacket with sparkling brass buttons concealed her features and a long-barreled pistol with an intricately etched handle knocked at her hip. She stared toward the horizon, head turned, and Isaiah didn't want to see more, he *shouldn't*, it wasn't *right*. He braced himself hard against the wood, but his hands found no real purchase on the damp surface as the panic held back in waking hours rose up to the surface.

Wake up, Chase. Wake up. Wake up, WAKE UP WAKE UP—
The boat was angular in its sides, and there was barely room
for the both of them. It was made of a lacquered wood, nothing like
the standard rough-hewn board that the boats were made of. The
interior was padded with a cloth lining, which struck Isaiah as
exceptionally odd. By the captain's booted feet, there was an odd,
boxy pillow.

Isaiah's mind caught up with what his eyes had recognized all
at once. He and the Captain had not been sitting too long inside
walls of the bizarre, tiny, dream-boat when it dawned on him that
it was, in fact, a long, floating casket. The vessel stopped, and the
woman's slender hand fell from the tiller. She scratched at the back
of her head, below her brown hair, and didn't turn to face Isaiah.

"I find this whole scenario exceptionally ironic. Don't you find
it funny? Knowing all this. All this pointless, futile cruelty."

" . . . No. No, Miss." *Wake up, DAMN you.*

"The thing about irony is," She said in a raspy alto, matter-of-
fact. "That it tends to only be truly *funny* from a bird's eye view."

Suddenly, a flicker of motion caught Isaiah's eye. It was dozens
of bundles, one bobbing to the surface after another, wrapped
tightly in canvas of different sizes, different shapes. Holding the
sum of the crew's existence.

"What a waste of life."

He suddenly knew he wasn't supposed to look in her face. He
had a feeling he shouldn't, no matter what she said, and the sliver
of panic had turned into a yawning chasm and *why couldn't he just
WAKE UP ALREADY,* except his hand stung where he'd cut it days
and days ago like he'd just drawn blood. It *burned*, and there was
something hard and round and nubbly in his hand, in the cut, just
under where the skin was and she was already turning to face him.

In her head, there was a gaping hole cleaving the left eye
socket, and he realized with a dawning, raw terror that she had
been scratching at the place where a bullet had exited.

He dove from the boat, mouth open to scream as he hit the
water, and Isaiah woke up coughing.

CHAPTER TEN

A **WHOLE DAY** passed by, and Isaiah didn't see the Captain once during his own comings and goings about the *Merciful*. Seemingly, no one had; Fallon claimed to have spotted the cook taking him rations at mealtime, but there was no real way to be sure. They all went about their duties, as best they could.

For his part, Isaiah avoided returning below to the brig at all. The nightmare and the ill omen he had scried hung over him like an axe inches over his neck. He felt the wholly irrational urge to run back to the officer's quarters and hammer on the captain's door, just to elicit some kind of response, to make certain that his vision hadn't immediately come true.

The next morning, another whale was scouted at least a league off in the distance. Coffin was called to direct the hunt, but he still didn't appear. Sharpe scrambled to command, but the haphazard nature of the call and of the crew's less than orderly assembly rendered the effort useless. The creature disappeared over the horizon well before the *Merciful* could give chase.

Resetting tools and steadying the sails once again after such a rushed unfurling meant more work, and less time to distract from stray thoughts that slipped in when Isaiah was doing manual labor. Such as what in all the realms the woman in the dream had *meant*. The thought swirled in his mind round and round like a whirlpool.

The route they'd taken in the attempt to hunt down the stray whale had chewed into their regular circuit, biting a wide gap into their plans. With Coffin still absent, Sharpe had done the best he could to mitigate the blunder. It could be corrected, Demir had insisted. It would just take a while. But everyone knew that on their return journey, toward the end, when they all were sick and tired of each other and ready to be free of the water forever, those scant days and wave-born miles whiled away chasing after a bum prize would be worth their weight in gold. Hendricks was grim, as she notified them that rations were very well likely to be cut in the end. Nothing to be done about it, Coffin had already made the choice for them when he'd thrown that good stock of fish over for no damn reason. If they weren't hungry now, they would be later—and you couldn't eat whale oil.

Isaiah could barely hear her words through the thick cloud of anxiety that wrapped around his head like a prickly woolen blanket. The image of the hanging body in the scrying pool lingered in the back of his thoughts, right behind every distraction he tried to ply his brain with.

That they'd heard no news about Coffin's condition made it all the worse, and a sense of desperation mounted silently aboard the ship.

"We'll be in deep waters yet," Sulaimi said.

"What's that?" Fallon called from where he'd been scraping away at barnacles off the port side of the *Merciful*'s hull.

"They *said* we'll be in deep waters yet." Isaiah called down, careful not to lean on the spot of the railing he'd been lacquering.

"How d'you mean?" Liu said from the other end of the railing. She'd almost begun to catch up to him, and Isaiah painted faster. "Don't be so cryptic!"

"Aye, Sharpe thought that we already were at lower latitudes, which was why that other bloody—whale—" Fallon paused to chip heavily at the shells. "Escaped us. Still got the worst to go."

"No, just the opposite," Sulaimi answered for their benefit. "It's why the whale was alone. We've not reached them yet."

"Don't be stupid." Fallon said, looking up to frown in their direction. "Sharpe doesn't know worth a—"

"You're wrong. And if we're to find more, we go where the whole families of them are," Liu said. "It'll get easier."

"Well, it's his problem now," Sulaimi appended loudly, cutting her off. "Whether we've a long ways to go or not."

"I'm sure he was just doing what he thought was right," Liu said.

" . . . If that's true, we're all in much worse trouble than we thought," Isaiah said.

"We've *been* in trouble," Fallon said. "This whole blasted hunt. We've been in nothing *but* fucking trouble." Isaiah heard the wet spatter of Fallon spitting over his shoulder, and muttering a word of a prayer below him.

"Hendricks has been getting to you. Her talk of running out of rations comes out of *fear*," Sulaimi said boldly, leaning dangerously close to part of railing Liu was covering with wet lacquer. "Fear'll burn a hole in your head if you let it."

"Sometimes there's things to be afraid of," Isaiah said, shooting them a look down the line of the rail.

Sulaimi met his gaze wryly. "Lay in some tokens. Do your devotions to the gods below." They called downwards. "You won't be stolen away in the night, Chase! A little hardship's good for you!"

They all heard the hollow knock of Fallon rapping three times on the wooden hull, warding away the very idea of something stealing away *anyone* in the night.

Sulaimi was off belowdecks before Isaiah could shoot back a response. He'd barely finished the lower half of the rail before Lice's voice clanged upwards from the orlop deck.

"All who were up and about with Calder while he was still working! Monteiro needs you, one at a time!" Her gingery head popped up, gesturing at Isaiah. "Chase, rouse Fallon. Him in particular."

"What's that?" Fallon shouted. "Chase, pull me up!"

Isaiah sighed, hauling up the rope that held his makeshift bench in place, and Fallon hopped off, still speckled all-over with black paint chips, salt, and crusts of barnacle bits. He looked a mess.

"What?" he said. Isaiah must've been giving him a look. "Oh, don't pull that face, they were half a dozen layers thick down there," he said. He laughed and tried to mop himself off, to very little effect.

"Monteiro wants us, you in particular. Something about Calder."

"Alright. Well, age before beauty," he said, holding his hand out with a flourish. Snorting at him, Isaiah ducked belowdecks.

By the time he reached the surgeon's quarters, he could already hear Hendricks' voice emanating from within the examination room.

"Any pain, shooting in your limbs? Do your joints hurt at all?" Monteiro asked.

"No, Doctor."

"Headaches, blurred vision? Metallic taste on your tongue?"

"No, not anything like that." There was a pause. "I . . . I've been having problems remembering things. Since Bellamy passed."

"What sort of things?" Monteiro probed, crisp and immediate. As Isaiah approached, he could hear the scratching of something being written down.

"The days are . . . I dunno. Blurring together. I can't really tell when I get up to wake and when I go to sleep." Hendricks continued, "I do things but I'm not sure how I got to doing them."

There was a brief pause. "If you are having trouble completing your duties . . . "

"No, *no*. I'm not."

"Are you certain?" Monteiro asked.

"'Course I'm certain, doctor." Isaiah recognized the tone well. He could tell a stonewalling when it was happening.

"And you were on the *Dolphin*. On her last trip."

"What does that have to do with it?" There was a low note of fear in her voice.

"Records are retained when the company experiences any sort of . . . loss of staff. In case of any need for an investigation or post-mortem review of the losses."

There was a beat of silence before Hendricks spoke again.

"I . . . I got off at port mid-hunt. Before."

"Before what, Miss Hendricks?"

There was another pause. " . . . Before the change in Captaincy." Her tone was tinged with a shade of bitterness Isaiah had never heard before.

"There's no record of your departure here."

"Isn't there?"

"And you experienced the same issue with your memory after Briggs' death."

"*No.*" There was another beat of silence, and the scratching. " ...No, *ma'am.*"

"I'm just trying to discern if this issue might cause similar problems aboard this ship," Monteiro said. "If so, I'd be obligated to report them back to the company."

"Of course. And there aren't," Hendricks replied.

"Well. If it does recur," the surgeon said, "I'd like you to come back and see me."

There was a rustling as Hendricks hopped from the examination bench.

"These things have been known to happen. When crew is lost suddenly," Monteiro continued. "Your mind is trying to protect you from the reality of the matter."

"You talk as if what's in my head's separate from me." Hendricks said.

"I do." Monteiro said, clipped. "And I'd advise you not to let what's in your head get too far away from you."

Hendricks emerged from Monteiro's quarters in a hurry, and startled at Isaiah's presence.

"Chase. You're up." She tossed a thumb over her shoulder at him, not making eye contact. He was certain that she realized he'd heard the surgeon's words, but she was gone down the hall, shoulders high about her ears before he could get a chance to flag her down. The doctor poked her head out of the canvas flap curtain, mouth pursed.

"Mr. Chase. Please do come in." With a rustle of cloth, she was gone, and Isaiah tentatively followed her.

The examination room, already usually the tidiest place on the *Merciful*, seemed even cleaner than it normally was, with a selection of white squares of linen covering various surfaces. There was a cauldron of still piping hot water, with surgical implements propped within. Monteiro returned to her perch atop a tall stool, glossy black hair pulled up tight, apron folded down neatly over her usual buttoned vest. The surgeon always gave off the impression that she was older than she was.

"Sit," she said, gesturing Isaiah toward a covered bench. "I've been charged with giving interviews to all those who came in contact with Calder recently." Her expression wasn't harsh, exactly. Just . . . chilly. He could feel her giving him a thorough visual once-over where he sat.

"Since he's sick, you mean."

"Since I've found an infecting agent at the site of his amputation," she said, taking up a pad of paper and graphite. "And as I'm the lucky soul who will be charged with cleaning up the problem, it behooves me to find the source and excise it before it spreads further, and endangers the rest of the crew." She didn't look up at him as she scratched a few notes in the pad.

"Right," Isaiah said. "I feel fine. Is Jerry doing alright? Is he—"

"Mr. Chase. Please leave the interviewing to me," she said, stopping him cold. She sighed for a moment. "He is not well. Hence my line of questioning."

Isaiah couldn't have put her at more than a handful of years older than his twenty-five, but something in the crispness of her tone put him right back in primary school. "Aye. Sorry, Doctor."

"Fret not, Mr. Chase. Most of those who've come in have expressed similar concerns. It seems Mr. Calder was—is not unpopular," she said, returning to her notepad. She was nearly speaking about him in the past tense. Isaiah was suddenly quite conscious of his fidgeting, and cast his gaze about the examination room for something to look at besides her.

"So. Have you had any pain anywhere in the past week or so? Muscle aches, bone or joint pain, metallic taste on your tongue?"

In the starkly tidy room, his eyes caught a series of brown glass jars lined up against the far wall. Instead of being filled with tonics, bandages, salve, and medicines as he'd expect, they were all empty.

All had blank paper labels on them, waiting to be filled with something.

"No, m'am."

"No warmth or fever, cold or stomach upset?"

He thought of the dream, of being trapped in the floating casket, of waking up sweating and gasping for breath. " . . . No."

"No headaches, images that aren't there, auditory hallucinations?"

"I . . . I'm sorry, what?"

"Auditory; meaning of the ear. Certainly you know what a hallucination is, Mr. Chase."

"No, no, I do. Sorry." The stark white and black outline of the tilted skull blazed in his memory. "I don't have any of those."

She shot him a look. " . . . You're certain, Mr. Chase?"

"Yes! Very certain."

"And you would inform me with all due haste if that were to change?" Monteiro's tone was incisive, honed to cut at him at a very precise angle.

"Of course, m'am."

"Have you been sleeping, Mr. Chase? You don't look particularly well-rested."

He tried to swallow the sudden lump in his throat, hard. " . . . As much as I'm able."

"And how much is that?"

"'Round half the night. Watch shift changing makes it difficult to stay asleep, most nights," he said, picking at a hangnail. He didn't dare look at her directly.

"Right," she said, in a way that implied he'd given the absolute wrong answer. "And this has always been the case, I assume."

"No, just . . . being on board, is all." The hangnail tugged at the edge of the bed, drawing a minuscule pinprick of blood. Monteiro scratched a note into her pad before peering over at him. "Bad dreams."

"And these are so bad they impede your sleep?"

"Not too often." He could tell he was edging up to something dangerous. His mother would wake him in the middle of the night, when he'd scream and cry out for help, or wake up stiff as a board, and tell him to never, *ever* speak of these things to anyone. His father had never told his own dreams to Isaiah at all, despite the fact that he could remember waking to hear his father's sobs and cries from his parents' bedroom. He had his mother's curls, and his father's dark circles under his eyes, and he knew that he'd been born with both. " . . . No more or less than most." He said, edging away from the precipice. "Am I free to go, Doctor?"

Monteiro set down her pencil and closed her notebook on top of it. She blinked placidly, and clasped her hands neatly over the notebook's leather cover.

"Yes, Mr. Chase. You are."

As he picked at the last of his food at dinner that evening, he decided to chance a return to the man from the belly.

Isaiah realized it was simpler to justify his curiosity as just doing the duty he was charged with before the captain's outburst. Coffin had said that the man didn't eat. How he could possibly know that was beyond him, but he decided not to take the risk of neglecting him, on the off chance that the man actually did need some kind of sustenance and Coffin was just being cruel.

He wrapped up some biscuit and salt meat carefully, trying to calm the churn of anxious anticipation that was only growing stronger by the minute. *Bellamy's gone. Nobody saw you scry. Who will know if you go find out what the hell he's done for Coffin to confront him like that?*

The brig was icy, as if the whole room had been permeated with the same rolling chill he'd felt when he'd eavesdropped through the crack in the door. The man was awake, kneeling neatly and facing the back wall. He'd threatened Coffin with a curse in that *voice*, and yet here he sat, pressing his forehead to the wooden bands running crossways across the breadth of the ship's inner wall. The sight was uncanny.

"Can you feel it?" Isaiah asked. "The water. Through the hull."

There was a lengthy pause, in which Isaiah approached the cell.

"Certainly. Can't you?" the man answered, not turning to look up at him. He could see raised lines through the worn and stained linen of his borrowed shirt. Old healed cuts and scars, certainly numbering in the dozens, scattered across his back. Through a gap in his curls, he could see an indented, angry line running around his neck, healed to a darker brown. As if someone had tried to unsuccessfully garrote him. Isaiah instinctively touched where the line would have been on his own throat.

"Not . . . not like that," he said. "Is it the way a fish feels water? The way an eel does, or a whale?"

"Hmn," the man said, finally twisting around to face Isaiah. "I suppose so," he answered, mouth twisting into a wry grin. It wasn't altogether distinct from the expression he'd worn when talking about Bellamy's death. It was the look of a man who only asked questions to which he knew the answer. "It doesn't hum to you like that?"

Isaiah considered. He supposed it *could*. Something about the sensation of it, especially when he'd scried, had a kind of vibration. A soft hum, separate from the regular motion of the waves, just as he'd said.

"Not exactly like that but . . . sort of." The question made him feel self-conscious, for some reason.

"How interesting," He seemed truly intrigued by him. "Most can't feel it at all."

Isaiah backpedaled slightly. "No, not like that, I just—"

The man sighed. "Come now. I wish you'd stop that."

Something about the man made him want to tell the truth. It was intensely frustrating. "I'll stop bullshitting when you do."

"Fine." The man was grinning again. "You tell me what you were doing the other night, I'll return the favor."

Even if he does try and sell me out to Coffin, odds are good that he won't believe him. If Coffin is bold enough to try and speak to him again.

"I . . . I have some strange dreams. Of things to come, sometimes." The truth came tumbling from him almost too easily, and fear rocketed up immediately to take its place. "But it's probably nothing, honestly, I don't put too much stock in it—"

He blinked. " . . . Things."

"I know it sounds insane."

"Not as insane as asking a man if he feels like an eel." The man's grin broadened, toothy in the dim light of the brig.

"And still not as insane as that man agreeing to it." He bit back, before reeling himself in. "Sometimes the dreams come true."

"Ah." The man's smile subsided, and he tilted his head. Considering. "Finally, some honesty."

"You haven't exactly given me much reason to be honest." Isaiah said, careful.

"I suppose not." He said, frowning lightly. "You wouldn't be the first I've heard of who had such . . . talents."

"What?" Isaiah blurted. "Who *else* have you heard of?!"

"Nobody you'd know. But where there are gods, there tend to be those who have ears open to them." He said, tapping his temple with his pointer finger. "I've heard of many such people."

"*Many?*"

"Without eyes to see or ears to hear, what'd be the point of speaking at all?" He replied, shrugging, as if that explained the matter. He stood, crossed the distance between them to peer down at Isaiah from between the cell bars. " . . . You thought you were the only one in the world." His tone was surprising. Gentle, even. Isaiah's heart beat hard in his chest.

"Aye."

The man reached through the bars, tilting his face up to him with a knuckle, and Isaiah froze. From this near a distance, he could see his pupils and irises, taking up a bit too much of the whites. He could see the faint blue-green veins around them, showing up a little bit too easily beneath his skin. The man's skin wasn't pale, but something about the quality of it made him seem translucent, as when you could see the places where bones had been in a fresh cut of fish. He found a tiny, curving scar running into the corner his top lip, pulling the skin in, a little. Isaiah did not think to flinch away.

"Were you lonely?" The man asked.

" . . . Aye," Isaiah replied, quietly, without realizing that it was the truth. The man's brow furrowed ever so slightly. As if he had been given sudden pause.

Isaiah didn't dare budge. "What do these other people do with their . . . visions? If they see something bad?"

He pressed his thumb to Isaiah's jaw, delicate as anything. "They tell those that would listen, I suppose," he said, eyes searching over Isaiah's face. What he was looking for, Isaiah couldn't tell. "But I'll warn you that once the gods have decided on a certain end, there's nothing above or below that can deter them from their purpose." The man let his hand fall back through the bars, and Isaiah very nearly chased after it. He was suddenly quite aware of the fact that it was his own spare tunic the man wore.

"What did you see? In this vision," he asked.

"I asked to be shown something of the end that's coming. Tried to scry it."

The man seemed fascinated. "Why might you do such a thing?"

"Because he's been absent from the crew since he came down here to see you. Something's happened. Or *about* to happen."

"And you overheard what he had to say that night, I take it."

"Of *course* I did," Isaiah said. "And I heard you threaten him in kind." The man's mouth opened, closed again.

"And what did you see?" he asked, no trace of the haughty assuredness that had colored his questions before.

He can't decipher exactly what's to come. Not like my father could, and not like I can.

What *did* he see? He saw a hanged man change into a casket. The fact that Coffin might one day die should have been no surprise at all. The end of things was often just . . . death. Nothing more, nothing less.

"I saw a dead man change into a coffin. And I dreamed of more dead after I'd gone to sleep," Isaiah ventured. The man was silent, and not quite looking him in the eye. "He *is* going to die, isn't he?"

Isaiah stepped up to the bars, leaning in, coming close to him once again. "Did you know that already? You said to him that this 'wasn't how this was to end'."

The man bowed his head, scruffy chin almost touching his chest. His hair fell in a dense curtain about his face.

Isaiah continued. "You were trying to scare him, I heard it."

"Only because he tried to threaten me first." Suddenly the man had drawn himself up to his full height to glare down his nose at Isaiah. He stood head and shoulders taller than him. "He cursed himself long ago with drinking. If Coffin dies, *I* won't be the one to have set it into motion."

Isaiah's gut curled in apprehension. He *felt* the half-truth as it tripped off the other man's tongue. "What did you do to Bellamy, then?" He asked quietly.

"I did *nothing* to him," the man snarled. "What could I do, locked up here in this cell?"

"You've done nothing but sell me lies," Isaiah said, tone souring. "I know you can . . . do things. I just don't know how."

"Bold accusations coming from someone who barely knows how to work his own craft," the man replied, setting his jaw.

"Not so bold if you saw how the whale that killed him behaved in its death roll. And you *still* don't deny it," Isaiah said, face heated. "I saw him drowned! The creature was dead, as dead as *you* seemed when we pulled you from inside the stomach of that thing!"

"Why should I deny it, if you're so sure?" The man's eyes were cold, his face half wrapped in shadow. Isaiah couldn't tell whether or not he was bluffing. "Any bad luck that comes of it will certainly be no fault of mine. He'll have brought that particular fate down on himself, as will the rest of the ship."

The man wrapped his arms in on himself, sinking back to the low mattress in the back of the cage-like room. Isaiah felt a tugging sensation at the back of his throat.

Perhaps there was a reason he'd asked Isaiah if his dreams made him lonely.

"Your Captain is as rotten as this ship will be. Mark me on it, Isaiah." He stared back at him from where he sat, in Isaiah's old shirt, hair lank, eyes burning into him. It made him feel wholly see-through; as if one stray word from him would lay him bare.

Isaiah turned, made to leave the brig behind, but something slowed his steps.

"You know my name, but I don't know yours," he said, schooling his voice into careful neutrality. "That hardly seems fair."

The man cocked his head to the side. "Call me Essex," he said.

Isaiah clutched the name tight, and made his way back to the deck, away from the brig and from the man from the belly. Essex.

"Call me Essex."

CHAPTER ELEVEN

THAT MORNING, after three days of absence, the captain finally appeared again, leaning heavily on Sharpe's arm. He seemed recovered enough from whatever it was that was troubling him to grab his own meals from the mess, and to carry a scanty plate back to his quarters. Isaiah nudged Hendricks' knee under the table, and he saw her cut her eyes over in the direction of the Captain's retreating form. She turned back to him, one eyebrow having shot up toward her hairline.

"You catch his face?" She asked in low tones.

"Uh-huh."

"Well?" She prodded, voice only betraying the slightest irritation, "What did he *look* like?"

"The same as he did three days ago. Maybe a little less horrible than last time."

"Gods, you're no use. Still drunk? Sober as a shrinehold?" She asked, exasperated.

"Couldn't see enough to tell from this distance," he said. "It just means he'll be back above decks soon enough." He shoveled a piece of dry biscuit into his mouth. "I'm sure we'll hear about it one way or another."

"I've heard enough to last me a blasted lifetime," she cursed quietly. He had to assume that the Captain had given her a hellish dressing-down when they'd returned without Bellamy. It wasn't fair. But nothing about Coffin was, after all.

He couldn't help but remember Essex's claim: that if Coffin was doomed to die, he had set the toll in motion himself long ago.

He and Hendricks hadn't spoken about the terse conversation he'd overheard outside Monteiro's quarters. She tended to keep silent about personal things, and the look of shame on her face as she'd left kept him from pushing the matter.

Despite all likelihood to the contrary, he'd slept deeply and soundly after his strange talk with the man . . . with *Essex*. He'd rolled around the name on his tongue. Reconfiguring him as someone who had a name that only he knew seemed strange, but intimate, somehow.

For what felt like the first time in weeks, he hadn't had any bizarre, disturbing dreams, and come morning, the only thing that had persuaded him from bed was Fallon, shaking his arm heartily enough to rock the entire bunk. He almost smacked his head on his way down.

Sulaimi was waiting for him once he left Hendricks and the mess hall behind.

"Well. Fancy seeing you awake."

"Yeah, yeah."

"*Yeah* yourself," they said, tossing him a belt with darning tools strapped to it. "Up you get. Heard something tear last night on watch."

"You're sure?" he asked, although he had already begun to strap the tool belt to his waist. He cinched it a good few notches tighter as Calder's torn arm flashed in his mind's eye.

They snorted at him, rolling their eyes and striding off down the deck. "Just find what's wrong with it, Chase," they called back, not even bothering to turn back to him. Isaiah exhaled steadily, starting his long climb up the foremast.

The roughly tied ropes of the rigging passed below him speedily, if a little less than usual. He made sure to grasp each hand-hold as he went, putting one over the other in even measures, willing him to not think about Calder, hanging from the cracked mast, a spear of wood through his arm. As he ascended he could feel the cool air filling his lungs to the brim. The ragged knot that had seemed to stick in his stomach since the dreams had started up had eased, if only a little. He could feel that Essex had still been less than truthful with him, but that at the same time, he'd also been more honest than before. And despite his admission of a name, of the gentle thumb on his cheek, he'd still barely tried to cover up the fact of his threat to Coffin, when the Captain had begged him for mercy.

It seemed more distant, up in the rigging. It was easier to let his mind wander to the humming sensation Essex had mentioned. If he focused, he could feel it in his hands and legs, where his body touched the ship that touched the water.

He spotted the tear in the sail: an odd, jagged looking thing that revealed itself to be not one tear, but three. Three long rips that had bled together into a larger one, almost as if a hand had reached down and batted at their foresail from the skies above. Isaiah reached out, measuring the space against his palm. He'd have to give Sulaimi credit for good observation, later.

Gripping the mast easily, he slung a leg over to the rigging itself, balancing his weight, letting the breeze sway him lightly to and fro. It was better not to fight against the motion of the ship; it was not a battle you'd be likely to win. Two hand-lengths of cut canvas square later, and he was sewing up the hole with waxed cording. It wasn't so much that Sulaimi couldn't have fixed it themself, they were just certain to do a worse job than him. Once one has sewed up the flesh of an injured animal, getting blood all over one's trousers, waxed canvas seems a much simpler task.

He wondered who had sewed up Essex's multitude of scars, had they been deft hands or inexperienced ones, or if the skin had been left to knit together on its own. The idea made his chest tight; it had to have hurt something fierce.

Giving the sail a pat for good measure, he turned to begin his long sidle down the rigging, when a flicker of motion caught his eye. The hatch to the orlop was thrown open, as it usually was upon someone's exit, but there was an odd wave of moving bodies as the other whalers darted swiftly out of the way of whoever was emerging. The person was Essex, being pushed along by Lice, with Sharpe close behind.

He scampered downwards a few feet before thinking better of it. They wouldn't dare put the man overboard.

Would they?

"Out of the way!" Lice called, her jarring voice ringing up the mast. Sharpe prodded the man along, and Lice fanned out to chide the rest of the sailors. "Back to work!"

Outside the circumscribed scale of the brig, Essex looked smaller than Isaiah remembered. He was still tall, but seemed

FROM THE BELLY

shriveled in the light of day. Tilting his head up to the sun, he shielded his eyes with a hand, and met Isaiah's gaze. Isaiah's heart dropped hard, and he ducked down behind a block and tackle instinctively. He couldn't tell if he'd just happened to look his way, or if he'd sensed him there, somehow.

Taking an even breath, he gathered himself up to peer back down at the surface of the deck. Sharpe had pushed him along to the end of the railing and was just standing guard. The rest of the crew were slowly scattering to mind their business, but he could tell that most were loitering, content to stare at the man from the belly from a relatively small distance.

Essex rolled his shoulders, stretched, and leaned down to meet the water. For a moment, Isaiah was sure he was going to simply slip overboard, like the fish Coffin had dumped over the side. The voice in the back of his head asked quietly if Essex would still be a man at all when he hit the surface.

Without warning, a heavy bundle of rope whacked him on his back and he wobbled, breath knocked clear out of him. For a second he was aware of just how precipitously off-kilter his footing was—when abruptly the once-gentle breeze kicked up into a stiff wind, buffeting him back on-balance, as if the air itself had wanted to set him back on his feet.

Pulse hammering, he gripped the rigging for dear, blessed life. Training his eye toward the sea, his stomach dropped. The same wide, pitch-black shadow that had lingered underneath the boat on Bellamy's final, ill-fated hunting trip was haloing the *Merciful.* Even at a distance, he could tell that Essex's head was bent down toward it, black-brown curls hanging around him like so many ragged lengths of seaweed. The waves bent their heads toward him.

Wind blew stiff and wild in Isaiah's face, and he watched as the first mate grabbed hold of Essex's shoulder, steering him away from the shadow, the side of the ship, and from the open ocean— propelling him back to the innards of the *Merciful.*

Isaiah's feet hit the deck with a light thud. "Did you see that?"

"See the man from the whale take his walkabout? 'Course I did." He found Fallon coiling rope not too far off from where Essex had been. "Can't imagine what moved the Captain to let him do that. He seemed in a real snit about him before."

"No, I mean—yes, that. But the shadow too. Around the ship."

101

He grabbed the other man's shirt, towing him to the side and pointed him forward, toward the ocean.

No shadow.

"Steady on there," Fallon said, peeling Isaiah's fist off of his shirtsleeve. "Did you knock your head?"

"Fallon," Isaiah hissed. "It was there. I saw it. It was easily twice the width of the ship around."

Fallon squinted. "Uh *huh*."

"I didn't imagine anything, promise."

"Sure you didn't," he said, voice thick with sarcasm. Isaiah ground his teeth, and left Fallon where he stood.

"Crew! Assembly in two bells!" Lice called out down into the mess area. "Cap'n's orders!"

"Finally," Álvarez said as he passed by, scratching at his scalp. Isaiah followed him along with the rest of the crew up to the main deck again. Most were groaning, stretching themselves, having been pulled from their midday tasks or from midday rations which were growing less and less satisfying as the days progressed. He hadn't been called back below to assist Moirah further, and he had no clue if the leak had continued, or what the state of their stores really were-only that they were growing less and less appetizing by the day.

Coffin, however, was already waiting above deck.

He was freshly dressed, crisp blue coat flapping in the wind, standing solidly at the mizzenmast. Sharpe stood close at his heel, with the air of someone who was waiting for the other to snap at any moment. He was best at catching him when he slipped and cleaning up the messes Coffin left in his wake. Less skilled at performing the tasks and duties of a first mate. Lice had taken to picking up whatever sundry duties he abandoned in the full-time job of making sure Coffin did not fly off the handle.

"Is that all? Good." He cleared his throat precisely, scanning the crew assembled. To Isaiah's view, he looked utterly exhausted. Bags ringed his eyes, his coloring seemed sallow and worn, and his face, normally square-jawed and just post-handsome, looked almost sunken, caved in. Isaiah could see the bones underneath, prominent enough to give him pause. Coffin drew himself up to continue.

"Crewmen of the *Merciful*. I would ask you to excuse my absence from command of late. I've not had my full faculties, and regretfully, some of my duties have been delegated to incompetents." A snicker filtered its way up from the crowd. "That ends today."

Sharpe tried his hardest to stand firm at the Captain's right hand, but even from where Isaiah stood, a few bodies deep into the assembled crew, he could see something in him crumple.

"While we should have been making hasty tracks to deep waters for the majority of our hunt, we've been distracted. By stray whales, prey gone loose, various oddities, and by a liberal excess of free time and a lack of *discipline*." Any laughter that might have burbled up before was now thoroughly squashed. "Beginning today, we are operating on double time. Our barrels have been empty for far too long, and we are going to get back the weeks we've lost off of our hunt. We are going to steal the time back from the gods below in oil and whales once we make it through to the Southerly Reaches." He took a grand step forward, looking crewmembers in the frontmost row in the eyes one by one, with an intent that Isaiah hadn't seen in weeks, no, months.

"The first whalers to take in viable oil will be rewarded. Handsomely." He put a hand into his jacket and withdrew a long-barreled pistol, ornate in its detail. The golden filigree touched the handle and stretched up to the muzzle of the weapon, gleaming and winking in the sunlight, and Isaiah locked his jaw tight to stop himself from gasping. "The personal pistol of Captain Johanna Briggs—a fine tool despite its history, to be sure. The hand that takes first blood will receive it as a prize."

The woman in his dream with the hole in her head. Isaiah swore a line of curses internally. How could he have *forgotten*. The new captaincy on board the *Dolphin*, the floating coffin that the woman had steered through the waters of the dead . . . the image interlocked in his head with a near audible click.

Isaiah whipped around, searching the crewmembers around him until he found Hendricks, a few feet away. She was staring resolutely at the deck, unmoving, as the other people around her jostled and whispered excitedly amongst themselves. " . . . And until that time, said prize will be kept with me." He stepped back from the now-buzzing crew, a satisfied expression on his face.

"Now. With that out of the way, *back to it*." He gestured for Lice with a simple nod and strode back aft toward the upper decks.

"Alright you dogs, *hands to work*—You, Toole, up on the watch in your time, Liu, take the rest of the haulers and get those sails tightened up . . . "

Isaiah would have jumped to work with the rest of them, but he was busy watching Hendricks make a direct beeline back to the lower orlop deck. Glancing around, he made sure that Lice and Sharpe were sufficiently distracted, and followed her.

She was sitting crouched on her heels at the far end of the last row of beds. Her shoulders shook as Isaiah approached with caution.

"Hendricks . . . ?"

"Go *away, Chase,*" she said, voice thick with tears and stuffed up with snot. He reached into one of his pockets and withdrew a handkerchief that was serviceable, if none too clean. He set it on the bunk nearest to where she'd curled into herself, and sat opposite her, saying nothing.

She rocked and pressed her face into the flat of her hands. Her cries seemed raspy, like she'd had more than a few nights of it. He realized with a guilty jolt that he had no clue how long she'd been in this state. He'd seen her every day along with the rest of the crew.

"How did he come by Briggs' pistol from the *Dolphin*?" He said, tentative. "You . . . knew her."

She nodded, not looking up at him.

"How?" He asked, as quietly as possible. She darted a hand to the bunk to take his handkerchief.

"Johanna's body was just sitting there. On the deck, the whole morning after," she said, voice raw and eyes bloodshot. "Nobody would touch her."

Isaiah didn't remark at the use of Briggs' first name. "I had thought her family would want it but . . . but they said it would bring bad luck." It was not an unheard-of thought. The bodies of those that died violently by their own hand were thought to bring bad fortune on whoever knew them in life. In some exceptionally superstitious cases, even their possessions were considered marked. Doomed.

"It's bullshit, but I had thought of selling it, and sending the money back to them. But the company was recruiting for this hunt quickly after I skipped out at port, and I didn't have the time to get a good price for it." She wiped her nose on the handkerchief, still not looking him in the eyes. "I didn't *want* it. Why would I want the thing that killed her?"

Something slid into place. "You loved her."

She stared up at him, watery eyes hard and defiant. "She loved me back."

Isaiah didn't know what to say. Relations formed between crewmembers were to be expected on occasion, but it was rare for a storied captain like Briggs to take up with a member of the crew. Even a seasoned one like Hendricks.

"How did he get it from you, then?" He settled on asking her the basics. Pushing her for reasons why didn't seem particularly kind. She wiped her face clean with the handkerchief and left it crumpled next to her.

"He knew I was aboard the *Dolphin*. When he took me aside that night, he wanted to know how Bellamy died. Threatened to thrash me in front of everyone for letting his best harpooner die in such a *stupid* bloody way." She replied. "I . . . I knew he wouldn't pass up the opportunity." She tucked a stray lock back behind her ear. "Offering something up, something worth good enough money to appease him in the moment, seemed like a good bet."

Isaiah sat back, dumbfounded. Hendricks' breaths steadied, and she stared downwards, letting her finger line the knots on the wood-plank floor. "Better it go to someone who wants it," she said hollowly.

Don't you find it funny? Knowing all this. All this pointless, futile cruelty.

"Hendricks, I'm—"

"Chase, if I wanted your sympathy I'd ask for it," she said, balling up the now-sodden handkerchief and throwing it back at him. "Go. Lice is on the warpath today."

He rose, uncertain. When he left her, she was still staring at the floor, tracing warps and divots in the wood.

It wasn't by chance that Isaiah heard the footsteps heading down into the brig that night. He had been too nervous to sleep. His near-fall from the rigging, the shadow ringing the boat like some kind of terrible halo, plus how easily he'd overlooked Johanna Briggs appearing in his dream just to taunt him gave him more than enough reason to stay awake, silently staring at the musty ceiling just above his head. Whoever or whatever Essex was, he hadn't mentioned anything about missing food or rations, and having never seen him actually eat, Isaiah didn't see the point in bringing him food unless requested. Besides, the last time he'd been caught doing that particular duty it had ended poorly.

Essex had to have been casting the shadow below the water. Summoning it. Doing *something* to dredge it up. Bellamy had died by that unnatural whale the first time and now . . . who knew what would happen.

As he contemplated what kind of hopeless idiot he had to be, a series of footsteps passed by the berth where the crew slept; light, tapping, and butting in on Isaiah's circling thoughts. Not Coffin's heavy boots, certainly. His eyes adjusted to the dark, and he tilted his head to squint in the direction of the noise. A long shadow disappeared down the hallway, out of his peripheral vision. Ducking from his bunk with one practiced swing, he landed lightly and crept past the sleeping crewmembers.

The figure tip-toed down, toward the brig, passing shadowy doorway after shadowy doorway. Isaiah ducked from dark spot to dark spot, avoiding creaky floorboards and bits of decking. He'd walked this same route to the brig enough times, after all. When the person passed through a spot of moonlight shining through a porthole, he realized it was Monteiro. The sight gave him pause; if she needed to see the man, she could just as easily request him to her quarters during the daytime. Unless Coffin had commanded otherwise?

She crept through the door separating the hallway to the brig from the rest of the ship, letting the latch fall quietly but propping the door open behind her. Isaiah waited until he could be sure of her remaining on the other side of the door, and crouching low, hovering just beyond the door. She faced Essex, back to Isaiah.

The surgeon stood in front of the bars, arms folded in front of her, and was already speaking to him.

Her normally crystalline tone wavered a little as she spoke. *She wasn't quite afraid of him,* he thought, *not like Coffin.* More likely afraid of what would happen if she were found out. He couldn't blame her. He edged closer to the doorway, straining to hear over the perpetual creaks and moans of the ship.

Isaiah could only see half of her, but the angle at which he found himself allowed him to glimpse Essex, leaning back on the floor, partly nested on his limp straw mattress. His hair had fallen over his face, obscuring it almost completely. He could have been awake or asleep, if Monteiro hadn't been talking at him directly.

" . . . How strange." Essex said, leaned back, tone light. He was the picture of disinterest.

"Have you ever seen anything of this nature, have you ever experienced any of these effects? Because if that's the case—"

"You'd need to take care of the whaling company's investment. Wouldn't you?" he said, drily. "I don't envy you your job, Doctor."

Monteiro took a step forward, her tone colored with a kind of thinly veiled desperation. "Nor should you. It is not an enviable one." She leaned in, and Isaiah could only imagine she was giving him the razor-precise visual once-over he'd been on the receiving end of yesterday.

The thought chilled him, and he recalled the jars. All empty and waiting to be filled.

"Nobody can seem to tell how long you were within that creature, or how you still lived post-extraction. I don't believe that you would know that you were infected, but if you are showing any signs of illness at all, I'd be obliged to—"

"I see," he replied. "I'm certain your Captain would be happy to have an excuse to be rid of me."

"And *your* Captain too, so long as you're aboard a Pyle, Thacket, and Coffin ship." She paused. "The mercy and superstition of some has just barely protected you. But it cannot do so forever."

"You seem awfully certain of that. I take it you're not a superstitious or merciful person, Doctor."

"I do not cast lots on belief," she stated flatly. "And besides, I have been busy with a variety of other crewmembers, all of whom must be checked as soon as possible."

"Does he know of your little theory?" he said, dropping the lightly quizzical facade.

"What does or not get reported directly—"

"I don't think that he would approve of your looking in on me one bit. Certainly not in the dead of night, and certainly with *nobody* else around." He tilted his head, almost lazily, and stared significantly toward the crack in the door. Isaiah gulped.

This was now twice that he'd simply been . . . aware of where Isaiah was.

"The Captain is . . . preoccupied, at the moment. And it behooves me to act in the interest of the other thirty individuals who take up rank on this ship."

Essex leaned forward. "You're an effective guard dog, protecting your masters' investment."

Monteiro stayed as firm as she could, arms folded tightly. "I cannot experiment properly to rule out other variables, and so I must ask you to be direct with me. For the good of the crew."

"The good of the crew? You can't admit that you're looking out for the company that happily mines their flesh like a blood harvest." The man had risen up from his seat on the mattress and stalked forward toward Monteiro.

"If the interests of one party happens to coincide with the other—"

"Then I cannot imagine what you think would move me to act on your definition of what is *good for the crew*, Doctor."

Essex spat the words back in her face from the other side of the bars, and as he turned away from her, glanced toward the door. He stopped for a beat too long, and for a moment, Isaiah saw his expression alter, shift into something almost sly. Like the fact of Isaiah's spying was some silly joke between the two of them. Before he could think, before he could return the look, Isaiah bolted. Back down the hall, away from Monteiro and the man, and back into his bed.

CHAPTER TWELVE

AFTER COFFIN'S REAPPEARANCE on deck, work was duller and more brutal than it had been in a long, long while. Lice was absolutely incandescent with the fires of productive rage, having been given the Captain's blessing to work the crew as hard as humanly possible. Not to mention the fact that the wind was now running crossways and the ship was making piss-poor time. Every soul on board was sour and bone-tired, and the majority of them threw up regular prayers begging for the wind to change, for whales to be spotted. Anything.

By the time evening shift took their rounds, the sky had turned blue-purple and was still bitter with wind. He caught Lice cussing to herself as he crossed past her on the midships. When Hendricks finally made an appearance, she simply nodded curtly in his direction and made for the upper mainsail. She was gone in the rigging before he could think to say another word to her.

"Chase! Back to it, we don't have all day," Sharpe barked at him. He could feel the first mate's eyes boring twin holes into his back, and he hauled faster. He ran to assist Ramsdell, and hand-over hand they hauled. "When you're finished with that, get below—Moirah needs assistance."

Strange. He'd heard nothing more, from neither the quartermaster nor Moirah about the state of the storage since the week before. Something in him tensed.

He headed down below, arms aching with recent exertions. The further down he traveled, the colder his extremities became. His feet were chilled at each toe, and he felt a hard wave of cold air roll down his spine. The storage was soaked with seawater, and tendrils of seaweed dragged and dripped from the ceiling, like so many limp fingers. The pools of water had edged closer to the ramp leading up and out of the hold, and he cuffed up the hem of his trousers to stop them from soaking through. He gave up the closer he came to the leak. Moirah was already hard at work, elbow-deep into the mess. She was pulling out clumps upon clumps of dense, blackish green seaweed, tiny eddies of leaked water circling her stocky legs.

"Over here, Chase. Bring a light from that barrel, I can't see a goddamn thing," she said, huffing. Isaiah hustled over to where she was working, lantern held aloft. The light from the oil lamp cast a bizarre pall over her, glinting off the pools of water, by now well over a foot deep, and exposing the rotting barrels. Where last week he'd been able to easily roll them away, they'd almost begun to melt into each other, the wood softened to an advanced state of decay.

"I thought that you'd found the leak some time ago."

"Well, clearly damn not," she said, peeved. "I've been plugging up the leaks as they've sprung, but no—*luck*—" She said, pulling up more and more seaweed growth between words. She had floated a bucket, attaching it to a pole with a rope. It was easily half full with the stuff.

"The whole thing needs to be damn well re-lined, but we haven't the tools, the time, or the trade to do so, and this shit just keeps coming on . . ."

"I've never seen such a thing," he said, as she yanked a long strand from the depths. It almost looked as if there were a full set of roots at the bottom. As if it was anchoring to the wood itself.

"Well, neither have I, but I don't just stand there, *do I*."

He complied and bent double, fishing his hands into the water, feeling around in the dim light for more growth. The water was like ice, raising the hairs on his upper arms as he went. His fingernails scraped along the rough wooden surface until they found purchase on a patch of weeds, and he pulled hard. Silt filtered from between his fingers and the plant flesh stuck between them, depositing a kind of slimy film over his hands and arms. Tossing the seaweed into Jackson's bucket with a rough thud, he wiped the film off on his shirt before diving back in for more.

"Sometime this year, Chase." Taking Moirah's lead, he rolled up his pant legs further, bunched up his sleeves, and dived back in, swallowing the sickening feeling that was gathering up at the back of his throat. "I've been pulling the blasted things from the damn hull all morning, and if you're feeling poorly you'd best get someone else who's willing to do your dirty work for you!"

"Sorry—"

"Sorry my left tit," she grumbled.

The slick, almost greasy texture, the cold . . . something about it made the whole enterprise feel deeply, spine-chillingly not-right. He imagined the sensation of rotting flesh, the cold lap of a dead man's tongue. The water pulsed and swam before his eyes. His head throbbed. This was wrong. Incredibly, fully wrong. He retracted his hands from the water, thinking about broken masts and Bellamy's decaying corpse leaking saltwater into his eyes from the bunk above him, and barnacles latching onto Calder, right underneath his skin. He must have dreamed it; he couldn't have imagined Monteiro speaking to Essex so directly. But it couldn't have been a dream, because he remembered the man catching his eye through the crack in the door, he remembered him seeing him and it was all much too strange to be happening—

"Chase!"

When he looked up, Moirah's normally quite solid form was wobbling in place. Or maybe he was the one wavering. He couldn't focus on her. She was anchored to the water with a dark cloudy shadow around her feet, clustering at the puddle around her bare legs and spreading out in inky tentacles throughout the hold, connecting to the weeds and reaching out through the water toward him . . .

Isaiah let out a choked breath, stumbled backwards, sea water splashing even further up his pant legs.

"HEY, get back here!"

Why was Moirah still down here, working at a leak from last week? And seaweed didn't grow inside boats; it wasn't supposed to grow within the ship, there wasn't enough for it to grab hold of within their tiny, blood-soaked island of iron and wood timber. Lice hadn't breathed a word of it to anyone. His head throbbed once more, sending a hot flash of pain across his face and down his neck.

"CHASE!"

He had to leave. "I'm sorry—"

He bolted back up the stairs, out of the storage, into the bright light of the main deck, and went crashing to the side to throw up over the railing.

"Hey now!" Demir grasped his shoulder, half clapping him on the back, half holding tight to him to ensure he didn't tilt too far overboard. "Chase, what's this? I thought you were helping patch the leaks below . . . "

"Felt . . . ill," he choked out, coughing up the last of it and wiping his mouth clean. The waves below him sloshed against the hull, clear and regular as always. There was no black shadow to be seen around the ship, and the sea foam carried away what little he'd coughed up. It soon dissipated into nothing. "Where's Fallon?"

"Fallon? I'm not sure," Demir said, with the even tone of someone speaking to a petulant young child.

"I . . . I need to talk to him," Isaiah said. He had to be sure that the things he was seeing weren't entirely his own mind working against him. If someone as even-keeled as Amos Fallon couldn't see just what was so strange and unnatural about the growth overtaking the hold, he'd know that the crew was far more compromised than he'd thought.

"Check the rope locker, I think he'd been sent there," he said, dropping Isaiah's shirtsleeve.

"Thanks." It would only be a matter of minutes before Moirah called Lice to punish him for dereliction of duties. He darted off, legs still soaked and wobbly.

He found Fallon not in the rope locker nor in the bunks, but in the mess, scrubbing up tables with such focus that he jumped about a mile when Isaiah grabbed him.

"Hey. When was the last time you went below? To the storeroom?"

"Come again?"

"Have you been to the *hold*, recently?"

"A few days ago, I think . . . " He knit his brow. "Chase, you look *foul*, what's happened?"

"I just . . . I need you to look out for something with me." He wiped a chunk of spittle from the corner of his mouth.

"I can do that, I suppose . . . " he said, setting down his washrag.

"There he is—*Chase*." Moirah's shout came like a thunderclap, and she was trailed close behind by Sharpe, who looked none too pleased.

He took a deep breath and girded himself. "I'm sorry, I was feeling ill all of a sudden and I didn't want to . . . "

"Slacking will not be tolerated, Chase." Sharpe said, tone poking at him in all the most irritating ways. "Monteiro just saw you yesterday, and you weren't ill. Or shall we let the good doctor know you're a liar to boot?"

"I'm no liar sir, it just came on all of a sudden," he said, pleading.

"I don't know if I much enjoy that tone."

"Enough, Jackson," Sharpe said, cutting her off before she could go any further. "Chase. Ten extra hours duty owing for slacking. Put it on the log, and any more falsehoods will go to straight to the Captain."

Isaiah swallowed hard, the acid tang of vomit still in the back of his throat. "Yessir." He tapped his forehead deferentially and watched as the two dispersed. Fallon eyed him skeptically as they went.

"What did you do?"

"Nothing. I felt sick as soon as I went below—"

"If it turns out you are full of it, Chase . . . " Fallon clucked disapprovingly, taking back up his wash rag.

"I'm not, promise."

"Yeah, it's the hold, and there's some water about. What's strange about that?" He rubbed hard at an ale stain that had crusted and gone sticky on the table.

"No, I mean, yes, but there's . . . there's things growing down there," Isaiah said, pivoting in front of Fallon as he went. "There's seaweed grown into the wood itself, the water won't stop in from who knows where, the barrels are starting to break down . . . " He could feel himself sounding as insane as he felt, but Fallon's scrubbing slowed to a stop.

"But the leaks only started last week, how could it already be rotten?" He said, considering Isaiah's expression, which he was sure wasn't exactly the picture of calm. "How much damage, then?"

Isaiah breathed a sigh of relief. "Enough. Once Moirah is out of the hold and you're finished up here, I'll show you."

As it happened, 'later' was no sooner than five hours after. Isaiah had been charged with making a long round at watch in case he stayed ill, and the fresh air cleared any remaining dizziness from his head. Liu was more than grateful to take a turn below, handing tools to Jackson and pulling up seaweed instead of swabbing the floor of the mates' quarters.

Fallon jostled him just as he was starting to nod off against a wall after supper, yellow speckles of lamplight swimming before him.

"Hey. You ready? Don't fall asleep on me."

"Aye—I'm ready, I'm ready," he replied. He cut his eyes about. The majority of the crew were at their leisure, tossing dice, a few writing or carving small charms of bone or wood or talking amongst themselves. None were paying a particular amount of attention to them. Moirah had headed off to sleep, looking utterly exhausted and soaked stiff, and neither Sharpe nor Lice were anywhere to be found.

"Let's move casual," Fallon said with a curt nod, and they strolled leisurely downwards. The doorway was bolted, as usual, and Fallon beckoned for him to unlatch it. No sooner had he cracked the wood and metal barrier open than a small wash of seawater flowed forth.

"Shit!" Fallon yelped, springing out of the way. Isaiah moved a touch too slowly, and gasped as the still ice-cold water hit his ankles. "You coulda *warned* me!"

"It wasn't this bad before! Stop yelling," Isaiah hissed back, letting the last of the water drain out. The entry to the hold was a slightly elevated platform where they stood which ramped downwards, leading into a still deeper pool of leakage, and the lack of light made the whole thing horribly, all-consumingly dark.

"You have a light?"

"No. Do you?"

"Didn't think to grab one . . . "

"Why don't we come back tomorrow, early, when there's light to go by—" Fallon said, starting to edge backwards.

"I don't think Moirah will let me back in after today," Isaiah said, sloshing down into the hold. "I said I'd show you, and I will."

The water had climbed another few inches deeper than last time Isaiah had been in the hold, and he held his hands out in front of him to grasp his way between the crates and barrels stacked chest high. The space was punctured by thin slivers of light, coming from the deck above, barely enough to split the darkness.

As his eyes adjusted, Fallon reached out, fingers wiggling, and snagged Isaiah's shirtsleeve. "Why couldn't they dredge it?" He asked, voice uncertain.

"Dunno. They were trying hard to find the leak, and they thought they would have an easier time of it, I'm sure . . . " Isaiah said, steadying himself as he took a few steps deeper. A long tendril of seaweed brushed his foot and he tamped down an aggressive shiver that ran up his spine.

"What the hell was that?" Fallon said, and Isaiah could feel him jump.

"I told you. Weeds have been growing down here and—"

"Something *touched* me, Chase!"

"Nothing touched you, come on . . . " Isaiah tried to sound conciliatory, but he felt nearly as panicked as Fallon sounded. He remembered his own sudden rush of nausea and steadied himself.

The water itself was just seawater, but the further they walked from the ramp and the exit, the denser the plant life became. The pools slapped and shifted against the barrels with the rolling and rocking of the ship itself, and in the narrow pin-pricks of light from the deck above, he could see that the water was a brackish blue-green. It was still as ice-cold as he'd felt it earlier that day, as if they were taking a quick walk into the deepest parts of the ocean floor. The scent of mildew and waterlogged wood was overpowering.

"Chase, this is *bad*."

"I *know*. Now do you understand?" Isaiah said. "Do you feel sick, woozy, at all?"

There was a pause, a stillness, as Fallon thought hard. "No. I don't think so, but this still isn't right, it shouldn't be like this . . . " Suddenly, the other man fell silent. There was a dull slapping sound and he dropped Isaiah's shirtsleeve. He could hear him breathing heavily through his nose, over his hand.

"*Something touched me,*" he whispered.

Isaiah sighed. "It's just the seaweed, stop being jumpy—" But was cut off by Fallon clapping his other hand over his mouth.

"Chase, *we're leaving, now*," Fallon whispered, and slowly dropped his hand from Isaiah's face, taking up his shirtsleeve again in a vise-like grip. He heard Fallon step back, and start up the ramp. His stomach heaved and clenched as the darkness pulsed in front of him.

There was something moving in the water.

With a cry and a heavy splash, Fallon hit the water. Isaiah sprung back with a strangled yell, dragging his hands back through the water for Fallon. Fallon, who had been right behind him, he couldn't have gone anywhere but *right behind* him—there was another shout, partially gargled with water, and a thunderous crash of boxes hitting the seepage, and before he registered what had happened, Fallon was running out at top speed, legs dragging through the nearly knee-deep water, back through the dark in front of him and Isaiah did not think twice or ask questions because Fallon was pushing him bodily toward the door out of the hold.

"*Move*, Chase, MOVE—" And they were both running, up the ramp, both soaked to the thigh with ocean water, and Isaiah slammed the door to the hold shut behind them. He panted, bent over onto himself, dripping heavily.

Fallon spat up a throat full of salt water onto the still-damp floor, near choking. "What in the ever-LIVING shit was that?!" he said, gasping for air.

"I . . . I didn't see what happened . . . " Isaiah pressed the heel of his hand to his breast, trying to slow his own panicked heartbeat. "Where did you go?!"

"I didn't go anywhere, as soon as I took my hand offa you, I felt something wrap around my ankle and pull hard, you bastard," he replied, one sentence bleeding into the next. "You didn't DAMN well say there was something living down in the *fucking hold!*"

"Keep your voice down!" Isaiah hissed. There was a clatter of rushed footfalls from the deck directly above them, doubtless roused by the shouting and falling boxes below.

"*Gods above*, they'll think we're fucking stealing. Get to the mess, we'll be keelhauled—" Fallon started in a rough whisper.

Isaiah's mind raced. The footsteps were right there. "No time for that, back in."

Before he could utter a word in protest, Isaiah dropped to a crouch, pulling Fallon with him, and they tumbled back into the hold and into the dark once more, huddled side by side in the space below the ramp. He grabbed the back of Fallon's neck like a mother cat with her kitten, and kept the both of them pressed firm against the wall. Fallon, clamped under his arm, breathed short and panicky. He was shorter than Isaiah, but stockier, and he could just barely hold him still. Just as Isaiah's eyes re-adjusted to the blackness, Lice threw open the door to the hold, and a beam of lantern-light shone high above them. The glow illuminated the murk beyond the door, but left them in deep shadow in their hiding place, and Isaiah held fast to Fallon with a wiry grip.

"Who in the hell . . . " she muttered. There was nothing but silence as the light swung wide in Lice's hand.

The *Merciful* creaked, and the water sloshed about the room with the regular motion of the ship. She must have come alone. After a long pause, the beam of lantern light disappeared back into nothingness behind the shut door, and Lice's footfalls faded back down the hall. He held his breath still, praying that Fallon was doing the same. He counted one, two, three, four . . . and on the fifth count, he let the hand he'd been covering over Fallon's face fall away slowly, and loosened his grip on him.

"What in the EVER-LIVING is *wrong with you—*"

"Shush," Isaiah hissed, jabbing a finger above toward the upper decks. "She might be back."

With no further encouragement, Fallon ducked out from Isaiah's spot and hastened back up the ramp, where he settled into a low squat and stared out into the dim water.

"Maybe you just slipped," Isaiah began in a low whisper, beginning to regret this whole venture. "I just had a bad feeling about it, because Lice hasn't said a thing about the condition of the stores and I *still* don't understand how it could have got in this state so quickly."

Fallon took a shaky breath in, out. Rolled up his left sleeve, to reveal his lower arm, which was ringed in a fresh, painful looking bruise that hadn't been there before. Isaiah could barely see it in the low light, but it wrapped dark and two fingers thick around his limb.

"I don't care. Let's get out of here, I damn well wasn't imagining things—"

Without any warning, there was a sharp cry followed by a wet thud as Fallon was pulled off the end of the ramp.

CHAPTER THIRTEEN

ISAIAH JOLTED AWAKE to the incessant clanging of an alarm bell, a gasp catching hard in his throat. The image of Fallon disappearing into the black shadows of the hold ran circles around his head. There was the sound of muffled screaming from somewhere else in the ship, and the crew mates in the bunks surrounding him popped out their heads, still sleep-bleary and confused.

"What's that?"

"Who's yelling at this hour?"

"It's coming from below . . . "

One by one, the crew shimmied into their clothes. Isaiah quickly swapped his trousers, still stained with brine from the night before, for his only other pair, and ran a hand over his face and hair for stray pieces of seaweed.

Hendricks hustled past him, and he tailed her closely. "What's happened?" he asked, careful to keep his face impassive.

"Nothing good," she said, walking faster.

The source of the screaming was Moirah, who was standing outside the hold, muscular figure squeezed back against the farthest wall away from the hold door. The entrance was cracked open like a gaping, toothless mouth, the shadows within illuminated only by thin strips of daylight coming in from the ceiling and two lamps. A small crowd had gathered, and all were craning over Sharpe's shoulder to try and get a look.

"Stay back, I say! *Back*, and let the Captain through!" he said, pushing hard against the first row of observers. Hendricks pulled the both of them to the side as Coffin strode down, face unreadable. He made it just in time to see Lice and Sulaimi carrying out a body, as limp and pale as a whitefish. Fallon's lips were blue with cold and trailing seawater, his unseeing green eyes wide open and glassy. The skin that was visible around his legs, neck, and jaw was banded with violet bruises, more than Isaiah could count. Dead.

Hendricks choked, and gripped his shoulder tight as a vise. A hushed gasp rippled through the crew, coupled by cries of shock and whispers of his name. Isaiah felt his tongue go dry and thick in his mouth.

The Captain stood, frozen with his back to the steadily growing crowd behind him, and stared into the small piece of ocean that had taken up residence in the very bottom of the *Merciful*. He did not turn to address Sharpe, or anyone else.

When he spoke, it was near to a whisper.

"Get the lot out of the way."

Sharpe's eyes were wide, but he nodded to his captain, and turned to face them. "Crew! To your duties."

Shocked into stillness and silence, no one could think to protest. They moved, almost as one, away from the hold and herded the other crew members out of the way. When Isaiah looked back, only Lice, Sharpe, and Coffin remained, standing over the body that used to be Fallon's.

He worked that day, just like he'd done the day before, and the day before that. He didn't know how. Then again, he didn't know what else there was to do. Hendricks had gone utterly silent, and didn't speak a single word to him, or anyone else.

That night he'd stood pressed up against the door of the hold, and listened to something long and dense slither back into the water. Fighting the urge to scream his lungs out, he had instead waded as far as he dared, and hissed Fallon's name over and over into the pitch-dark that swaddled him until he grew hoarse. Fallon never responded.

Isaiah had crept back to his bunk in a daze in the blind hope that it was a dream.

The following afternoon, the funeral service for Fallon was one of the worst held on board the *Merciful*.

The crew assembled before the quarterdeck, with the body already wrapped up in canvas. Someone had stitched him shut, once Monteiro was done with him. She had been tasked with inspecting the body and finding the cause of death, and she went about her work behind closed curtains, without anyone to aid her. Sulaimi, who had been dismissed after pulling Fallon from the hold, mentioned that they'd seen Coffin go into her dissection room, and that they'd stayed talking for a good long while. About what, they couldn't be certain, because they'd kept their voices hushed.

Now, she stood up on the main deck with the rest of them, no longer wearing her apron and sleeve-covers, brow knitted and deep in thought. Calder had been walked up to the deck to pay his respects—somewhat awake, this time, but looking dazed and sitting limply in a chair, his hand cradling his wrapped-up amputated arm gingerly. Hendricks kept her eyes down and trailed along next to him. The Captain said some loose, ineffectual words about the nature of death and life at sea and promised life eternal for Fallon no matter what circumstances had led to him passing to the realm below. It was nearly as discomforting as his service for Bellamy.

When the wrapped body went over and hit the water, with a dense splash, the heavy sound made Isaiah's stomach lurch.

Taking Hendricks' cue, Isaiah didn't say another word on the matter to anyone, and settled with occupying his hands with what he could do. The rest of the crew, not knowing how to digest the bizarre loss, went about the remainder of their tasks with all the enthusiasm of the dead, dragging their feet in a kind of daze.

The picture of Fallon, bruised, swollen with water, and dead, hammered itself into Isaiah's mind. It was forged into shape and he couldn't loosen it, no matter how quickly he finished his duties, or how much he wanted to work until he dropped.

He'd done all he could. Hadn't he? The moment they'd entered the hold it felt like they'd both slipped into the world of one of his own dreams, one from which he had awoken from but Fallon hadn't.

If he'd just let Lice find them, accepted the punishment and assumption of thievery which was sure to come, hadn't held Fallon back . . . or would whatever was living in the hold have let them escape at all, no matter what they did? *You   certainly   weren't hurt, at any rate,* the small, sly voice in the back of his head supplied.

There was no possible way for some kind of creature, big enough to drag a fully grown man to his death, to get into and lie in wait inside the hold on its own. Not without Moirah or Liu or Lice or *someone* noticing while they spent hours fruitlessly trying to clear the water. It was as if it appeared from thin air that night, when he'd descended below with Fallon.

Besides that, he'd felt woozy and disoriented when he'd been in the hold below, when no one else had. Perhaps the creature, or Essex, or both together hadn't wanted him to be there? But why? And was this Essex's doing?

The questions circled his brain like so many vultures, picking his nerves raw, leaving behind only guilt, and a cast-iron sadness.

That night, when he slipped out of bed, there was a new watch route. Isaiah waited silently as Ramsdell made a short round past the kitchen, by the bunks, before continuing up to the main deck. There had been mutterings that Fallon had somehow killed himself in the hold, and Isaiah had done nothing to curb or correct the rumor. He supposed, out of everyone else on board, he could have told Monteiro—but Essex was right. She hadn't tried to warn a single other member of the crew about the infection, or about anything else. For her and the rest of the crew to believe Fallon had died in any other way would have been far too frightening for them to contemplate.

He ducked behind a high stack of trunks and waited. Ramsdell didn't return. He took the opportunity and jogged as quietly as possible down to the stairs leading to the brig. Since Coffin had seen him bringing rations to Essex, Isaiah had been committed to visiting him at odd hours. It would do no good to change that now that he was on even higher alert.

The hallway was empty, and the door was bolted soundly. Sliding the latch open, he ducked inside, closing it behind him. Essex was standing flush to the bars, long fingers grabbing hold of the iron and eyes unblinking, an unsettling grin on his lips.

"Isaiah." His voice was gentle, but the look on his face made

Isaiah want to bolt from the room, as fast as his legs could carry him. The man was close up on the bars, too close. Isaiah could see how wide and black his irises were. He seemed hearty, color high in his cheeks.

"You look . . . healthy," Isaiah said.

Essex's grin broadened slightly. His teeth, for a moment, seemed a touch too sharp, but when Isaiah blinked, they appeared as square as any regular man's. His skin crawled. He stepped closer.

"Do I?" Essex replied. He looked flushed, almost. More solid than before, although the cool-colored veins around his eyes still remained, just barely visible underneath the skin.

"Yes," Isaiah said, pushing down his apprehension. "A man died last night. In the hold."

"Oh really?"

"Yes. Amos Fallon." He continued. "He was a good man. A friend."

"Ah." Essex schooled his expression into something approximating solemnity. It was not fully convincing. "My condolences. For your friend."

"Yes, thank you *so* much." Isaiah felt his temper balloon out of his control. Why in the hell did he look so . . . well-fed? He set his jaw, and jabbed a finger through the bars to prod Essex's chest. "There was *something* in the hold that killed him."

"Well that seems unlikely," he said, cocking his head. "And you think I had something to do with it?"

"Of course you did!" Isaiah hissed, his face growing warm with anger. "Who else would?! The whole storage keeps flooding with no leak to speak of, there's seaweed growing from the ship, and SOMETHING pulled Fallon in, and killed him!"

"Did you see it? When you were below?"

The chills returned, worse than before. Isaiah dropped his grip on the bars.

"How did you know I was below when it happened?"

The man's mouth twitched and something in his expression shifted. " . . . Ah."

"'*Ah*' what? Did you or didn't you have something to do with it?!" He said, voice growing rough with anger.

The man was silent and dropped his gaze to the floor.

"*Answer* me!"

"Like I said, it's easier for me to . . . hear things. Onboard."
Suddenly, the flush on Essex's face faltered, and he seemed more
human. Sadder, and less fired with an uncanny energy. "I noticed
you were with him. But I didn't know you valued him so highly. "

"Of course I did. Why in the hell shouldn't I?!"

"I thought . . . " He trailed off, eyes still cast down. "I'm sorry
for your pain. Truly." His brow furrowed, not meeting Isaiah's gaze.

Every other time they had spokes, Isaiah had the sense that he
was telling him a half-truth, that there was something slightly off-
kilter. But this was the first time he seemed truly contrite. It was
the apology of someone who hadn't considered that there were
other human beings in the world besides Isaiah. If the thought
wasn't so terrifying, it might have been almost touching.

He moved before he could think, and slid a hand back to the
bars, resting it on top of Essex's. The other man's skin was
surprisingly warm. Not cold and fish-like, as he'd feared. Essex's
eyes widened, and darted up to where Isaiah's hand rested on his.
Seeing his expression change so freely tugged at something in
Isaiah's stomach.

"Here," he said, taking Isaiah's hand in his own and pulling it
just barely through the bars. "Please don't be afraid."

Isaiah stayed still and tried not to flinch, but the man's grip
was gentle. He flipped Isaiah's palm skyward, and with his other
hand, placed a small jumble of objects upon it. Essex curled his
fingers shut over the objects, looking down at him through long
lashes with a serious expression. He pushed Isaiah's hand back
through the bars.

Peering down at his own hand, Isaiah realized that the objects were
tiny, smooth-backed cockle shells. They were perfectly clean of grit and
sand, and shone in peach and tan colors in the low light. He shifted his
hand to and fro, and they clinked together lightly in his palm.

"They're yours. I really am sorry."

Isaiah could see the deep furrow still cleaving Essex's brow and
something in him tore and stretched out of place. It was as if the
perpetual background noise of fear, of wrong-ness had been
muffled, buried below this new sensation.

"Alright," he sighed, and breathed deeply. They were still close
enough that he could smell Essex's skin. Salt, and a metallic smell,
mixed with the familiar earthiness of linen. He felt raw, exposed.

"I need you to *promise* me," he said, the tearing feeling yanking hard behind his sternum. "No more people will die. Not like that, not on this ship."

Essex looked at him and his expression was sorrowful. There was something like pity in his eyes. "You want for everyone to be safe? For nothing else to befall another soul on board?" He sounded reluctant.

"You know what I mean," Isaiah pleaded. "*Please*, Essex." He extended his free hand back through the bars, pulse beating hard when he made contact. He pressed his hand flat against his breastbone, a small animal part of him savoring the contact. Isaiah could feel the warm solidity of it seeping through Essex's shirt.

"It's a near impossible thing to ask," he responded, tentative. He peered down at where Isaiah's hand met with his chest. Isaiah could not feel a heartbeat. "Whalers deal in death. They go bloody wherever they travel. They revel in it."

"I don't."

"No. You don't." He placed both hands over where Isaiah had pressed his. He cradled it, as if it were a living thing that had alighted on him. Delicate, careful. "But the crew does not take the care you do. If something befalls them, it won't be out of spite. It will be because they've gladly been party to a world that's earned it one hundred times over."

He let Isaiah's hand fall in the space between them, back between the bars. A small, sharp note of fear cut through the man's words. "I can't just stop what's been set into motion, Isaiah." His hair hung over his face, painting it in long, wavy streaks of shadow, and Isaiah couldn't read him any further.

For the first time, it occurred to Isaiah that the man may not be entirely in control of what happened around him. No more so than a strong gale meant to crack their mast, or a tidal storm meant to crush a house.

He stepped back from the man in the cell and felt some bodiless part of himself stay with him. Isaiah latched the door leading to the brig as he left, quickly and quietly. The sensation of Essex's breastbone, warm and solid and silent under his palm, stayed with him as he fell asleep, paired with the roll of the ship rocking him into unconsciousness.

CHAPTER FOURTEEN

HIS DREAM THAT NIGHT wasn't quite so direct. No strange Captain appeared, no foreboding warnings were spoken from the mouths of the dead.

He simply slipped overboard the *Merciful*, dropping easily into the sea as easily as a seal might. He dreamed that he was paddling at the surface, the boat having disappeared as soon as he left it, and watching the sun go down over the horizon. As Isaiah saw it dip lower and lower in the sky, he knew unerringly that he had to follow it as it fell below the horizon. The burning ball traveled fast, looming huge in the sky above and plunging into the sea with a splash, like a boiling rock being dropped into a pond. In the dream, Isaiah took a huge gulping breath as he dived below, chasing the heat, heading toward the bold light of the sun as it rippled and hissed in the cold waves. It descended, and Isaiah chased after its radiating warmth, paddling faster and faster, but the drag on him pulled him back for every inch he gained.

He could see the sun going out as it neared the ocean floor and fear clapped heavy around him—bodies were sinking, falling past him, weights tied to them hand and foot to ensure they made the trip to the bottom. The bundles drifted and melted together and fused into the bare forms of both Fallon and Bellamy. Their eyes closed, they lay as if they were simply asleep and dreaming, just as he was. The harder Isaiah swam, the more distant they grew, the harder Isaiah's lungs burnt with the effort of holding his breath. Even in a dream, he couldn't avoid the crushing weight of the water surrounding him.

He awoke knowing that he'd died a few moments ago, his lungs aching.

Above, the clouds had shifted the dark grey of the underside of a gull's wings, and the air was still as the grave. The *Merciful* sat nearly frozen in the water, and the crew was sour to match. Demir was twining rope together, one hand over the other, as Liu took up what they'd twined together, and coiled it up for storage. The deck creaked with the slight rock of the waves below them.

"When was the last time we moved?"

"Not some time now. Not since last night," Demir said flatly.

"Not since before Fallon's funeral, at least," Liu supplied.

"Should think not," Demir said, quickly spitting over his shoulder.

Isaiah shook off the creeping, skin-crawling feeling that rose up his neck at Fallon's name, and set to his watch, where Álvarez was waiting to be relieved, looking antsy.

He gave him a curt nod, before the other man caught his shoulder, pulling him back.

"You've seen that Ramsdell is guarding the hold, right?"

He had, but he wasn't about to admit it. "I . . . no. For what?"

"Aye," he said, raising an eyebrow. "Cap'n dearest set him to it earlier. No word about it, and Moirah was locked in there when she was set to fixing the leaks in the hull."

"Have you seen her since?"

"Absolutely not. I get the feeling we're not supposed to be asking those questions."

"What are you on about?" he asked, squinting at Álvarez.

"Come on, Chase," he said. "You know full well that Fallon wouldn't have offed himself, let alone in that stinking hold, of all places. Why the hell would he?"

Isaiah didn't make eye contact. He couldn't bring himself to lie so boldly about Fallon, even in death. Speaking ill, or even false, of the dead was the last thing you wanted. Their spirits tended to hold it against you.

"I—I don't know."

"Exactly." Álvarez crossed his arms over his chest, only a little smug. "So how the hell did he die down there?"

"I don't know, Álvarez," he said, beginning his round on the watch and leaving the other man behind. "Why don't you tell me if you find out?"

He heard Álvarez make a 'tsk'-ing noise and took his leave.

126

Isaiah stared out hard over the static, grey sky, over the clouds as thick and dense as sheep's wool and thought of wind and rain and dry land, with nary a drop of salt water in sight.

"All hands to lower deck, we're taking on water!" A panicked voice—Moirah's—shouted out. He jumped and darted amongst the crew.

Buckets were passed and Isaiah sprang into action with the rest of them, feet already running, heart thundering against his ribs. By the time he reached the hold entryway the whole thing was sodden, Demir, Ramsdell, and Phelan already there and passing buckets back, heavy rivulets of blackened water coursing forth from underneath the door. Moirah burst out of the hold, gasping heavily, trousers hiked up over her knees and soaked through.

"It's taking on water faster than I can bail—we need hand pumps, NOW." Handfuls of people ran past him and the skull cocked itself to the side behind his eyes as he slowed to a halt. The end of things was not supposed to be like this. It was not supposed to end, now, on this ship, simply taking on endless water from below. He turned and ran.

He made it to the brig and slammed open the door full speed to find Essex kneeling at the back wall, hands on his thighs, back turned to him, and staring at an invisible spot on the far wall.

"I need—I need you to do something," Isaiah panted.

"What could that be?" he said, not turning.

He took a steadying breath, trying and failing to temper his panic. "We're taking on water. I need you to stop it." He was at the bars in two strides, and placed a hand against the metal. *"Please."*

Essex shook his head, oil-slick curls shaking to and fro. The panicked footfalls of the rest of the crew, bolting to put hands to pumps, fetch more buckets for the ceaseless water echoed above them, tamping out an irregularly frenetic drumbeat. The ship was rolling in its death throes, about to dive down deeper than it had ever been, and his father's voice rose to the back of his memory unbidden.

The sea will never love you back.

"Essex, *I'm begging you*, there are people on this ship who don't deserve this, they don't deserve to die—" Desperation bled into his voice. Essex finally turned, fixed him with a look that was equal parts mournful and pitying.

"I told you, I can't stop what's been started," he said. He paused, as though catching a thought as it came to mind. " . . . Not entirely."

"I'll do anything, *please*. Just tell me how."

Essex leaned over to him. Isaiah tried not to be intimidated by the look in his eye. "You mentioned that Coffin holds a key. I'd like it."

Of course. Isaiah should have known.

Dread surged forth, but he nodded quickly, reaching through the bars to brush his fingertips against Essex's chest. He turned to run, not waiting to see the look on the man's face.

Emerging back topside, Isaiah twisted through the oncoming throng, weaving between panicky crewmembers tossing rags and materials. Someone shoved a bucket into his hand and he took it with him, as he darted back through the mess, away from the line conveying the water, back to the upper back deck with its hallway to the captain's quarters. Coffin was nowhere to be found, but if there was anywhere a Captain should be in a crisis, it certainly wasn't hiding away in his private quarters.

The sound of the crew's rescue attempts faded behind him as he moved further and further away, treading quietly along the oak-paneled hallway, heart thudding. He abandoned the bucket in an open doorway that might have been Sharpe's. He had no way to tell, other than the fact that it was almost as far away from the rest of the crew's bunks as you could get.

There was another door that *was* the furthest from them. A heavy, meticulously constructed dark wooden barrier closed off what must have been the Captain's quarters loomed impassive and foreboding. In a world dominated by a distinct lack of privacy, it seemed the only people that were allowed a closed door were those in charge and those kept prisoner. He tugged the wrought-iron latch open with a terrifyingly sonorous clunk. Pressing a palm to the surface, he eased the wood open in one smooth motion, and the following creak made his stomach turn over on itself.

The prevailing thought as he looked in Coffin's quarters for the first time was disgust. Papers, bottles both empty and full of liquor, old trays of food, maps on every surface, brass navigational instruments used as paperweights: clearly Sharpe had been an even worse steward than he was first mate. The broad, heavy-legged table in the center of the room was covered with the mess, and Isaiah darted in to get a closer look at the minor mountain of debris, skittish as a cat. A half eaten apple rolled over onto an open logbook as the waves shifted slightly—if it was the regular motion of the sea, or the *Merciful* taking on more water, Isaiah couldn't say, and he sprung into action.

He pawed through the first layer of detritus on the table, every nerve on edge. With no sign of a key, or anyplace where a key would even be kept nearby, he replaced the things he'd moved as best he could and tried the shelves lining the wall. A dozen half-filled drawers, another dozen filled with maps, smoking implements, spare buttons and bits of cording, endless bullet casings in one of them and, finally, *blessedly*, a ring of keys. Isaiah muttered a quick prayer to the god of lost things and pressed the keys to him as he turned to leave.

The door snapped shut with a sudden heavy crash, and Isaiah was no longer alone.

Coffin stood, a dark shape outlined by the dark stained wood of the door. He looked murderous. Before Isaiah could move a muscle, Coffin was upon him, fist clenched onto his shirt collar tight enough to hurt.

"Thieving little shit . . . " His bright blue eyes were bloodshot and a potent mix of musty seawater and something metallic rode on his breath. "What've you taken from me?!" he hissed through gritted teeth. "*Well?!*"

"Nothing, I- I didn't mean to!" Isaiah fumbled, the keys dropping from his fist. They hit the deck with a rattle.

"I'll have you hanged for this!" Coffin pushed him away, and Isaiah stumbled backward, nearly falling into the refuse-covered table. The Captain ducked to pick up the keys, a look of realization dawning on him. "Oh, I *do* see."

Isaiah had begun to scramble upright when Coffin darted forward once again, this time making for Isaiah's neck. The Captain's hand crushed his throat and Isaiah gagged. The room pulsed for a moment and he scrabbled at the man's hand.

"*Please*, sir, please I'll . . . "

"Shut up. Take me to him," Coffin said, dropping him. He propelled Isaiah backwards to the door. "Move as if there is nothing amiss."

"Yessir." Isaiah said, through gulped mouthfuls of air.

"Walk. Pick that bucket up."

There was an unmistakable click of a revolver's safety being unlocked and, through his shirt, the cold press of the muzzle against Isaiah's spine. The memory of the skull he'd scried so long ago turned to face him. Or was it looking over his shoulder?

The muzzle disappeared but he was under no impression that it was gone. He could feel its cyclops eye trained on him as he picked up the bucket from the doorway—stupid, *stupid* of him to have left it in full view—and marched, not daring to look around or make eye contact. The place where Coffin had choked him stung and pulsed something fierce, his nails had pricked half-moons into the skin. Coffin barked a few curt orders to Lice as they passed by the bailing proceedings, still in full frenetic force.

The Captain pushed open the door to the brig, and Essex was waiting expectantly, pressed up against the bars. As soon as Coffin appeared behind Isaiah he shrunk back like a kicked dog, hair curtaining over his eyes. Isaiah caught something close to hurt twist in his expression, before it disappeared.

"I take it this . . . " Coffin jingled the keys next to his ear, loud and abrupt enough to make Isaiah jump. " . . . is what you wanted." He felt a hand press on his shoulder, and then push him slightly. "Or was it this too?"

Isaiah was frozen, stiff-kneed, unable to say a word even if he'd wanted to. Essex's face started off wounded underneath all his curls, but as his eyes darted to Isaiah's neck, it snapped from betrayal into something else entirely.

"Well?" Coffin goaded, and the boat slipped to a truly precipitous angle. The Captain kept his footing. "I tried to deal with you equitably, so SPEAK."

Something hard and metallic made contact with the side of Isaiah's skull. His ears rang and another blow rained down. The butt of Coffin's revolver had landed squarely on his temple. Isaiah tripped to his knees, hands going to cradle his head automatically. He felt the ship or his head sway, but Essex was still standing and staring death at Coffin. The veins around his eyes had popped and darkened and the obsidian color that made up his irises had inexplicably widened.

Before he could think, a long, booted leg made contact with Isaiah's ribs. A harsh gasp escaped.

"ANSWER ME. WHAT DO YOU W—"

Coffin was cut short and, no, Isaiah was certain now that it was the boat rolling, not him. He squared himself on his hands and knees, turning to look up at Coffin, clawing and scratching at his own throat. It was being pressed, compacted by an invisible hand. Essex did not blink, did not move an inch as the *Merciful* shuddered and stumbled in the water.

No sooner had Isaiah had realized what was going on, than the Captain desperately slammed a fist on the bars. Coffin's mouth opened and shut, fishlike, his lips growing purple.

"*You have had enough time to live,*" Essex said in a warped, multi-timbred voice that flooded the tiny brig with raw, claustrophobic terror. "*So let this end.*"

Isaiah clamped his hands to his ears. "*ESSEX!*"

In a blink, the man from the belly dropped Coffin. He fell to the floor of the brig in a heap beside Isaiah, taking massive, chest-filling gulps of air.

Isaiah tried to cough, but coughing hurt, so he simply stayed on his knees and tried to breathe, focusing on the dusty bits of straw that littered the planks underneath him. He was vaguely aware of the hubbub of footsteps and surrounding panic above them subsiding. In a moment, Coffin was scrambling to his feet, clawing his way upright. His eyes were wild, crazed. He panted, stared back at Essex for only an instant, and threw open the door to the brig, running out as if chased by wolves, keys in hand.

"Isaiah."

Essex's voice was soft, and closer to his head than he expected. He looked to see him knelt down on the other side of the bars, irises still wide and dark, but brows knitted together in concern, fingers knotted around the bars and halfway reaching for him.

"You . . . you can't cross iron, can you," he managed.

"Not in the way you could, no." Essex said, with a quiet exhale. If Isaiah hadn't known better, he might've thought it was a sigh of relief. "Makes things quite difficult."

"Can't even free yourself but you can—" He paused to catch his breath. "—Nearly choke a man to death," Isaiah said, dropping his gaze back to the floorboards and trying hard to focus on not throwing up.

Essex didn't dignify the comment with a response, and the ship slowly grew level, as if the water that had been flooding the hold was being pulled back out to the sea, where it belonged.

"He'll kill you. He'll hang me." Isaiah laughed, wobbly. The weight of what he'd done started to cut through the shock.

"I don't think so." Essex said, leaning back. His irises were shrinking. "There's been too much blood spilled by his kind. There's still a debt to be paid here, in full."

After a long moment, Isaiah rose, head still throbbing, neck and side aching.

"I don't *understand*." He said. "Debt or not, you can't just . . . why can't you just stop it?"

Essex looked almost pitying. "I keep forgetting that you're still one of them."

"What, *human*?! Yes, Essex, unfortunately I still have to live inside this *damn whaleship* and hope not to follow in my fucking father's footsteps—" He coughed again, throat complaining. Essex was quietly observing him again, and Isaiah could have screamed.

"Your father's . . . ?"

"*Yes*, my father's footsteps." He scrubbed a hand over his eyes, not wanting to watch him watching him. "Whalers aren't the only overzealously superstitious ones. He was caught back home. Hanged."

By the time he opened his eyes, Essex's mouth was twisted into something between disappointment and sadness.

"And you still can't see why I have to finish what's been started here? Despite what they've done?" Essex said, drawing closer to him again, eyes warm brown, nearly human. "Despite how you've had to live?"

Isaiah stared at him, willing himself not to cry. He gingerly felt the place where Coffin had held his windpipe shut, and something in his chest snapped cleanly in half, leaving only the empty space of where certainty used to live.

" . . . I know. I know."

CHAPTER FIFTEEN

SAIAH WAS IN the hallway leading down to Monteiro's dissection room.

A thin sliver of light emitted from under the canvas that cut the room off from the rest of the hallway. Something thrummed and itched at the back of his brain, telling him to open it. Telling him that he *wanted* to open it and see.

Before him sat Calder, seated by the surgeon's table. Monteiro's glistening silver implements, boiled clean, laid next to him. He had been propped up in a chair, grey and sallow as a haunted shade, heavy bags below his eyes. His skin, upon closer inspection, stuck to his bones with a shocking stiffness. His intact arm rested upon one of the well-worn supports of the dense wooden chair, and his heavy-lidded eyes rolled wide, barely conscious until they settled on Isaiah.

Calder's mouth fell open, as if the tendons holding his mandible from the rest of his skull had been severed. A voice emitted from his throat, rattling and caustic.

"...*Next come.*"

He recoiled, motion slow in the dream, and backpedaled as if he were tripping through glue, his feet dragging no matter how hard he strained. Calder lifted his arm upwards, pointing it directly toward him, the flesh taut and Isaiah could *tell* it was near to splitting, stretched white and thin.

Isaiah opened his mouth to cry, to scream, to be sick, but his mouth was full of water—hadn't they been safe inside the *Merciful* moments before? But the ship had been sunk down deep, deep below the waves the entire time, and he was intrinsically, unerringly aware of the fact that he couldn't draw breath. Something kept his feet attached to the floor even as he tried to step backwards, swim away, anything at all to get away from him, to escape that room.

It was only when the skin peeled back from Calder's fingers that Isaiah began to choke and gag on the water that engulfed them.

He woke curled in on himself, shivering. They were far enough south that the wind had turned cold, the chill biting through the layers of wood, canvas and iron to reach him, feeling like he had barely slept at all through the night. The image of the dream-Calder's lolling tongue sticking out of his mottled mouth danced in his brain and he couldn't bring himself to close his eyes again. Even hours after the incident with Coffin, he could still tell that he carried some kind of external mark from the struggle.

But still, as he made his way to the mess for breakfast and was made to scarf down his food by an irritated looking Morrow, he found that nobody called for him to be hauled in front of the Captain, to be beat or keelhauled for attempted thievery. Instead, the crew breathlessly discussed the close call that they all had prevented. Moirah was preening, content with the knowledge of a job well done in preventing further damage to the hull.

Even still, Isaiah could barely draw breath all morning. The steps up to the main deck were wobbly under him, and his footfalls were less than stable.

He rubbed out the gooseflesh that raised on his skin from the chill in the air, making his way over to the upper deck. When he yawned, his ribs still ached from where Coffin had laid into him the night before.

Someone was scrubbing. It was far too early for any of the other deckhands to have roused from sleep, and yet the stiff, scratching sound persisted. He crept forward, peering around the far mast, behind a near wall of crates and boxes that had been evacuated from the lower bilge, in an effort to save some of their rations from the wet.

Coffin was nearly bent double over some of the crates, a scrub-brush in hand and bucket of wash-water beside him, working ceaselessly at the wood. The Captain was doing deckhand work, and in his regular clothes. He still wore his clean-pressed linens and black leather boots. The coat had been discarded next to him as he scrubbed, arms straining, working at a nearly infernal pace at the same spot. He was well on his way to working a hole clean through the softened wood.

Isaiah hemmed for a moment, and the bruise on his ribs twinged. Pushing the ache aside, he stepped out from behind the pillar.

"Captain?"

Coffin didn't react, arms still working tirelessly against the wood. Back and forth, beating out an even, scuffing beat against the planks. Chips had begun to wear off from the crate, falling in his hair. A vein in his forehead stood out prominently.

"Sir?" he repeated. No response, no indication that Coffin had registered a solitary thing he'd said. "Captain Coffin, *sir*."

The bits of wood crate decked his shoulders in a light dusting of mildewy shavings.

After briefly considering his lack of options, he pushed forward, and lightly tapped at the Captain's shoulder, stepping back immediately to snap back to attention.

The Captain looked up, eyes narrow. "Back to your post."

"But sir, allow me to—"

"I cannot *allow* you," he said. "None of you can be trusted to get this damned infection out, can you?"

Isaiah's mouth fell open.

"Ah . . . let me help you, at least?"

"No. To your prior post, or to your own spot to scrub," Coffin snapped. His arms didn't stop moving once while he spoke. The wrong-ness of it was overwhelming. Upon closer inspection, his previously pristine pants had gotten soaked through and torn at the knee. His bleached white shirt was stained as well above the cuff, a dark grey-brown line of muck marking at what depth he'd plunged his hands into the murky water in the wash bucket.

Isaiah stepped back slowly, carefully. Coffin didn't budge, and didn't so much as look at him when he darted off to the mates' quarters.

Sharpe was already awake and eating when Isaiah found him. He looked hollowed out, like someone had come along and scooped out the substantial percentage of him. He did seem unusually thin, and Isaiah found himself wondering how often he could eat alone, uninterrupted. A twinge of guilt poked at him as he approached.

"Mr. Sharpe," Isaiah said, ducking his head. "Apologies sir, but there's—"

Sharpe closed his eyes and rubbed his jaw. "Just show me what's the problem, Chase."

In the time it took them to return to the aft-wards sail, Coffin hadn't shifted position in the slightest. He had, however, cracked one of the planks of the crate with the force of his cleaning and a small shower of grain had sifted out and was falling through cracks into the decking. Sharpe sprung forward, kneeling beside him and trying to take hold of one of his arms.

"Captain—"

"*Back*, begone from me!" Coffin barked at him, spittle flying as his arms still moved. The motion drew Isaiah's eye to his knuckles, which had begun to bleed.

"What are you—"

"I already said, fool, I do not trust a single damn one of you to clean the infection from this ship!"

"What? Erasmus please listen to me, you *must* allow the crew to—"

"Fool!" He spat. "*King* of Fools! You'd let this ship fall to ruin! You'd let me be chewed down to skin and sinew and bone and . . . and . . . " He trailed off as his arms worked, voice fading and eyes growing distant, staring down at his own still-scrubbing hands. Sharpe grabbed at Coffin's hands, seeking purchase. It was horrible, as if Isaiah was witnessing some terrible struggle between an unwilling child and a schoolteacher. He ducked behind the mast, averting his eyes.

"Chase! Fetch—ah—just *get Monteiro!*" Sharpe yelled, and Isaiah ran, leaving the First Mate to wrestle with his Captain.

It took Sulaimi, Álvarez, and Sharpe all together to transport Coffin from the main deck. They bundled him up in a not-insignificant length of rope, his arms tight to his body so that he couldn't take anyone's eye out as they went. He cursed and screamed bloody murder all the way to his cabin, only falling silent once the door had been shut for a long while, with him left inside.

"ALL HANDS, CALLING ALL HANDS."

The all-hands order, as it turned out, was a true all-hands. Even those who were supposed to be sleeping were hustled toward the main deck where Sharpe was standing before them, at attention. He'd cleaned up since his bizarre, stilted battle with Coffin, and after his removal from the deck. He had the look of someone who'd been diminished, had been whittled down to the sparest of parts.

Something was incredibly wrong. Coffin was not a *good* captain, by any stretch of the imagination. But even when he took to the bottle, he was comfortable ordering the men to work harder, push for more whales and at least the crew feared him enough to obey. Sharpe was something else, something worse: he was just as afraid as the rest of them.

And now, Sharpe stood alone at the head of the crowded crew, and the panic in his face sent a chill running down Isaiah's spine.

"Alright, gather 'round." Sharpe said, clearing his throat. "Some of you might've noticed that—that the Captain isn't well." He could see him looking about the crowd even from a distance.

"Until such a time as he's recovered, I am going to be taking command." His voice broke on the final word.

"I also wanted to tell you that we've got a new charge." Sharpe said, looking back to Lice for assurance. She frowned in response. "All hands are to put aside regular tasks for the foreseeable future. We are, ah . . . "

Lice piped up instead. "We are to holystone this ship, top to bottom, until this damn rot is cleaned out, once and for all." Sharpe seemed frozen in place as Lice bowled him over. "The ship's leak has been stopped for now, and supplies have been well diminished, but we won't continue South if we aren't able to suss out the cause of the rot." She folded her arms in front of her, glaring out to the crowd, as if daring one of them to disagree. "Restocking won't do much good if we aren't able to stem the leak from ruining fresh rations."

Sharpe took the opportunity to finish. "Quartermaster Stowe will assist you all in the distribution of materials with which to clean. I expect every member of this crew to be well occupied with their own duties." He gestured for Lice to step forward, and cleared his throat awkwardly. "All hands, um. Form two orderly lines please, by the brush locker and we'll distribute supplies and let you know where you'll be cleaning."

There was a long moment of stunned, blistered silence. Not a one of them so much as breathed. Isaiah had to wonder if *this* was how the ship would be destroyed, not by sickness or by dead crew or water in the hull, but by something as mundane and material as mutiny. There was a long, pregnant pause in which friends looked at each other and shuffled in place, seemingly unsure as to what they should do. Each one wondering who would be the first to break rank and either jump to obey or voice dissent.

"WELL? You heard him!" As it turned out it was Lice who, characteristically, broke the silence. Her shouting jolted them out of their collective stupor, and one by one, the crew began to part in two, forming a ragtag cleft in what had once been a united group of disgruntled, silent whalers. Sharpe took the opportunity to get well away from the mess he'd made, making a good attempt not to look at anyone in particular. His coattails flapped in the chilly breeze as he went back below. Isaiah shivered.

This was the first real admission, that they were losing a critical, potentially deadly quantity of their stores of food. That the flooding had been bad wasn't a surprise. That they would be going brutally hungry, and sooner rather than later, *was*.

He must have been staring something fierce, because before he knew it Hendricks had yanked him to join her line. He could hear Álvarez grumbling in front of him.

"I knew they were bloody lying about rations," he said. "And now keeping us busy for no bleeding reason."

"Shut it, Álvarez," Hendricks replied.

"I'm fucking serious—"

"They're making do with what they can," she said. "Now shut up."

" . . . Have it your way," he said, with no small amount of salt in his voice.

Something had been, was *still* deeply wrong with Coffin. He'd been working away on some imagined rot like a man possessed, and Isaiah was certain if the captain had really been himself he would've gotten a thrashing that would've made his violent encounter in the brig seem like a walk on the promenade by comparison. He shuddered at the thought, and the line moved forward slowly, dragging step by dragging step. Lice had taken his line, and Flores had taken the head of the other, with Lice looking each person in the eye with a thunderous certainty. Flores seemed to have committed themselves to the polar opposite, and was sheepishly distributing scrub brushes as fast as possible. When Isaiah made it to the front of his line, he only barely met the Quartermaster's gaze. She waited until he looked at her to hand him his brush and deck-cloth. Her green-brown eyes darted to his neck, and he ducked away before she could say another word.

He laid into scrubbing down a patch of deck next to Liu, who had found a particularly crusted-over part of the bilge and was washing it down diligently. Her shoulders jumped up to her ears with each scrub, and she seemed determined to work in quiet. Normally he would have tried to find Hendricks (*or Bellamy, or Fallon*) but since her tearful admission about Captain Briggs and her gun, she seemed hesitant to speak to him about anything at all, let alone make small talk. It would be all the better he kept to himself, just in case Coffin somehow came to his senses anytime soon.

The chill made the tips of his fingers ache fiercely, and the bucket of wash water supplied by a mournful-looking Demir only added to it. And still he and Liu scrubbed in dutiful silence.

After the first half-hour, his knuckles were raw and cracked. After a full two hours, they'd started to bleed, minuscule pinpricks of red blooming on the lines on his hands. They were all of them used to work. Every soul on board was used to enduring and enduring more, for the shining promise of an end to their signing debts, for a return home to be envied by every other whaler in Shaliston. But something about the *quiet*, the blood dotting his hands and the wind blowing through the still sails above them as they labored was unsettling. Preternatural.

A voice broke out in a ragged, warbling scream from the direction of Monteiro's surgical theatre. Liu whipped her head around, bangs falling into her eyes. "Who was that? It sounded like—"

"Calder." He set aside his brush. There was a patter of footsteps as those closer to the surgeon's offices hurried to investigate. "Wait, I'm gonna go see what's happening."

The image of Calder-in-the-dream, terrifying mouth unlatched and sour tongue rolling from between his teeth flashed across his brain up unbidden. Liu's eyes were wide. "I . . . I'll be right here."

Not a moment later, Monteiro darted past, faster than he'd ever seen her move, returning quickly with Sharpe in tow, Moirah jogging close behind. There were a series of shocked gasps, full-on curses emitting from down the hall. Dark curiosity fought with a riptide of fear. There was another scream, even more raw and unhinged this time, and curiosity won.

Crew members had clustered immediately, and he ducked up next to Flores, standing on his toes to see over his shoulder.

"Get back! BACK, I say." Sharpe was fighting a losing battle against the swelling crowd behind him. From Isaiah's inconvenient spot, he could see Calder's leg through the parting in Monteiro's drape. It was shaking, frantically spasming in place, and he spied Moirah's forearm leaning on him, and Morrow's low, uncertain, "Easy, easy now old boy. *Eeeeasy.*"

"SHARPE," Monteiro called back through the curtain, as Calder let out another unholy wail. The assembled cringed as one, and someone daring called out, " . . . He alright in there?"

No one responded from beyond the entryway, and the mutterings continued until there was an unmistakable scrape of an implement being rapidly sharpened.

" . . . *Alcohol*, Morrow, once you're finished with that—"

Demir began muttering a long prayer.

"Many a man would nigh assume
A bit o' light of a high-god's moon-
But not by blood, but yet by blade
Can break the magic of the low-god's make"

Álvarez joined in, and then Howell and Demir. Another muted scream from Calder punctuated their mutterings. Even as someone dared to look underneath the curtain again, heavy footfalls appeared at the end of the hall, and the quartermaster advanced on them once more and the collected group scattered, like so many rats into their nests. Isaiah followed Liu as she darted back to their post.

The both of them returned to scrubbing the deck with a vengeance, Liu trying to talk at him from under her arm.

"I . . . couldn't see . . . anything—" She continued, out of breath. Isaiah gripped the brush tight, about to respond, when an even more feral scream came from the room, followed by a sharp crack that echoed like a gunshot.

Sharpe came rushing out of the room, only to be sick in a bucket of dirty scrub-bucket water, which nearly overflowed onto his shoes.

"What the *hell*." Liu breathed.

Lice followed, even paler than usual under her freckles. "Back . . . back to work," she said, voice warbly and barely carrying. Once again, nobody moved.

There was another stiff-sounding cracking that resounded through the deck, followed by an animal-sounding moan that was only partially in Calder's voice. It trailed off into silence, as a third crack came, followed by a fourth.

"What are they doing to him?" Flores called from somewhere behind him, voice growing rough with alarm.

Lice wheeled on him, eyes blazing. "*Take that tone again* and I'll see your shifts tripled."

"Aye. Quartermaster, miss." He said, now quiet. There was another crack, and a corresponding moan, and Isaiah winced hard. He backed away slowly, clenching the brush in his hand. The canvas divider swished open and Monteiro exited, bloody to the elbow, eyes flinty.

" . . . Do not let your compatriots deter you from your work, crew," Monteiro said, to no one in particular. "It's important work we do aboard this ship. Do not forget it."

A light chorus of weak-sounding 'ayes' followed her as she turned heel, and returned to the operating chambers.

They scrubbed until night took the sky once again, and Monteiro didn't emerge for supper.

CHAPTER SIXTEEN

"**S**O. DID YOU see it?"

"See what?" Isaiah said. Sulaimi's voice was overeager behind his left ear.

"See . . . y'know. What was happening with Calder belowdecks," they said, ducking around him to sit at the seat opposite his.

"No," he said, gruffly. " . . . Heard more than I saw."

"Shame," they said, clucking their tongue. Bile rose in Isaiah's throat. They didn't need to know that he saw far worse when he closed his eyes.

"Why don't you go bother Morrow about it, since you're so curious?" he said, finally looking up from the task at hand. Rather, the task that was his hands. Applying the fatty balm to both sides when both left and right were equally cracked and aching was a delicate business.

Sulaimi sniffed. "Won't say a word about it."

Isaiah simply stared at his bleeding middle knuckle with intent. "Some things are best left that way, Sulaimi."

"What, like how you got those bruises the other day?"

Isaiah startled, blinked quickly, recovered. "What're you talking about," he said, flatly. Unconvincingly.

"I mean that you look like you got double-garroted, or else someone did a piss-poor job of strangling you."

"You're seeing things," he said, resolutely returning to his careful application of the balm. It went on thick and nearly-astringent smelling, and had cost him a truly despicable 6 coins.

"I'm fine. Just got tangled the other day when I was patching sail." Bellamy's line about him being a godawful liar floated to mind.

There was a pause, which, for Sulaimi, was unusual. " . . . Sure,

Chase," they said, rising from their chair with a sigh. "At any rate, what d'you think's happening with Sharpe."

"I dunno."

"You *dunno*. A man of many words, I see." He could tell they were prodding at him. It made him anxious.

"I'm sure he's doing his best given the situation."

"His best. And what does that look like, y'think?" they needled.

"I couldn't begin to guess that, Sulaimi."

"I'm sure you could guess," they said, tapping an irregular rhythm on the low wooden stool next to them. "If *I* had to guess . . . probably not very good."

Isaiah made a point of ignoring them, but an alarm bell rung loud and clear in the back of his mind.

"Think about it, Chase," they said, hopping up and vanishing off gods knew where.

The post-dinner crowd that filtered in after them was nearly silent, bordering on morose. The chill had only gotten worse as evening bore on, and even with the whole of the crew at work on the task of scrubbing out every plank on the *Merciful* top to bottom, they hadn't had occasion to switch out the watch or maintain any of the other more regular functions of the ship itself. Besides, the admission about dwindling stores weighed heavy as a storm cloud above the lot of them.

When Hendricks had ventured to ask Lice about it, she'd gotten a ripe earful, and a resounding threat that if there were any further questions, she could direct them to the Captain himself instead of bothering her. Hendricks, needless to say, had not taken her up on that offer. Even if she had, Isaiah couldn't have said what state Coffin was in. He hadn't appeared for dinner just like Monteiro hadn't. He wondered if they were together, discussing things. Plotting what to do with a ship falling apart underneath them, losing money, and a crew that grew more and more uneasy by the day. If he even was able to discuss things with the surgeon, or anyone for that matter.

Isaiah darned a tear in the lining of a vest in silence as Hendricks whittled away at the totem she carried. She was like a cat—easy to be around, but it would be on her own terms or not at all.

In a rush Morrow wandered past the two of them with a pocket-size grinding stone, and needle, looking ghostlike, wide-set eyes distant.

"Hey," Hendricks called, setting her carving aside carefully. "Morrow, come sit."

". . . Can't," they replied, not looking back at them. The tools were clutched to their chest, protective.

"Just for a moment?"

"Can't. Sorry."

Hendricks gingerly placed a hand on her shoulder, tugged a little. Morrow cringed away at the contact. "I *can't*. Let me be."

"We just wanted to know . . . how Calder's doing," she said, haltingly. "Please? Everyone's in a right state."

Morrow paused, closing their eyes, tilted their head backwards, as if expressing some kind of fundamental exhaustion that had nothing to do with Sharpe's work orders. They breathed in, out, slowly. "Calder is alive. If you want to know so badly, go ask Monteiro. I won't be recounting it."

Prodding them for more would clearly be a losing battle. And Morrow looked as if they'd been dragged from the grave besides.

"Thanks, Morrow," Hendricks said, dropping her hand from their shoulder.

Given the sounds they'd all heard echoing through the orlop deck, Calder still being alive was, admittedly, surprising. Morrow hustled down the row of bunks to an area where they'd set up a small ink boil-plate and steel quill. They began to kindle up a small pan fire, controlled licks of flame brushing up the kettle of ink.

Whatever they'd seen in the surgical chamber, it was bad enough that they were tattooing in fresh tokens. Needing protection from the waves and beasts of the deep was one thing, but an illness so foul that it required cosmic intervention was quite another.

"You regretting your blank canvas yet?" Hendricks asked, when Isaiah sat down across from her.

"Hmm. Not really," he replied, considering his arms, mid-brown color unpunctuated except for a few moles, which seemed to grow in number each year. His father had insisted that the act of laying in tokens for protection was rank nonsense. 'Why go writing your prayers in ink?' He'd said. 'The gods love to laugh, and you're just setting yourself up as a good old joke for them'. He didn't say what they both were thinking—since the gods were just as able to speak to them in dreams, there was no need to emblazon your fears and wishes for protection on the skin. They *were* listening, whether Isaiah liked it or not.

"Fair enough," she said. "What are the odds on Morrow letting slip what's happening?"

"Couldn't say," he said. "I don't blame them for not wanting to dwell on it. Not after this afternoon."

She hummed, considering. "Monteiro must be doing something drastic."

"They didn't look none too confident. And to be laying in tokens too . . . "

"Aye. Wouldn't make sense if things were going well."

They both craned necks out to peer down the row, where Morrow was adding in the vial of squid ink to the wood-ash and iron shaving mixture. Smoke bloomed from the small mixing pot, and they didn't lift their gaze from the spot where it burned, muttering what Isaiah knew to be repeated prayers into the vapor.

"Has anyone else started with that, you think?" he whispered.

Hendricks pursed her lips, considering. " . . . Not yet. But between the Captain's fit and this? Only a matter of time."

"Even if Calder recovers and Coffin comes back?"

"Especially then," she said. "Even if he does, it's bad luck to carry sickness back with you from the grave."

"That's a new one on me."

"Bad luck to come back from the grave at all," she said, not looking at him. "Like that man below did. Unnatural stuff."

"Hmn," he hummed, swallowing.

Isaiah took pains to pick at the frayed fabric, putting extra effort into fixing his sewing. Focusing all of his attention on what was ahead of him, like a horse wearing blinders, seemed the best course of action, given how often he'd been told that his face told the truth even if his words were intent on doing otherwise. Soon he'd sewn a rapid whip-stitch into the vest and made sure it laid flat and clean. He tied it off, stretched, and tried to cover up a wince—he'd managed to wrench the very place where his ribs hurt the most. Luckily Hendricks seemed to be engrossed with the wood in her hand.

"Be back soon." he said to no one in particular, and to his surprise, Hendricks actually nodded, tapping the side of her brow. She didn't look up from the long, sleek carving of a whale that was gradually taking shape in her hands.

The vest was Phelan's, and Isaiah successfully traded the rushed job for a small quantity of extra balm and gauze. Phelan was still half-drunk from ale and exhaustion, and he just grunted in his direction, pointing out where he'd left the material and stowed it away for later, picking his way back through the various crewmembers.

Liu usually slept sprawled out like an oversized house cat, at ease in her height and agility. Tonight, however, she'd curled up shell-tight in the dead center of the bunk. Isaiah thought to reach out to tap her awake, let her know about Calder's survival. He paused, indecision winding up his gut.

There was the question of what the hell Monteiro had Morrow doing in that surgical chamber. And what if the surgeon was right, and Calder's infection was Essex's doing too? Better for him to figure out what in all the gods' names was happening himself. After Fallon, it felt obvious to Isaiah that he didn't need to drag anybody else into it. He let Liu sleep, and moved on.

The ship, much like it had been at dinner, was graveyard-quiet. The crew's collective exhaustion had made quick work of any individual who harbored an urge for mischief. There was less late-night carousing, no whalers gathered on deck to throw dice or threaten the others with accusations of cheating at cards. On the whole, they had been subdued by labor and fear.

As silently as possible, he crossed the hallway leading to Monteiro's cabin. The telltale low glow of lamplight seeped out from the gap between the cloth curtain and the doorframe, and there was the sound of labored breathing coming from the other side. Isaiah tilted his head close, careful not to push out the canvas divider too far, just enough to get an eyeful of what was going on in the exam room.

It looked as if a miniature earthquake had touched down. Brass tools, clamps, and implements he didn't know the origins or use of were scattered everywhere, and ledgers and notes layered the free surfaces. Multiple sets of gloves and surgeon's aprons spattered with dried blood had been scattered haphazardly atop of it all, and in the eye of the storm was Calder. He had been laid back on Monteiro's exam table, half-propped up on a pillow, sheets covering his lower half. Whether it was for his own dignity, or to cover up some bizarre effect of the infection, it was impossible to say. At the furthest end of the bed, as far away as was possible in the small cabin, Monteiro was slumped back in a much-abused, rickety chair, clearly passed out cold. Her chest rose and fell evenly, arms crossed protectively over each other.

Before he could think better of it, Isiah was through the curtain, and registered the scene all at once: the other half of Calder's body, finally, was in full view. The amputated arm looked ragged, nearly macerated. The left arm was half wrapped, half abandoned, and the flesh at the end of it was a bloody, pulpy mass. His mind couldn't parse what it was, and he just . . . .stared.

His brain caught up to his eyes, and he realized that skin had been cut away manually, to reveal a layer of dark, onyx-hued shells that had fused themselves into the muscle itself.

He felt the acrid sting of bile in the back of his throat as he registered what was between the sleeping doctor and Calder. A pail, half filled with bloody, sizable barnacles. Clumps of excised flesh were still attached. They mixed with pieces of stained, discarded linen wrappings. The bottles had been taken down from their spot against the far wall.

Some part of him registered Calder's stomach, slowly rising and falling. The motion was shallow, but he drew breath, still, despite the mangled remains comprising his left arm. Isaiah couldn't break away from the grated pieces of flesh where the barnacles had once been, like someone had been pulling up stones and pebbles from a garden. Whoever had done the pulling left little behind. Reaching down to the bucket, he picked up one of the dozens of small, bloodied barnacles from the bucket.

Head throbbing, Isaiah gripped the piece of shell, and ran as quick as his legs would carry him, back to the end of the hall, no pretense of quiet left.

That was what what had Lice and Sharpe so terrified: they didn't know any more than he did what Monteiro was doing with Calder. Or what she would do to cut out the rot in the crewmember's still-living body. *She might be butchering him, slowly.*

He should have felt as disgusted as he had in the dissection room, but the bloody speck resting in the dip of his hand transfixed him. The edges were rough but rounded, and there was still a fleshy piece of Calder attached to the base where it had clamped on.

Suddenly, Isaiah was aware of the place where he'd made contact with the barnacle, now sitting innocently in his pocket. He scrubbed the flat of his hand against his trousers, hard.

He sat heavily on his own leather-bound trunk. Fishing out a small flask from his things, he uncorked it and took a hefty swig. His throat shuddered and he dumped out a small amount into his palm, and scrubbed with his fingernails as the abrasive tang of liquor filled his nostrils.

Better safe than sorry.

Returning the flask, he closed the trunk gingerly. *Maybe Morrow was right to start laying in with the tokens. Or maybe they were just afraid and don't know what else to do.* They couldn't protect themselves from an illness, a rot that's already under the skin.

Essex had created shells from nothing and placed them in his palm, delicately. His alcohol-dampened hands prickled. It stung where his skin had cracked from working the floors.

He was still shaky. He grabbed the flask back from his trunk and threw back a mouthful, letting the liquor burn slow and warm on its way down. It settled in a pool in Isaiah's stomach, and he imagined it burning away at his insides. He let the warmth spread from within, burning away any sign of infection, any indication that something foul had taken root inside of him. He took another heavy swig for good measure, followed by a third, and then a fourth. He drank steadily, seated on what used to be Bellamy's bunk below his own, in numb silence, until he could no longer feel the hum of the sea around them.

By the time he felt moved to lie down, he could barely feel his legs underneath him. If he wasn't unmoored enough as it was, the ceiling wasn't staying put, and as soon as he had fixed his gaze on a certain point, it slipped out from under him like a panicked fish. He shrugged out of his shirt and did his best to get comfortable under his blankets, which seemed determined to slip from his grasp too. Cool fabric ensconced him, and the seasoned oak planks above him swayed back and forth, divorced from the motion of the waves in a way that made Isaiah let out an audible groan.

It was far too much effort for his eyes to stay open. After a few moments of fighting with them, he admitted defeat, rolling straight into sleep and into a dream.

He stood on the main deck of the *Merciful*, surrounded by the usual machinery of slaughter. Someone must have finally won the prize of Briggs' gun and spotted a sizable whale. One less thing for Hendricks to worry about, he supposed. The creature had clearly already been hunted down and slain, and for a moment he felt the urgent anxiety of a missed appointment. Who would have been able to assist Hendricks in the hunting party, without him there?

Preoccupation slipped away as he realized that the try-pots were manned and working already. They had done well without him.

Billowing smoke rose up from one of the massive vessels standing like twin statues on deck. Two men stood on the elevated step leading up to them, both hunched over the cask, backs straining with the effort of stirring and manipulating the huge quantity of oil. Their long oar-like stirring implements cut through the vapor gusting upwards, and clouded the sky with black smoke, thick as a woolen blanket. It was only when he looked back down did he realize that the deck was empty of other people, and he stared as a particular mark caught his eye—a wide eye of the gods, staring back at him from the reverse of the larger man's neck.

He did not have long to ponder the question of why Bellamy was alive because on the wrists and lower arms of the other man he saw ringed bruises, in the shape of suction cups.

"Fallon," he called, feeling his voice fall short and fail him. " . . . Bellamy?"

Neither man turned to meet him. They didn't so much as flinch at the sound of their names. Through the dark, particulate smoke he could see a surgical chair, propped up. This time, empty and unoccupied, as if Calder had never been there at all. There was no sign of his amputated arm, nor of barnacles, nor anything at all but a dark stain coloring one of the arm rests, the sight of which sent a chill ripping down his spine.

Bellamy and Fallon stopped stirring the massive try-pots simultaneously, without signal or warning. Smoke continued to billow forth, burning off fat and impurities from the material. Heat rolled off of the surface. Even in such a dream, Isaiah could feel sweat begin to bead on his brow.

Above Bellamy's pot, however, the column of smoke wavered, just slightly. Something stirred him to move closer, and he leaned over to observe the surface. Ripples appeared: concentric circles, rolling out from the center, sending boiling hot oil rocking up against the metal sides of the barrel. Isaiah stepped back so as to not be burned as the source of the ripples revealed itself.

The top of a head cleaved the surface of the boiling hot oil, peeling upwards steadily, like an anchor being hauled upwards from its place in the depths.

The head gave way to long curls of nut brown hair, hanging over-long and soaked through, which parted to revealed a bowed head with strong nose, followed by shoulders covered in scars and old healed cuts from wounds past, which led to a broad chest and strong hips—

Isaiah tried to move his legs, to back away, but was tethered where he stood. Essex emerged from the boiling hot whale oil and let the liquid run off of him in thick rivulets. It trickled down his bare legs to seep through the boards of the *Merciful*'s decking. He could see, through the spot where his curls had parted, that the whites of his eyes were nearly entirely flooded black-brown, irises blown wide. Isaiah walked closer, and Essex smiled at him with teeth pearlescent white and canines a bit too sharp and mouth still shiningly wet with whale oil. Something unconscionable coiled in his gut at the sight of it.

The man from the belly reached to him and swiped a thumb across his mouth, leaving a warm trail across his lips. The thing in his stomach curled taut in on itself. It sat right next to where he'd poured all the liquor from the night previous.

"Isaiah . . . " Essex said. The end of his word trailing off as he traced Isaiah's bottom lip with his thumb once again. His wide, black eyes raked over him hungrily. Isaiah couldn't speak, couldn't respond, could only listen to the way the syllables of his name rolled off of the other man's tongue and tripped into the air between them.

This wasn't the sharp revulsion he felt from staring at the surgical chair, or the sick fear that had accompanied Coffin's appearance in his dream, or the raw terror he'd felt when Calder had peeled back the skin on his arm. He could do no more and no less than lean into Essex's hand, drawn in by the heat rolling off of him in waves, pulled in toward his mouth—

He was vaguely conscious of an ambient, heavy, knocking sound moving in the air around him, sending the atmosphere rippling around him. The image of Essex before him shook and trembled. He closed his eyes, and when he opened them again, there was nothing remaining of him but smoke, dissipating and drifting off into the sky. He fell through the dream, all the way back to his bed, and saw no more.

The bell clanged for the early watch, and Isaiah rolled out of his bunk feeling stiff and cotton-mouthed and absolutely thrashed by the alcohol that had swept through him the previous evening. Whether it was the liquor, or the vision of Essex in his dream, or a combination of both that made him hesitant to leave his bed, he couldn't say.

CHAPTER SEVENTEEN

S CREAMING WRENCHED HIM upright faster than the watch bell could. The bunks were alight with moans and cursing, crew mates springing into pants and fresh shirts, and running for the upper deck. Isaiah swiped up the shirt from yesterday and bolted with the best of them.

Moirah was screaming bloody murder. She had fallen back against a wall of boxes, staring up at a body that dangled from the mizzenmast. A rattle of fear ran through Isaiah's body like a poison. The body belonged to Captain Coffin. It was a mirror of the vision he'd scried days ago. He couldn't stop staring at it, the tension of the rope and the subtle roll of the ship sending his body flapping like a piece of clothing left out to dry, to bake and calcify in the morning sun. He was conscious of the fact that he was not shocked. Was not surprised, even. Still, he couldn't stop staring at the body in the rigging.

Voices called out in many dissenting voices, but through them all a loud, "Cut him DOWN!" could be heard.

"Axe coming by, I *say* AXE COMING BY," Lice darted through the crowd with a wild-eyed vengeance, holding a dagger between her teeth and a boat axe in her hand. She elbowed bodies aside without a second thought.

Someone behind Isaiah had already begun calling out a plea to whoever might be listening. *"All-lords of the deep, please—"*

Lice scaled the better part of the mast in record time, hands flying over one another, quickly reaching the spot where the captain dangled from a noose. High above them, his polished boots swayed and flashed in the morning sunlight.

"He's gone . . . " Demir murmured beside him. Even from this distance, Isaiah could see that Coffin's head was cocked to the side, snapped neck letting his skull roll loosely in place. His mouth had fallen open, tongue lolling out, swollen and greying. Phelan began to scale the mast to assist Lice with her work, as she was already consumed with hacking off the rope that held his body aloft. The whaler gingerly took hold of Coffin's lower half, and slung the body over his shoulders as they began the descent. The captain's long limbs dragged, knuckles brushing against the whaler's calves as he carried him. His body was laid down on the decking with a thud. The rope still hung about his neck and Sharpe received the body on the ground below. He scrambled to remove it, tossing it aside. The crew dodged, as if touching the rope would burn them. Isaiah ducked down, and threw it overboard.

There was a brief moment of shocked stillness, before the prayers for protection began again.

"Lords keep us . . . "

"Good gods. Oh good gods." Yesayan spat behind him, muttering out the words to protect them into his shingled fingers, hands shaking.

Isaiah had always assumed that the end of a captain would come with more pomp and circumstance. Some kind of grand gesture to indicate the death of a great man, an important man. Coffin's now slightly less than spotless clothing was the most distinguished thing about him. The only thing indicating that anything had gone wrong was a coin-sized spot of blood and spittle sprayed on the collar of his jacket, nearest to where his head had fallen as the neck snapped. It still looked moist.

"Someone fetch Monteiro!" Lice barked.

"I'm here, let me through." She shouldered her way across the assembled crew and knelt next to Coffin. Her deft hands prodded at the back of his neck, where his spine met his skull. Shaking her head, she sat back on her heels, facing the crew with darkly circled eyes. "He's certainly dead."

"How . . . how did he . . . " Sharpe said. Almost as one, the rest of the crew seemed to immediately remember that he was First Mate. Now, Captain.

Monteiro appraised him quickly, hands moving across his head, prodding at his ribs and torso.

"I can't say, sir." She blinked, rising to her feet. "If I may, we should wrap him up and bring him to my offices, quickly. Calder will be moved elsewhere."

Sharpe nodded curtly, stepping out with what appeared to be unsteady legs. "You . . . you lot heard her. Phelan, take one end. Morrow, you take the other."

The two moved silently to each end of the body. As Morrow reached down, Isaiah spotted the intricate tangle of lines across their hands.

Sharpe turned to address them, shell-shocked and hollow-eyed.

"Alright . . . We're going to be asking every one of you to go about your business for the day. This ship still must sail, and we must stay the course." A rough, anxious tension lay thick on the deck, peppered through with muttered prayers and pleas for protection from the crew.

Sharpe looked shaken. "You heard me!" he shouted, voice hoarse, wild. He took out his pistol, unlatching the safety with a quick motion and the first row of men sprung backwards in a disjointed wave. "Move!"

The crew shuddered backwards. Someone's elbow crashed into Isaiah's chest, and someone else pushed up against his back to edge him out of the way.

"*Move*, I say."

As one, they backed away, away from the corpse, away from Sharpe, still half-hunched protectively over what remained of Coffin's limp body. Some turned away as if ashamed, sensing that this was something that they shouldn't bear witness to.

When Isaiah dared to look back, Sharpe had sunk to his knees, the pistol abandoned at his side. He reached down to cradle Coffin's head. Isaiah averted his eyes before he could see them make contact, and edged backwards, down to the brig.

He flitted down the hall and toward the door, hands scrabbling to undo the latch. He found Essex already at the bars, eyes bright and peering over at him expectantly.

"Isaiah." He sounded warm, almost relieved to see him. Isaiah's stomach tugged, and the vague memory of how Essex had looked in his dream, emerging from the whale oil, bubbled up unbidden. He felt blood rush to his face, despite himself, and tried to shake off the pent-up feeling that was mixing with dread in his gut.

"I thought you'd forgotten about me," Essex said, sly grin creeping across his face. "Some things have been fixed for you," he said brightly.

"*Fixed*—" Isaiah took a deep breath and gathered himself.

"So that he won't touch you ever again."

"Essex, Coffin was just found dead!"

"And you would rather Coffin be permitted to just carry on?" he said plainly. He certainly didn't make any effort to sound repentant.

"No, that's not what I meant, but now *Sharpe's* in charge, Calder is way, *way* worse, Monteiro has Coffin's body, and everyone is in disarray—" He stopped. Gathering himself, he stared hard at Essex, as firm as he could be.

"Did you kill him?"

"I did not. Guilt and despair are close cousins, especially in the mind of someone like Coffin." He stared right back at Isaiah. "And how could I, when you still won't find a way to let me out," he said. His irises were preternaturally wide again. He wasn't as charged with strange energy as he had been just after Fallon had died, but the similarity was a touch too close for comfort.

Isaiah turned from him and pressed his heels to his eyes until he saw spots. Essex's talking in circles around him was too much. Too irritating, too *strange,* and what good was being shown the future if he wasn't able to do a single thing to stop it.

He stepped forward, less than a foot and a few strips of iron separating them."You *said* to me that no one else would suffer. Like Fallon did. Like Calder suffers now."

"I told you that I cannot stop what's been set into motion." Essex set his jaw. "The crew aboard this vessel are already well on their way to devouring themselves whole."

Isaiah groaned. "Essex, *please.* Just be honest with me."

"I'm not being dishonest," he said, looking down his nose at him.

"That's not the same thing!"

"What would you have me say? That Coffin well earned the death that found him?" Essex said, matter of fact. "He was soaked in blood and cruelty by virtue of his all but unearned position, and he reveled in it." He raised an eyebrow, jaw still set firm. The more Isaiah spoke to him, the more he was certain that he was dealing with the most stubborn creature on earth.

"What's done is done."

Isaiah paused to take a breath. It wouldn't do to snap at him when he was only shakily aware of what Essex was capable of. Or, at least, capable of inciting.

"*Fine.* Coffin was a bad man and a worse captain. He's gone now, so stop this." He could hear the bitter twinge of desperation creeping into his voice. "You righted the ship."

"The balance that must take place . . . .it can't discriminate," Essex's tone was mournful. Nearly. "That was . . . different."

"Different *how*?" Isaiah stared. "Is it that you can't or won't stop it?"

"It's not . . . It's not something to be stopped, or allowed." He dropped his gaze down, clearly dodging the first part of his question. His eyes lingering on the planks below their feet. "Humanity believes itself to have mastered the will of the gods above and below. They think they *know* things."

"But they don't?"

"They put names to forces beyond their control in the hopes of taming them, of understanding and measuring the inevitable." He shook his head, and he looked almost regretful. Essex stepped near to rest his fingertips on Isaiah's collarbone."And they would punish anyone with any knowledge of these things outside their power." He tapped a finger gently on him for emphasis.

Isaiah felt his face flush warmer but couldn't bring himself to pull his eyes from him. The stubble on him somewhat disguised the long-healed cut on his upper lip, but at this proximity he could see it trailing upwards, light scar tissue ghosting into the coppery-olive of his skin as it met his cheek.

"And you have to be the one to do it?" Isaiah asked. For a moment, he almost stopped himself from reaching upwards, to brush the spot, but didn't. He could feel Essex's breath catch.

"I—" He huffed a small breath inwards, seemingly unable to continue.

" . . . Or do you have a choice?" Isaiah finished softly.

As he spoke, Essex shrunk back, suddenly and without warning. He let his hair fall back in a dense curtain about his face. "I certainly do not."

Isaiah let his hand drop back through the bars, and took a small step back in return.

"What will you do about it?" Essex asked, apprehensive. There was more than a touch of sadness in the question.

"I don't know."

He had just told him that it was out of his control, wasn't it? That he couldn't put a stop to anything that had begun on the *Merciful*. Isaiah couldn't just throw him to the wolves. They would tear him apart, and then him afterwards for not telling anyone sooner. He had let him get too close. Let *himself* get too close.

He would be lying if he said that his dream wasn't rife with wishful thinking.

Essex peered over at him through his hair, brows knit together in concern, and the guardedness in the other man's face made Isaiah's chest ache. It was nearly enough to make him forget the death that trailed behind him like a bridal veil.

He blinked, leaned closer to him from behind the iron between them, and Isaiah left him there, before he could do or say anything else he might come to regret.

When Isaiah returned from the rest of the day's work, back aching, he nearly walked straight into Álvarez.

"Meeting. Near to the bow. Be there in half an hour." He said, barely looking up at him.

"Meeting? With who?"

"Just be there." He said, and stalked off toward the upper deck without another word, his shoulders tensed up about his ears, back stick-straight.

As it turned out, the meeting was more of an impromptu huddle. The group clustered around the bow, clutched around each other like a group of nervous hens, bobbing about to check for foxes outside the coop. Álvarez poked his head up at Isaiah's approach, and the group parted to admit him into the fold.

"Alright. That's all the ones I admitted. For now," Álvarez said. "We'll go it in shifts with the rest of them."

It was an odd group seemingly selected at random; Flores was there, as well as Sulaimi, Morrow, Phelan, and Toole. They looked grim, serious, and Morrow's eyes kept darting over their shoulder. Álvarez cleared his throat for an uncomfortable moment, but powered on, addressing them like he was supposed to be in charge.

"I'm sure we all know why we're here—"

"I don't," Isaiah said flatly. Phelan shot him a sour look.

"Did you or did you not see Coffin hanged and Sharpe nearly lose his mind just this morning?" he asked drily. "Unless there's a different Chase on morning watch."

Isaiah fought hard against the instinct to roll his eyes, too exhausted to hold back much. "I did, thanks. What are you doing? Or is this just the far Lower Seas' most elite sewing circle?"

The group around him was deadly silent. Sulaimi's eyebrows had shot far up into their hairline.

"Oh."

"Keep. Your voice. *Down*," Toole hissed.

Álvarez carried on, one eye warily trained on Isaiah, as if he was already regretting his decision.

"Sharpe isn't equipped to lead. This much is certain." Scattered nods and hums of assent followed. "Remaining are Lice, Monteiro, and Moirah. They are obstacles, but not insurmountable ones."

Morrow nodded. "Monteiro belongs to the shipping company. The situation with Calder has her thrown, and if she can be shown reason, she may not put up any fight at all."

"Aye."

"Monteiro's on commission, just like Coffin is though," Flores said, tentative in his dissent. "If I were her, I'd be worried about the legality of it. Once we make it back to Shaliston."

"Desperate times." Álvarez leaned over, using all his over six-feet of height to his advantage, and laid a warm hand on Flores' shoulder. "And that's if we make it back to home port, Bennie." He looked up at Isaiah, meeting his gaze. "*If.*"

Isaiah swallowed the lump that rose in his throat, Essex's assertion that the crew was already close to devouring itself ringing in his ears. *There are a dozen, no, a hundred ways this will go south.*

"Lice won't be so willing to upend what she's helped build," Sulaimi said.

"That's where you're wrong," Álvarez said with a sigh. "Morrow here doesn't want command. Moirah can't. I damn well don't. Someone will have to take the captaincy if we're to restock, hunt for further whales, and make it back home in one piece."

" . . . And it can't be Sharpe?"

"It damn well can't," Phelan said. "He's more of a steward than a proper mate. He was too attached to Coffin to see sense and take command, before it's too late."

"Too late for what, exactly?" Toole asked.

"You saw the lower deck." Álvarez intoned. "How long do you think those rotted supplies are going to last? With that man in the brig as well not earning his keep, and still needing to feed anyone that falls ill or injured as we go?"

"Even if every soul aboard fishes for his supper day in and out, even if there are any fish around the cove? Which there likely won't be, because we're hunting for damned whale oil instead of good catch," Phelan said.

It wouldn't be enough. What they suggested was mutiny, plain and simple, no matter how dire the straits. The image of the skull twisted in place, outlined stark white against the deepening cover of night. The reality of such a plan sunk in.

"You would upend things, risk angering the gods—" Isaiah finally asked.

"We risk *nothing*," Morrow bit back. "We'll be protected."

"How? By who?!" He asked, growing desperate.

Morrow thrust forward their hands, palms facing skyward. Slowly, they rotated them, bottom to top. The arrows and bands which had seemed confusing and tangled from a distance had a pattern this close up. They were intricate bowline knots. Each arrow was plaited in circuitous paths, so that they appeared tangled; if you pulled the right thread, however, the whole thing would go straight, leaving only one long rope behind.

"Everything will come clean. In the end." Their hands were still puffy and swollen with blood from where they'd laid them in the day before. It looked raw, like meat left out in the sun for too long. Their eyes were bloodshot, lingering someplace else entirely.

Isaiah didn't say what he was thinking. Bowlines were notorious for looking secure, holding weight, but could come untied easily if you pulled right. Before you knew it, an overeager deckhand would tug the quick release, and what you'd been trying to secure would be lost to the waves.

But the crew around him looked upon him with eyes that

hungered and faces run hollow with bad food and Isaiah didn't have the heart to tell them any different.

Álvarez stared at him. "If there had been any other option? Trust that we'd be doing it."

"I understand," he replied.

"Do you?" Phelan asked, fixing him with a long stare.

"Enough." Álvarez sighed and ran his hands through his inky hair, which had seemed to lose a bit of its luster as it went. The ends were ragged where he'd tried to take off some of the length. "We'll reconvene tomorrow, different location. Speak to the others as quickly as possible. I'll alert everyone individually where and when it's safe to meet."

The group nodded and mumbled words of assent, and they dispersed one by one across the deck.

Night had crawled up on them from the distant horizon. The clanging of the watch bell chased after them as they returned to bunks and cabins, to lay still and pray themselves to sleep. Isaiah knew deep in his bones that Morrow's upturned hands would only hold back their bad luck for so long.

CHAPTER EIGHTEEN

A SORT OF GRIM, rote cycle set into them all over the next day, and a few crew members went about the watch without being told. They simply donned jackets against windy weather and walked out, not chatting or whistling, barely speaking at all. There'd been no further word from Sulaimi or Álvarez, even though he'd seen them stalking about the upper deck, leaned in close and talking amongst themselves. As soon as he approached, they'd fallen quiet, or moved off to do something else. He spotted another group of them, this time led by Sulaimi, gathering by the aft. They all looked hungry for something, and whether it was blood, food, or just violence, he couldn't say.

Isaiah had taken a round at watch, waited for supper, and ate quietly while the others talked amongst themselves, as Hendricks tried to make some small conversation with him. She was picking at her food, same as he was.

"What do you think will happen? Now that it's Sharpe's ship?" he asked, pushing around a piece of dry, crumbling hardtack into a meager portion of watery stew.

Hendricks chewed and considered. "Well, it's never been Sharpe's ship. Everyone knows he's an acting substitute. It doesn't matter," she said. "None of it matters."

"So long as we find some catch, sure."

"I meant what I said." She looked at him, with something close to pity in her eyes. "It just doesn't *matter*." She set down her spoon, carefully balancing it on the edge of her dish, and stretched her right arm out across to him. She rolled the sleeve of her shirt up past her forearm, and in the crook of her elbow was a bump. Small, innocent looking, and still covered in deep brown skin. She tapped at the surface. It seemed hard beneath. Isaiah's breath caught.

" . . . Everybody knows about Calder's condition. Morrow isn't good at keeping secrets." She quickly rolled her shirt sleeve back down, her tone bleeding sarcastic. "Especially with the good doctor not executing any miracles anytime soon." Taking up her spoon again, she dug back into the food in front of her, not looking back up at Isaiah.

The number of times that they'd all been in tight quarters blurred together in his memory. Suddenly, he felt a phantom itching on his own palm that he knew wasn't real, and yet he reached down to scratch it anyway. Any trace of hunger for the food in front of him seemed like a laughable memory.

"There are others, too," she said, evenly. She still hadn't tore her eyes from the food before her, even though it was nearly gone. Her even tone was holding down something even worse.

"Does Sharpe know? Does Monteiro?" He asked, trying to keep his voice down.

"No, and no."

"Why not?"

"She damn well hasn't been able to help Calder. Why should she be able to help me or anyone else? Besides, after that procedure with Calder, Morrow's not telling her anything, regardless," Hendricks said, setting the spoon back down with a hollow clink. "They're a good student, but not that good."

"Maybe she'll be able to . . . ..I don't know. Learn something about how it's passed so that nobody else'll get sick," he said. Hendricks finally stared up at him. The look she wore was one that you'd give an inquisitive toddler, who suggested a visit to the moon or that fairy tales were real.

" . . . Your trusting nature will do you ill one day, I'm certain of it."

"I'm serious."

"I know you are." She sighed. "The only reason why Calder hasn't been thrown overboard or left on some godforsaken rock is because Monteiro's intent on studying him. One lab rat is reasonable, but two?" She laughed humorlessly. "At best? I join that man in the brig until I get sicker and sicker."

She looked resigned, like an echo of her former self. The loss of Bellamy, Calder, Fallon, not to mention Briggs and her gun had taken something fundamental out of her. This was just one more

162

weight, one more horrible, terrifying accident in a line of many that had consumed them, that had been eating them alive for some time.

And Monteiro had to have a plan. Even if it was just in service of putting the crew back to work, or getting them to the next port to restock their stores. *She has to know something.*

Determination cut into the shock. He made his apologies to Hendricks and left her where she was at the table.

This night, Isaiah noted that there was no light shining out from beneath the canvas divider. He lifted the flap and ducked inside, dropping the cloth smooth behind him.

No Monteiro sleeping in her work chair—instead, the captain's body was laid out on the exam table. He looked as limp and cold as a gutted fish, body beginning to swell. The ring of bruises where the noose had run taut around his neck made Isaiah shudder. He had never been allowed to see his father after he'd been executed, except in his dreams. He nearly reached out to touch the mark, but only made it halfway.

" . . . Chase."

Isaiah jumped back, barely restraining a thin yelp. The sound had come from what he had first taken to be a pile of worn aprons in the corner, but instead, was a man.

In a chair appropriated from the mates' quarters, Calder sat. Bundled linen rags patched up what remained of his arm, his shoulder and left pectoral. Bandages had been slung around his neck too. Some were splotchy with what looked like dried blood and antiseptic, others were only a day or so old. The patchwork of fabric didn't conceal the fact that he was awake, eyes gleaming wetly in the dark with reflected moonlight.

"Chase, help me." His voice was somehow both sawdust-raw and wet with fluid. Isaiah tried to steel himself.

"Calder, you're . . . "

"My skin hurts, Chase. She left me in here with . . . with . . . " The sentence broke in his mouth, whether from stress or physical pain, or both. "I can't . . . can't sleep with a *corpse*," Calder choked out, voice shifting scratchy and strained. He hacked a brutal, chest-rattling cough, once, twice, three times.

Not for the first time, Isaiah was wracked with the familiar pang of guilt. "I'm not big enough to carry you, Calder," he said. "I'm so sorry." He darted over to a pile of notes and rifled through them, scanning rows and rows of Monteiro's minuscule, slanted handwriting.

"No, no," he said, voice still shredded but growing louder. "Won't let you."

"Please, it's going to be okay, I . . . I . . . promise."

"Help me," he said, voice elevated to as close to a yell as he could get in his state. "*Chase* . . . "

"*Please* stop, you'll only strain yourself," Isaiah hissed under his breath. "He's dead, he can't hurt you—"

"NO," Calder shouted, chest heaving. "Not him, the other man will make sure I die, he'll—"

Sudden, creaking footfalls approached them. Isaiah whirled around, throwing himself to the ground, and getting as low as he could, inching on his hands and knees underneath the tall surgical table where Coffin decayed. He held his breath as Monteiro's boots made their way into the room at the edge of his peripheral vision.

Calder fell silent as she entered. The doctor walked over, inspecting him, moving from one side of his prone body to the other. Prodded at his bandages for a moment, adjusted something. She didn't address him, or try to speak to him. Isaiah finally had to draw a shallow breath.

"*He's here, he—*" Calder said, voice strained and cracking.

"Quiet. Nobody's here," Monteiro said. There was a muffled wheeze from the chair where Calder was seated. His feet, barely in view from where Isaiah hid, grew lax and still. Monteiro set down some implement on the counter with a metallic ping, and left without another word. Calder's shallow, rattling breathing had grown slow, rasping as it regulated and moved through his chest.

Isaiah crept forward from his hiding place, and slowly rose to his feet. Calder was out cold and a metal needle with a tin cylinder attached lay on the table next to him. How long the sedative would last, he couldn't tell.

Isaiah pawed through the discarded papers even more frantically than before, but his efforts produced nothing that looked remotely like a cure, or an admission that treatment was futile.

FROM THE BELLY

He stopped and nearly groaned aloud. Of course. Her most precious notes wouldn't be left where just anyone could find them. Not if she was attempting to conceal from Sharpe and the rest of the crew what she had or hadn't discovered from Calder's failing, infected body. Isaiah ducked out of the surgical chamber and skirted back away from the cabins as quickly as he could. He kicked himself for not thinking of it sooner, and for waking Calder.

Isaiah skirted down past the cooling room and what used to be Sharpe's room. It was dark and empty, the divider ajar; he had the right to sleep in the captain's old rooms now.

The doctor's personal cabin was next, with a canvas curtain fully drawn across the doorway. Only the captain was allowed a locked door. Common wisdom was that such privacy was a privilege that not just anyone could be afforded, after all. Pressing his back to the wall next to the opening, he peered inside at an angle, silently trying to pick up any sound, any hint of movement from within.

Other than the sound of snoring coming from Moirah's room across the hall, there was nothing. No sound of someone taking late-night notes, no light glancing out from between the curtain and the floor, no movement at all. Careful not to lean too far, Isaiah reached out a tentative finger, to crack the curtain just a few inches wider.

The bunk on the opposite wall, clearly visible through the gap in the canvas, was empty. The quarters were neat as a pin, bed done up, tiny folding writing desk in the corner orderly, with ledgers and ink stacked up on the surface. But empty. He ghosted inside, fear trembling high in his chest—Coffin had been predictably erratic, in the way that a bite-mad dog could be depended upon to do the cruelest, strangest thing possible. Monteiro, however, was much harder to read. Measured, restrained, and unnerving in a way that Isaiah couldn't quite parse. She'd been so quick to knock Calder out with gods-knew-what, and that wasn't even taking into account the strange conversation she'd had with Essex days ago.

Isaiah circled from bunk to desk to trunk to desk again. Hovering a hand over a leather-bound ledger that rested on top of the desk, he pulled back. Compared to the disarray of the surgeon's quarters,

165

her personal belongings were almost perfectly neat. She'd be certain to notice if anything was even slightly out of place. He hovered over the log, hand shaky. His palm prickled, and a chill ran down his spine.

Swiping the ledger's cover wide open put a stop to it. Isaiah thumbed through, rifling through orderly pages until he reached the log where Calder's injury was first named. It was a long entry, punctuating a variety of other notes about mundane hurts the crew had experienced: from split domes obtained from falling down wet steps after dinner to an abscess where a tooth had been. He steeled himself.

Day 188—Midweek logs caught up to date, Morrow informed on all necessary details about removal of infected nails.

Accident occurred after a storm [Jeremiah Calder] while mending cracked mainmast, received massive puncture wound to forearm. Potential for recuperation of appendage exceedingly low. Results of procedure yet to be seen. Wooden matter removed from the puncture, disposed of. Bone heavily damaged, sedative well in use and topical salve applied. (Note: Morrow suggests prayer and supplication by crew may be helpful in healing. As Calder has yet to regain consciousness, odds of this functioning are slim. Won't currently consider the suggestion, as Morrow never seemed to take much stock in common ritual before. Will discuss further to assess if they are experiencing some kind of distress.)

A few days of updates followed, almost casual in nature. Isaiah flipped backwards. In the space before Calder's injury he landed on a page, mostly blank.

Day 184—Logs need updating, ask Morrow to re-bottle and decant more cleaning alcohol for general use.

An adult man, of indiscernible age, was retrieved from the stomach of the day's hunt: large grey whale, ~20 meters in length.

Man is alive. Recommended to the brig by Capt. after initial exam. Unable to move him to speak, although he appears uninjured. Somewhere between 25 and 30 years of age, although impossible to tell precisely as no opportunity was given to conduct a comprehensive exam and molar count. Various scars and old injuries visible on the surface of the skin, with aged scar tissue. Source(s) of injury unknown, but seem to comprise various different types of entry wounds. Breathing is superficial, but he is otherwise physically intact. Behavior toward myself and the crew is inscrutable. Recommend he be given regular treatment, although Capt. disagrees with the necessity. If he lives, he may be integrated into the crew, given some sort of further emotional/mental assessment of his capabilities for language and for following work orders.

Anger jabbed at him. Essex had truly only been useful to them in such capacity as he was willing to work like the rest of them. And now, Coffin was dead, and Monteiro was given full access to him.

He flipped forward, returning to Calder's line of treatment. The entry was short, seemingly scrawled in a hurry.

Day 193—Amputation's been difficult to care for. The shells within Calder's muscle mass keep returning. We pulled forth about a dozen of them last night alone, and by the next morning there were buds where new ones had sprouted, seemingly overnight. We'll have to amputate further up the arm, but not sure how much more he can take. The least of our problems at this point.

A few blank pages followed. Most were scraps of thoughts, notes here and there that broke off mid-paragraph.

Spoke, finally, with the man who was recovered from the whale. Seems divorced from reality. The foreign nature of the infection cannot be unconnected—timelines nearly identical. Coffin will not give permission to investigate/take samples. Further steps must be taken. No recourse to get word to Messrs. P/T/C wrt. infection or Coffin's degenerative state

And then, on the most recent page:

Request urgent re-entry into crew population so as to test infectious capacity. Specimen of a physically transmittable infection via a singular carrier. Fetch a very good sum.

"Infectious capacity . . . " Isiah mouthed the words to himself as the entry trailed off. No more notes, no further entries followed, and Isaiah closed the log cover neatly. She was still convinced that Essex was causing the sickness, somehow. And that she could isolate it, auction it off to the highest bidder.

The irony of the fact that he had, in fact, infected the ship, just not in the way that she assumed, was not lost on him.

As he left Monteiro's cabin, he heard the low rumble of voices emitting from the captain's quarters, and darted back into the depths of the *Merciful* before morning broke.

There was no question that Monteiro intended to do *something* with Essex, and with Calder alike. The question was when, and what Essex would do to fend her off. If his first threat to Coffin was anything to go by, the idea of Essex, cornered, was not a comforting one. Isaiah had only heard the many-voiced presence that had emitted from his mouth twice, and even locked behind bars, the voice had instantly itched and tore at the inside of his skull. He couldn't begin to imagine what Essex would do, if Monteiro truly tried to dissect him.

Isaiah darted up to the main deck once again, avoiding the place where Coffin's body had been brought down from his noose. He grabbed up a pail of seawater and drew it up. There was no hint of a moon up in the night sky, but the starlight poking pinpricks through the clouds above would have to do.

He had been able to see Coffin's fate. Risking doubt, wasting a chance to keep Essex safe . . . it simply wasn't an option.

Isaiah set his teeth and looked into the sea water. It stung his eyes just as bad as it had the first and second times.

This time, he was able to lapse into that kind of loose unfocus that made it easier for the visions to come, and he stared deep into the pool. A shiver ran up his spine, exiting at the very top of his head, and he shook. He realized with a start that he hadn't spoken the usual incantation before he began.

Instead of fuzzy shadows, the shapes gained form and dimension in shining black and crisp white. He was tempted to sink into them, to pick through the pictures that floated to the surface like so many intricate etchings. They fanned out in the rough wooden bucket and his eyes watered.

Blinking. Blinking is important. Focus, Isaiah.

Was this what Pa used to see?

Another chill ran through him, this time crackling through his fingers and clearing his vision further. Despite the risk, this was the use of seeing what the future foretold. If it meant keeping Essex from Monteiro, the danger of it would be good for something.

Instead of sifting through the images, he tugged on a filament-thin, invisible string in his mind, pulling forward the question. He spoke the question into the ether without uttering a world. He was being heard without prayer, without tokens or murmured devotions or coin paid to a shrinehold. It felt *good*.

Show me what is to come for Essex.

why. Why WHY why w hy w h y?

The returning voices beat into his brain like hammers on hot iron, molding the words into his very mind over and over again. It was a fair question. He froze as he searched for the answer and one surged up unbidden.

Because he's mine. I want him.

In an instant, something washed over him and an image swam up from below. The starlight bled together and coagulated, forming something just as crystalline as the other images and twice as sharp.

It made the silhouette of a person, lying down on a table. Strapped to it, flat on the boards. His hair splayed over the surface and falling off to the sides. He knew, innately, that it was Essex. He could see the contours of his form where they lay. As his mind caught up to the vision, Essex's arm began to fall off in chunks. Square dissections, grafts of skin. Pieces of him were coming apart, being pulled off by someone, or something, until he was left with almost nothing but bone. And yet, he still lived.

The next moment, the image dissolved into a different picture. This time, Isaiah saw a body, wrapped up tight in canvas and weighted with iron ball and chain at its feet.

The same body, dropped off into the sea, still wriggling, struggling against its bonds. Stuck inside the taut canvas.

Isaiah emerged from his trance. The lightning-swell of power rolled off his back and into the night air, and dread filled its place.

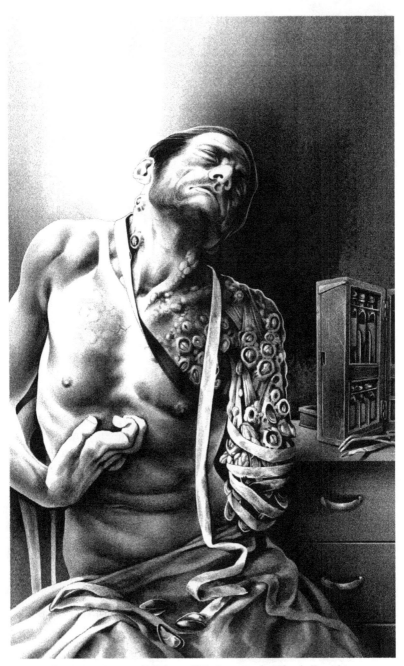

"Day 193 - Amputation's been difficult to care for. The shells within Calder's muscle mass keep returning."

CHAPTER NINETEEN

"**U**P!" **LICE'S VOICE** rang out through the hold. "Up, you dogs!"

She marched up and down the rows of bunks, snapping an arm out to hit those who were still sleeping. Isaiah jolted awake, head smacking on the upper ceiling, and he rolled out of bed. His foot made contact with something wet on the floor of the deck.

"Sulaimi! GET!" Lice shouted with a dull slapping noise as she made a hearty attempt at rousing them before hustling back above decks to check on the morning watch.

Fewer whalers had risen than Isaiah expected, and as he looked down to see what he'd stepped in, he sprung back.

There was a not-insignificant sized puddle of vomit, slowly rolling down the deck with the motion of the ship. He shook his foot off quickly, the source becoming clear: two bunks away, Flores was bent almost double, leaning out of bed.

"Flores, what the hell—" Isaiah started. He caught himself at the last minute. One arm barely held Flores' forehead clear off of the floor, and the other strained for a cloth just out of reach.

"What's going on?" Álvarez was vertical as well, and he reached down to touch the back of Flores's head. Just as his fingers made contact, Flores heaved a terrible, raw choking sound and retched violently.

"*Augh—*"

"Gods above!"

As Isaiah dodged the sick, a few small metallic specs carried on the tide of stomach acid and half digested dinner caught his eye. They were alive and wiggling.

Down the row, Sulaimi let out a loud groan.

"What are those?!" Álvarez asked, eyes like saucers, tracking the writhing, cigarillo shaped fish as they flopped in Flores' vomit.

"Minnows." Isaiah said. Sulaimi's groaning turned to a full-throated moan.

"Help . . . stomach hurts . . . " Flores moaned, rolling over onto his side on the bunk. Someone down the row had the presence of mind to grab a sizable bucket. Sulaimi coughed wet and ragged, and soon enough followed Flores' lead.

Isaiah felt raw panic rising in his chest, but he quickly snagged a few rags from the bin, helped Álvarez clean Flores up.

"Save a few of them." Isaiah said.

"What?!" Álvarez said, lip curling.

"Lice will need to know," Isaiah said. "Don't look at me like that. I'll do it."

Breathing carefully through his mouth, he scooped up two of the now limply-wiggling minnows into a small square of cloth, and wrapped them up tightly. The packet was warm, still. He felt himself gag momentarily. He swallowed hard instead, slipping the packet into his jacket pocket.

Lice was just beginning to rearrange a set of boat axes when he found her.

"What is it now, Chase?"

"I'm sorry but—"

"Sorry nothing." She wiped the polishing cloth over the surface, the metal of the blade making a subtle *sshek* sound as she went.

"There's been another rash of sickness, down below. Sulaimi and Flores," he said, and she snapped up to look at him. "They were spitting up . . . this." He gingerly handed over the packet, and watched her hands move as she unwrapped it. From the motion of the wax cloth, he could tell that the minnow was still wiggling lightly, shaking the fabric in her palm. Her nose wrinkled and she immediately set down the packet on the deck.

"*Alive?* Like that?"

"Yes, miss."

Lice spat and crossed herself in quick succession. "Get it all out of view of the crew, no more of this. I'll notify Sharpe."

Isaiah darted back to the bunks and pulled Álvarez from where he was patting Sulaimi's shoulder ineffectually.

"Orders are to get them out of sight. Don't let anyone else see this."

"We're just supposed to cover them up?"

"They're trying to avoid a panic," Isaiah cut him off. "Álvarez, *please*. This is bad, and it can get worse."

He grimaced hard, jaw tense, but did as Isaiah said. The two of them had cleared out Sulaimi and Flores from the bunks and to Monteiro's surgical quarters in a matter of scant minutes. Álvarez stalked off as soon as they did, trailing back above decks just as Sharpe was sweeping downstairs, eyes wide as dinner plates. Only a few of the crew seemed to realize what was happening and began to drift out of bed, curious.

"Up and out of here. All of you!" Sharpe barked. His face betrayed what his voice tried desperately, to cover up, and his eyes were still glassy and fearful. Those that were still in bed scattered. Isaiah didn't realize he'd been itching the palm of his hand until it began to prickle and sting.

If the crew moved quickly about their tasks that day, it wasn't due to Sharpe asking them nicely. Those that had business above decks stayed well out of the mildewy air below, and no-one would go back toward Monteiro's quarters. She'd disappeared back into the cabin and hadn't been seen since. Calder hadn't been brought out, but then again, neither were the other two patients. Unlike when Calder had first been taken in, there was no hint of sound to be heard from her rooms. No cries of pain, no sound of cracking bone. Just quiet, and a smell like stomach acid and rotten fish.

Isaiah had been tasked with re-coiling rope that'd gotten tangled, luckily, on a far end of the port side deck. Hendricks approached skittishly sometime after mid-morning. She walked up without really looking at him and leaned lightly against an already-tidied pile. He reached out a hand to steady it without thinking, brushing against her arm that had had the hard lump under the skin. The whole thing was awkward.

"Ah- sorry," she said.

"Don't, it's—" he replied.

"No. I didn't realize."

"It's fine." She looked at him, eyebrows cinched. "You saw the two of them this morning. How were they?"

"They were in a bad way."

"Chase."

"What?"

"You know what I mean," she said. Isaiah felt his stomach clench. He hadn't exactly had the spare time to check their skin for nodules.

"It . . . wasn't that kind of sick. I don't think," he replied, as evenly as he could. There was no telling if Hendricks would be the next one to start spitting up bite-sized sea life, but if she wasn't, there was no use in worrying her ahead of time. She seemed relieved.

She quirked her mouth. "Alright. So long as you're sure." She alighted from the freshly coiled pile of rope.

Over her shoulder, she called back to him. "You'd better be, Chase."

Not for the first time, Isaiah wished he could write to his father. He composed the letter in his head as they returned to scrubbing down the ship again. Sharpe flitted about the deck between them all, uncertain of what to do, of how to move with people dying onboard and the already cavernous gap between whale oil obtained and whale oil owed to the company growing wider and wider by the moment.

Dear Father,

No, the sound of it was too formal. He'd always called him Pa, when they were at home. In public it seemed too casual, so he'd called him Father in front of company. It had made his mother laugh, to see her small, mop-headed child talking so stiffly in front of neighbors and shopkeepers.

Dear Pa,

Some strange things have been happening recently. I've been having dreams like yours.

A part of Isaiah was distracted, turning over the image he'd scried last night, of Essex being taken in, taken apart, killed by the crew.

I know you never spoke much of these matters, and Ma never much liked to hear about it either.

From where Isaiah sat, he could see Álvarez eyeing Sharpe as well, from his position on the upper deck. He was crouched in place, carefully swabbing the floor in front of him, dutiful and unmoving. His eyes tracked Sharpe in turn, as he moved about the deck and Isaiah remembered his hard, determined look.

. . . But I have been seeing things I'm not supposed to be seeing, and some of them have come to pass.

As Sharpe passed about the deck, Lice took his place, watching them. Briggs' intricate, silver-inlay pistol sat comfortably on her hip. Sharpe hadn't even tried to claim it after Coffin's death, had hardly put up a fight.

Did you ever worry about the things you saw? Did you ever see your own end? Ma's?

Isaiah dropped his gaze just as Lice turned to stare over at him. He kept his eyes down on the dark oaken boards below him, and let the wash-water run over his fingers.

Mine? And what would you do if you had?

Sharpe summoned Yesayan to him, and passed something into his hand, and Isaiah could spot him speaking low and urgent into his ear. He nodded, darted off, and before long, Essex was being led up onto the deck. Not in shackles, not corralled in by anyone. Not contained by anything at all. Yesayan pushed him up the steps and he stretched like a cat in the mid-afternoon light. Sharpe stepped up and cleared his throat.

"Men, we . . . we will need more hands if we're to continue southward. It's been recommended to me that we make use of all able hands as we carry on." He looked even less sure than usual. Essex peered toward Sharpe, curious. "Make this gentleman at home amongst you."

Isaiah stared, slack jawed, as Essex shot him a wry look. Essex squinted against the briny spray for a moment until he was interrupted by someone handing him a bristle brush and pail. He ambled over to where Isaiah had been working, and knelt next to him, as if it was the most casual thing in the world. Isaiah could feel the eyes of the rest of the crew trailing him as he moved freely about the deck of his own volition. He had nearly forgotten that almost nobody else had seen him walk around or speak, aside from the solitary other instance in which he'd been allowed to walk about and take in some fresh air.

"Isaiah." Essex grinned, wide and toothy. "What *were* you ever up to last night?"

"*Don't,*" Isaiah hissed, horrified. He forced himself to look away and returned to the task at hand with a vengeance.

"Well I certainly felt something," he said, lackadaisically mirroring him. "Whatever it was."

"We're not talking about that here," Isaiah said, under his breath.

"Oh, *right.*" Essex seemed far too amused by the whole turn of events. "I'll let it be, then." And now he had just . . . been released. And was just sitting *chatting* with Isaiah as he worked, with nothing between them but air. He could feel the eyes of the rest of the crew present boring into him with an unprecedented ferocity. Not to mention Essex looking over him hungrily as he worked.

"But I am curious, Isaiah." He chanced another glimpse at Essex. He seemed nearly as fired with an unnatural energy as he had after Fallon's death. The thought of it made Isaiah's gut churn, and he tried not to consider the fact that Coffin, cruel and misguided as he was, had been the only thing holding him back. "What did you see?"

That night, Isaiah bypassed the bunks and headed straight up to the upper deck. Essex had taken the hint and refrained from questioning further, and as they'd worked throughout the day, it became more and more apparent that most of the other crewmembers felt strange about him. They avoided getting too close, skirting around him and avoiding making contact. He was given menial tasks, things that didn't require much skill or prior knowledge, and he wouldn't speak to anyone unless spoken to. Isaiah had tried his hardest to keep an eye on what Essex was doing, but doing so unnoticed was tricky work. He hadn't sat for supper with the rest of them, and Isaiah had skirted up to the main deck after dinner. It seemed unimaginable that he'd want to be anywhere else.

Isaiah couldn't tell who was on watch, and the moon hung big and pock-marked in the night sky. The breeze that had filled their sails after Coffin's death was still blowing fresh and clean, and he shivered against the chill. Leaning against a railing, he felt the wood beneath him shift and he leaned off of it, arm smudged with wet, partially rotten slivers of wood. A rank feeling slunk through him. The rot had spread through the body of the *Merciful*, as quickly and impenetrably as the infection had. He brushed off his sleeve and stood back, skin crawling. There were wet patches dotted along the railing and along the surface of the deck, where they'd just been scrubbed down on Sharpe's orders. They were well on their way to rot, and a pillbug curled out of where he'd been standing, milky white, and with antennae wiggling. Isaiah scrubbed at his eyes, keeping them closed tight until he saw stars.

When he opened them, the railing was intact. Just one long, well-worn piece of wood, intact and dry. He held back a choked, shocked sound, conscious of the fact that the deck was quiet enough for him to be noticed by anyone who was still awake. The breeze blew, and the canvas of the sails flapped gently in place, but there were no further sounds, no birds called in the dark, and the sound of the waves lapping seemed far off. Distant, as if he was hearing it from a great height. When he looked down, the moon was reflected on the water preternaturally large, illuminating the surface of the water with white silvery light, and the waves themselves didn't dare interrupt the reflection.

Essex appeared next to him at the edge of the ship and Isaiah jumped. For a man of his height, Isaiah had learned that Essex was extraordinarily quiet.

"Are you ready to tell me what you've been doing?" he asked. To Isaiah, it felt easier to be around him at night like this, lit by the moon above. He seemed to meld easily into the darkened sky.

"You know why I couldn't earlier," he replied. He leaned closer, a part of him relishing the fact that he could stand so near to him.

Something faltered in Essex's face. "You're that afraid of what they'd do." Anger brushed over his expression, like a shadow cutting below the waves.

Isaiah couldn't find the words to tell him so. *Yes, and now that they see that I'm the only one you speak to, I'm twice as afraid.* He settled for ducking his head and continuing on without answering him.

"I scried again. The surgeon isn't finished with you."

"I thought not." Essex searched him over, interest piqued. "I felt it, whatever you did."

"Felt it? . . . How?"

He shrugged. "Whatever you spoke to, whatever window you open up to see. It's a part of—" He gestured up and out. " . . . All this. So I could feel it."

"I heard some kind of . . . voice. A number of voices."

Essex nodded, eyes bright. "So you're *listening*," He looked so . . . enthralled. Interested in him, unafraid. Isaiah could have basked in the feeling for a very long time.

"I just wanted to see what might have been coming. For you," he supplied.

"For me." He blinked. "Why?"

Isaiah scrambled, pulse hammering. How honest was too honest, when Essex already knew more about him than nearly anyone else? He had told the strange, many-voiced thing that he had wanted him. He had. He *did*. The truth of it thrummed in his breast like a trapped bird, batting its wings hard and incessant.

"Because Monteiro's up to no good. As soon as Coffin died, she went to Sharpe to ask after you." Still, it was too difficult to say it aloud. To crack himself open like this and hope that the man from the belly, certainly not a human man at all, would treat him gently. "She still believes that she knows how to rout out this . . . sickness. And if not, that she can make a study of it, bring it back to port."

"I see." Essex's nose wrinkled. " . . . Let her do what she thinks she must."

Quick as anything, he brushed a bit of hair off of Isaiah's forehead, and he was off down the deck before Isaiah could think to react.

The break of day that morning was blustery, and growing colder by the hour despite the sun rising high ahead of them. The *Merciful* had finally been returned to the route first charted by Coffin, despite the diverted path to chase the last whale sighted. They'd crossed their final planned meridian around the lowest part of the coast and were passing by the furthest parallel on their chart before the final leg of the journey. The whales were known to be rarer here, and so there was nothing for Isaiah to do but work, sleep, and worry. The nearer they came to the south, the lower the air dropped in temperature to match.

As they crossed the furthest Southerly parallel, all bells on board were rung, and the whalers made small tributes, burning little finger-sized wooden poppets and dropping them overboard, as was customary. The cinders hissed and expired completely as they hit the surface of the waves, leaving small bubbling pockets of smoke in the surf. They dissipated near-instantly, as if they'd never existed at all, and Essex watched the proceedings with a kind of pointed curiosity from the far end of the deck.

Liu took Isaiah aside not long after the crossing, her fingers still a little sooty from dropping in her offering.

"Did you get a chance to speak with Sulaimi?" She asked, rubbing her hands on her pants distractedly.

"No, why should I?"

She clucked her tongue at him. "Because they and Flores were released back to the crew just now. I thought I saw them talking to you just the other day?"

It made no sense at all. "Wait, released? *Why*?"

"Don't ask me, I've no clue. Doctor gave them something and said, apparently, that there was nothing else to be done at the moment. I saw them both lying down but how long that'll last I don't know." She added. "Don't seem right, to have them out and among everyone and still being so sick."

"No. Certainly doesn't."

Isaiah considered the notes in Monteiro's logbook. A shiver ran through him and the wind carried the smell of burning wood back into his nostrils and Liu was off again. *She's still experimenting with them. Maybe with all of us.*

Slate-colored storm clouds began to gather overhead by the end of the afternoon, and despite what minimal preparations the ship needed for a cold-weather storm, Morrow was escorting Sulaimi and Flores back up to the main deck, just as Liu had predicted. Lice was directly behind them, prodding them along with not much delicacy.

"C'mon. Let's get at it, we've got a foul front headed our way and we can't have you lazing about while there's things that need doing," she said, batting Liu on the shoulder as she went.

Isaiah was busy re-affixing hard-weather batting to the foremast, but could see their heads bobbing along and Lice's voice floating upward from not too far below. Normally, Flores and Sulaimi couldn't look more different, what with Flores' bulky stature and dusting of black-brown hair, and Sulaimi's lanky frame and sleek black braid hanging down their back. From Isaiah's view, however, they were nearly identical in posture. Both were moving along on the deck at a snail's pace, shoulders rounded, clearly in some kind of hard pain; whether from infection or fever of some other kind of ailment, it was impossible to tell.

Sulaimi inched themselves along, body tilted in on itself, with one hand grasped tight to a railing, the other pressed to their stomach. For a moment, it seemed as if Morrow had just tripped. In the next moment it became clear that something was horribly wrong as they took another shuddering step, and fell to one knee. Lice bore down on them as they sank to the deck and Sulaimi stared, horrified and speechless.

"Get up. Now!" She hauled Morrow up by the back of her shirt, setting them to rights with a resolute hand. Isaiah flinched as they wobbled in place, trying to get their footing.

" . . . Sorry, I don't know what's wrong with—"

Sulaimi, in a blur of motion, hit the deck, moaning in pain. They scrabbled in place, legs working uselessly against the planks as their arms clenched around their midsection.

Monteiro had appeared from below, staring keenly over at the group of them. Waiting.

In the instant in which Lice was distracted, Morrow fell to their knees a second time, nearly crumpling entirely.

"Demir, to me!" Lice called out, and he dutifully came running from somewhere in the fore at top speed. Isaiah gripped his tools fiercely, and held tight to his seat above as the two hauled Morrow off of the deck, and returned to Sulaimi.

A small group of crewmembers had gathered nearby, close enough to be able to see and hear what exactly was happening, but not close enough that they'd be at risk of coming into contact with either one of them. They moved in place like ants or bugs, rife with nervous energy.

Sulaimi still moaned, heaving dry and ragged onto the deck, coughing fit to crack their windpipe, with each cough curling their body in again like a millipede under a muddy rock. The surrounding crewmembers drew back as one body.

Isaiah realized that it wasn't unlike the horrid, rasping and hacking sounds Calder had made.

"Fetch Monteiro!" Someone shouted, and the surgeon emerged, rushing over like for all the world she hadn't just been sitting and watching the two collapse, one after the other.

No sooner than Morrow was gone from the deck, from the back of the crowd, Yesayan fell, barely catching himself on his elbows. Isaiah caught the flurry of motion as a few of the crew nearest to him jumped, as the man too started vomiting dark-colored bile. Like some kind of awful joke, there was a beat of stunned silence before everyone started shouting and moving all at once.

"Blast the whole—"

"—Fucking GODS above man!"

Isaiah shimmied down the mast where he'd been working, elbowing through the crowd. On the other side of the crowd from him, Flores too fell, and opened his mouth as if to scream, grasping at his stomach and chest, his hand scratching at the place where his shirt met his skin frantically. Panicked, Álvarez lunged to hold back his arms before he could tear his own skin bloody. Suddenly everyone was moving, roiling on the deck, either to aid or to run, and the bile that had come from Yesayan was an unnatural, black-green color staining the wood the color of char.

Sulaimi's hands flew to their neck. "It's crawling—something's—*it's crawling up me!*"

They choked, convulsed where they lay, and grew still. Foam bubbled to their lips, and from the corner of their mouth, a long, slender eel the color of kelp slipped out. The creature writhed and squirmed from the slack corner of their mouth to the dark oaken deck, its body slick with stomach acid and seawater. It glimmered dimly against the light of day, mouth gaping open and shut, and forest green body hitting the deck with rapid, fleshy thuds.

Essex was perched far above Isaiah, a dark spot high on the mainmast, sitting easily as the ship moved under him. Isaiah could see him watching as Monteiro, with gloved hands, picked up the eel, and carried it below deck. The rest of them were left to pick up the bodies.

CHAPTER TWENTY

SHARPE DIDN'T LOSE the frantic, hollow-eyed look he'd been sporting in the morning after the sudden bout of sickness had taken both Morrow and Sulaimi in one. Isaiah hadn't spotted Essex since. He'd been pulled in by the mates to help move them back down below, to the sick bay, and when he had returned up top Essex had disappeared, gods only knew where. His sudden absence wasn't noted in the rush of calamity and sudden, brutal death.

Morrow passed belowdecks, not soon after Sulaimi had spat up the eel living inside them. Monteiro simply told Demir to help bundle up her things, and to prepare to deliver the both of them overboard along with her crew-mate. He'd conveyed it in hushed tones, felt the callousness of it drift and spread over the remaining crew. Yesayan and Flores disappeared too, to be kept in one of the darkened cabins attached to the growing surgical wards. Word had been passed down from Sharpe had said that they weren't to be allowed visitors. That the rest of them were to carry on maintaining their regular rotations of watch, washing up, and rest, regardless.

After all, they all still had debts to assuage that no sickness could wipe clean, and so they continued at pace.

That day, Isaiah pulled at the head of a haul line while backed up by Liu, who wasn't capable of pulling it much by herself. Phelan had tried to back her up before Isaiah did, but he had stumbled away moments later to throw up over the port side.

"—Careful there, careful—" he said, as Liu bent to pick up the slack, and she cringed as her knees bent in turn.

"Mind yourself, Chase." She crossed herself and gingerly took up the weight. They strained against it as long as Liu could hold out until the sail was hauled up full-mast. When it was done they stumbled back, Isaiah bent double and Liu falling back onto the deck with a dull thud and hissing through her teeth with pain.

"What's wrong with you?" Liu said under her breath, picking herself back up.

" . . . Nothing, nothing," he said, stowing the end of the line. He moved quickly on to his next charge, picking up the washing that one of the sick had dirtied earlier that day.

He looked away from her for moment, and as he did, there was a crunching sound. Liu hit the deck on her knees, howling. Isaiah bolted to her side, where she had fallen backwards. Her scream of pain and terror had turned to heaving sobs.

"Liu—LIU. What happened, what—"

"Back away! Don't touch her!" Lice shouted as loud as she was able. "Give her air—Phelan, fetch the surgeon!" Still looking pale, he stumbled to the bowels of the ship and disappeared. Monteiro came up without him and as quick as anything pulled out a blade to shear off the lower legs of Liu's pants.

A spur of bone-white coral jutted out just underneath her kneecaps, breaking up from below the surface of the skin. Monteiro's knife fell to the deck at her side and the onlookers shuddered back from Liu's body. She turned it, inspecting it round.

"Help—help—" She gasped. She grabbed at the surgeon's arm, clawing at her sleeve, barely able to breathe. The coral was mottled with blood and plasma, the skin stringy and split in two, and Liu just gasped for air, gulping it down as if she would never breathe again.

"Can you feel them?" She asked.

"No . . . I can't, I *can't feel them* . . . "

Isaiah's insides churned. Monteiro turned one coral spurred leg over in her hand, and grasping it tightly in her fist, snapped it off. Liu shrieked, arms winging out above her head, and the assembled gasped as one.

"Hold her down, Chase," she said, "On our return, samples will fetch a good price."

He obeyed, eyes like saucers. She pressed down on the other leg, and snapped the second spur of coral. It broke uneven, and she chipped away at it with a small knife drawn from within her vest.

"There," she said, matter of fact. "Don't let it spread further."
She pocketed them, addressing the crowd.

"Pyle, Thacket, and Coffin expect the use of all resources. Don't
waste what shouldn't go wasted." She seemed wired with a terrible,
fierce energy. "Bring her below if it's warranted."

Dinner that night was sparse, watery stew and cracked bread that
seemed well on its way to dust. Isaiah figured that it was for the
best that Essex didn't eat like the rest of them.

Álvarez was peering around the supper benches, roving around
between the tables for what, it wasn't clear. Maybe seeking further
signs of infection, or a kind of pallor among them. He must not
have found whatever it was he was looking for, because he
eventually picked his way over to Isaiah and Hendricks' table. He
sat next to Hendricks, leaning in and addressing the both of them
with a kind of measured calm.

"I take it you both understand how dire our situation's getting."
He ducked his chin at their meager plates. "We'll be meeting again
soon to discuss things further." Hendricks set down her cutlery
gingerly, nodding. She'd begun to move with a kind of ache, a sort
of stiffness that spoke of something bad growing even worse. She
kept her sleeves rolled down all the time now.

He eyed Isaiah. "If you're ready to follow us down this road,
then get prepared. If not . . . " He trailed off. " . . . you just stay well
out of the way, if you have so many concerns about it." He pressed
his lips together.

Isaiah leaned back on the bench, casting an eye around the
mess. Sharpe was seated in the customary center post of the
captain's table. He seemed small, diminished in the intricately
carved blackwood chair that used to be Coffin's seat. Sharpe
scanned the assembled, seemingly counting the remaining warm
bodies.

Álvarez was staring daggers into him.

"It's been near on a month straight of no catch, no whales, no
nothing. Sharpe lets Monteiro do whatever she likes when we take
ill. If we don't take action, we'll never be able to pay down what we
owe on the charter. Not a single one of us." Álvarez jutted his chin
in Sharpe's direction. "If I manage to escape the surgeon's knife, I
want to get some more coin to send back to my family before I die.

Don't you?" And without another word he was up from their table, striding back to his bench, now half empty with the spaces of where his friends had been hollowed like knocked-out teeth.

There was a heavy pause as Hendricks stared after him, hands empty of her utensils, dinner growing cold on the plate.

"He seems . . . serious."

"Why in all the realms wouldn't he be?"

"Coffin had just died when they first started bringing it up," he replied. "I didn't think they would still be going on about it. Assumed they were mostly just dissatisfied with the ship's . . . mismanagement."

"And you thought that kind of idea would just *go away*?" Hendricks said. Her tone was even-keeled, but just barely. "Easy for you to go along to get along. Being perfectly healthy, and all. With that man to keep you company."

Isaiah winced. She was right. He was hungry, tired. Exhausted-anxious with the idea of what Essex might do, of what Monteiro surely planned to do. But healthy. And now anxious at the thought that Hendricks was paying closer attention to Essex than he had thought.

"No, I'm not sick. And you are, so what's the point, right?" He said, more harshly than he meant to. "You'd just go along with this plan just to what? Get a few more barrels of oil in before . . . whatever this is spreads?"

"I am not going to 'just go along' with it, Chase."

"Gods, I know. But this isn't . . . it isn't right." Isaiah said, sudden defeat overtaking him. "It's just not. Nothing about this run has been right." He felt the familiar sense of doom hovering in his chest. "It can't work out the way they think it will."

Hendricks fixed him with an unyielding stare. "Why do you say that?"

It would be so easy to just explain to her. To tell her calmly that the man from the belly was not human, that this journey had been blighted by greed from the moment they set sail. Instead, he took a bite of his own now-cold dinner.

"Lice is just too loyal to the way the ship is *supposed* to run," he said, not looking up at her. "Monteiro will report to Pyle, Thacket, and Coffin. And we'll all be jailed on return."

"Not if we live long enough to return with a full ledger of oil."

Her deep brown eyes looked bright, with either fever or anticipation it was impossible for Isaiah to tell. "I'm not like you. I don't want to wait around to die, Chase." She stood shakily. "It's not what Johanna would have wanted for me."

Hendricks cleared away her now barren plate, leaving him alone with only the empty space where she had been for company.

There were fewer and fewer able bodies among them to send out on a skiff to harpoon any unfortunate creature that happened to cross their path. No fresh catch, and no whales either. A few of the lesser-ill had made a valiant attempt at looking out for fish, to supplement the dwindling stores of food. They had only come up with tiny nippers and skinny sea eels. Nothing worth the energy it took to reel in. It didn't stop some of them from trying anyway, and those that did came back exhausted and frustrated, stomachs just as hollow as before.

There should have been fish around them, he'd thought to himself.

Besides the hunger, the worst part of the coming days wasn't the fact that everyone was ill and getting worse, it was the speed at which people were dropping dead. The ocean's sickness came on like lightning, and passed through the crew like a fetid, sickly wind, and took all souls with it.

When Toole woke up ill with a horrid, familiar, wet-sounding cough two mornings after Morrow and Sulaimi's twin deaths, everyone greeted the fact of his sickness with something verging on open terror. His cough led to him choking up a chunk of slick, balled-up seaweed the size of his fist. No sooner had Toole been taken to Monteiro's sick bay, than Demir fell sick, gums bleeding and peeling back from his teeth like moss receding from an old tombstone. An old wound on his back had begun to open, the flesh previously conjoined by scar tissue running open like a ripped seam and revealing a round, knotted contusion within the muscle. It simply wouldn't heal. Isaiah and Phelan had to hold him down as Monteiro administered the sedative. There were more and more notes taken, and with every crew member that fell ill, there were more tests, further procedures to do.

Demir was barely out by the time she'd bent over his spine,

wax-threaded surgical needle in hand. Isaiah couldn't bring himself to look at what she was doing as the skin was pulled taut back over itself, but the dull, metallic smell of old blood hung in his memory for hours after.

That evening, he went back to his bunk and bent to shuck off his shirt. Nothing could have been sweeter than to sleep, just sleep, and to not have to think of anything at all. He would rather take his chances never waking up again than spend one more moment remembering a single thing about dying men hung from masts or eels wriggling from the inside of living people or the rusty, perpetual scent of blood. As he tossed his shirt into the trunk by his feet, a strange buzz of motion caught his eye.

"Be quick about it, right?" A voice said.

"I'm going, I'm going . . . "

"Bear with me. Nearly set."

A small group had gathered at the end of the bunks where Morrow's old spot had been, and were huddled over a set of implements. The acrid smell of iron and squid ink burning coiled down the passage between the beds. A handful of them were huddled together over Flores, prone on his front and near motionless. Another crew member was nearly bent double over him, long needle in hand. His face was turned to the side, but his bony shoulders went taut with every jab of the ink-dipped tool.

"Steady on. Hold still."

Isaiah couldn't see exactly what he was imprinting on Flores's skin but a few of the other crew members who sat in waiting muttered prayers over their body. One of the group even pressed hands to the closest of his folded arms as the laying-in of the token progressed. An occasional visible cringe rolled through them. Something about the scene was grotesque, desperate. It was the look of a ritual held in someone's dying throes, the work of their spirit rolling and shaking through their body like a brutal exorcism. Isaiah stood facing his bed, not able to look at it further.

And yet, as Hendricks had pointed out, he remained healthy.

Most days, he felt sick to his stomach with pure, unadulterated worry. He could barely eat much of the tiny portions that were left, and when he did it rolled uncomfortably in his gut, but the reality of it was that he saw no such strange lumps underneath the skin. He felt no chill setting in, he wasn't dizzy with fever. The place where Essex had instantaneously, mysteriously healed the cut on his hand so long ago remained soundly scarred over, never peeling back open on itself to reveal the delicate muscles underneath. He had taken to rubbing at it occasionally, just to be sure it was still intact. He looked at it in the low lamplight, then put his shirt back on to head up to the main deck.

Isaiah found Essex standing on deck, looking for all the world like he owned every last inch of it. Out in the night air he looked even less like a shadow than ever before, and a sliver of moon intermingled with the light shed from a lantern on the deck, and cast his features in a kind of warm glow. Isaiah could almost be convinced that he looked human.

"Essex?"

When he finally turned, Essex's eyes were wide.

"Isaiah." His voice had a rounded edge to it. Softened. Isaiah took in the shadow of just-sprouted sea-moss that was scattered by his feet that had definitely not been there that morning. The green ruffled with the breeze. Casting a glance about, he suddenly felt exposed.

"What are you looking for?" Essex said, voice low and more than a little bit amused.

"Nothing. Couldn't sleep."

"Dreams?"

Isaiah searched his face for some hint of mockery, and found none. "No. For once, no."

Before he could think too much about it, he crossed the gap between them. The light emitting from the oil lantern on a stack of boxes next to him was scattered by a thin fringe of newly sprouted ocean reeds. They looked preternaturally damp, as if a tide had just washed back from them.

"I've been put on watch. Apparently."

Isaiah let out what must have been an incredulous-sounding laugh, because Essex cocked his head.

"Sorry. It's just . . . the idea of it is—"

"What, you don't think I'm capable?" he said, and the question came out more sarcastic than earnest. Isaiah couldn't even bring himself to laugh, this time.

"More than capable. Just a bit contradictory," Isaiah said.

"Given that you'd be happy to see everything and everyone on this ship torn to pieces."

Essex shifted and, in an instant, had turned unnaturally still. Whatever trick or illusion he'd be using to keep himself breathing as a regular man fell away.

Essex's eyes tracked his warily. Isaiah had seen that look on wild dogs who were used to being kicked. Something he'd said had picked at an exposed nerve.

"Not everyone."

The memory of what had felt, at the time, like the wind holding him back from a near-catastrophic fall in the mainmast. His escape from the hold without so much as a scratch, even after Fallon had been pulled below by some creature lying in wait. He hadn't gotten sick, he hadn't been hurt, not *once* since his accidental cut at work alongside Demir. Essex was looking at him cautiously, and Isaiah felt a tangle of an ache behind his sternum.

"Why would you tell me that?" He replied, quietly. Isaiah couldn't stop the exhaustion from seeping into his voice. "As if nobody else on this ship matters?"

"Because they're . . . not like you," Essex started. "Not to me."

"And what am I to do with that, Essex?" He could feel his voice rising. "*Why* me?"

His eyes pricked angrily, and Bellamy was being pulled down to the cold bottom of the ocean again, and Hendricks was showing him the infernal bumps on her inner arm, and Coffin was rotting, rotting, rotting away, and Isaiah did not know if he was still alive or dead, or something else entirely. He felt the deck swell underneath him, and his vision went fuzzy for a moment.

When he blinked, Essex was directly before him. Holding him steady.

"I was waiting for you to treat me like the others did," Essex said, temples shot through with greenish veining. "You were the only one who . . . " He took a heavy, intentional breath in, and another out. Isaiah supposed even not-quite-human men had to steady themselves somehow. " . . . Who cared. For me. When I first came up from below."

When Isaiah looked down, the deck rail next to where they stood had sprouted a thick layer of lush green moss, and when Isaiah dipped a hand to it, it was soft as velvet.

"I had to." He said, voice coming out more tender than he'd intended. "You looked hurt—"

"It's just how I come back, each time." He cut his eyes away from Isaiah's, as if he was close to nervous. Isaiah automatically ran a soothing hand along his collarbone.

"Each time what?"

The even rise and fall of his chest ground to a halt again.

"Each time I'm killed." Essex tapped lightly on the aged, horizontal scar that banded his neck, healed dark and slightly raised against his normal skin.

Isaiah stopped breathing himself, for a moment.

"Killed?"

"As soon as the body is dropped into the sea, it starts again." His hand drifted from the scar on his neck to Isaiah's hand, still resting, frozen, on his collar. He picked it up and kissed the place on his palm where the cut had been. Isaiah felt himself shiver. "Merchants or hunters of all kinds will find a body. Anyone whose greed is fueled by killing or consuming, they can't help but pull it up. Take it in as theirs."

He closed his eyes. Maybe when he opened them this would be a dream too. Not that he could much tell the difference anymore.

" . . . And as soon as they realize they're doomed, they look for the closest unnatural thing to blame for it," Isaiah said. "Like Monteiro and the sickness on board."

"Yes."

He paused, something clicking into place. " . . . And Coffin knew that."

"Yes."

"So, they can't help it. But neither can you."

Essex searched Isaiah's face; for what, he couldn't be certain. He brushed his lip with the pad of his thumb, just as he had in Isaiah's dream, and the memory bounced forward in time and become flesh.

"And you don't have to be one of them," Essex said, voice rough. The aching feeling turned to a curling strand of want that unspooled deep within him. "I hope you'll remember that. When the time comes."

Essex was pressed close, and Isaiah couldn't gather himself enough to ask what he meant by that. The lantern guttered as a cool wind rolled in from the water, sending the yellowy lamplight playing about his face, glancing across the arc of Essex's brow, thumbing under his eyes, tracing along the long downward line of his nose. Isaiah leaned up to kiss him, and his mouth was firm and alive, curving toward his and returning the motion.

Essex laid back against the mast and gripped his waist tight, holding him close and drawing Isaiah down with him.

CHAPTER TWENTY-ONE

ISAIAH MADE THE trek back to his bunk at some unknown hour early that morning, just as the sun was beginning to seep orange up from the horizon. Mouth raw and body aching, he crept back into his own bed. His head was still buzzing, swirling with a distracting kind of warmth, and the sensation carried him into a fitful, brief sleep.

He was only awoken by the creaking of somebody passing closely by his bunk.

Recently, Monteiro had taken to peering into the crew's sleeping quarters to check who had fallen ill during the night. In the first few days or so of the progression of the illness, she had occasionally appeared above-decks looking haggard, aged beyond her years. After a while, she began to take in the sick with gusto, to pore over the bizarre symptoms they exhibited with a renewed kind of vigor. Nominally, this was tolerated, but it meant that there were mutterings that the whalers felt watched. Observed, and at her mercy.

When she re-emerged from her cabin early that morning, Isaiah was one of the few fully awake.

She crept among them, light-footed and vigilant, and at a glance Isaiah could see that she wore the long gloves she'd used to pick up the eel that had grown inside Sulaimi's gut. He squeezed his eyes shut, not daring to move, trying to steady his breathing. He felt her pass over him, and he couldn't help but think that it was a very good thing that Essex hadn't been sleeping in the bunks with the rest of them. If he slept at all.

Gods above and below, let Essex have listened to me and made himself scarce. Please don't let her find him. Not now.

But even as the crew rose for the day and began to go about

their duties, there was no indication that she had found Essex, or had taken in anyone else that morning. He ate breakfast at Hendricks' side and focused on making his paltry serving last as long as possible. They both spooned in small bits of mash with care. After Álvarez's interruption and their argument thereafter, he was surprised that she'd continued eating with him. Perhaps it was the fact that he was, seemingly, the only one who knew about the gun and twin looming ghosts of both Coffin and Johanna Briggs that haunted her.

"Just thought you ought to know. There're more of them," she said in a low whisper.

"Them who?"

"More of what, actually." She shrugged the arm which had been afflicted with the small pebble-like lumps under the skin. He eyed the spot by her elbow where she'd pointed them out to him last. There were numerous points below the cotton that pushed against the fabric of her shirt. Isaiah's mostly-empty stomach rolled.

She glanced up at him from her plate. "More of the same."

"Gods below."

Her eyes looked distant. Glazed with the beginnings of fever. Isaiah had seen that look on a number of the crew, by now. It never got less perturbing.

"And what's worse is that I keep wanting for salt," she said, picking at the food on her plate.

" . . . Salt?" he said, broken-up biscuit abandoned in hand.

"In my water, on food," she said, dropping her gaze back to the table. "S'been getting worse all the time. Alone with these things." She shrugged her shoulder again. "Keep wanting to scrape it off the side of the ship, or something."

Isaiah reached over to lay a hand on her wrist. Beneath her sleeve, lumps were solid, and had nearly doubled in size. He retracted it immediately in shock.

"Happy?" she said, tone souring.

"Gods above, *no*, that's not—"

"I can feel them move," she said, voice wavering. "Do you know what that's like?"

Isaiah's stomach churned once more. The image of the grimy metal bucket on Monteiro's surgery table and the raw, bloody, clumps of flesh and barnacle sat in his mind's eye.

"You've got to do something."

"I can't very well go run and tell the surgeon," she said. "With what's happened to Morrow, to Calder, to Sulaimi?"

"I know, but there has to be *something*—"

"Stop that. I haven't paid down signing debts, and that bloody gun was the only thing I had that was worth anything. Even if we make it to land . . . even then . . . " Her voice began to crack, seeping desperation.

"Easy, *easy*," Isaiah said, steeling himself and taking hold of her wrist. "We'll . . . I don't know. But I won't tell anyone about it if you don't want to." The texture under his hand was knobbled like buried stones exposed by the tide. "I'll try and see Calder," he said quietly. "If there's some treatment Monteiro's been doing to keep him alive, even with the sickness, he'd know about it."

She looked down, nodding silently by way of response, hair fallen over her shoulders.

Waiting until he spotted Monteiro making her rounds to the bunks, he stole back to the quarters where Calder was still kept. The last time Calder had been dazed, if coherent; he couldn't have possibly gotten *better* in the time since he'd tried to steal into the surgeon's quarters.

The fear in him fought hard against the nervousness he held for Hendricks. He made it to the smaller cabin attached to the main surgical chamber, picking his way between Flores and Yesayan, who were out cold in cots opposite one other. Isaiah moved with the gentle sway of the ship, careful not to bump into either of them.

Isaiah couldn't immediately discern if Calder was awake or asleep. He was propped up as he had been before, when he had been scared of someone entering the quarters. The pile of bandages had been pared down. He was missing pieces. Guilt began to chew at Isaiah.

As Isaiah moved closer, his eyes fluttered open.

"You . . . " Calder rasped. "You returned."

"Jerry, I'm sorry I couldn't stay," he started.

"How many . . . how many others are left?" He wheezed, voice muddled by the fact that a good-size chunk of jaw was simply gone from his face, scooped free of the rest of the bone.

What is she doing?

"Of the sick? Enough to man the ship. That's all."

It was then that Isaiah took in the jars around him. JC 2. JC 3. JC 7. Racked together on a long wooden shelf, carefully and neatly labelled.

"Calder, what's happened?"

"I . . . can't," he said. "Can't remember."

Suddenly his eyes grew wide and hazy. He looked somewhere behind Isaiah, and he whipped around to see nothing but empty air.

"He follows you," he croaked.

"He *who*?"

"The man who was dead—"

"What?" Isaiah said, startled. "Calder, *no*, Coffin is gone, his body isn't—"

"No! Not him, not the Captain," His words degraded into a ragged cough. It was somehow even weaker than the before. "He follows."

Essex.

" . . . Follows?"

Calder choked, coughed, and spat up a dense pellet of blood. The skin visible on his face was mottled with green veins and purple bruises.

"What's dead doesn't truly die. Not here," he said, voice barely reaching above a whisper. "Not . . . not on this ship."

A chill ran through him. Isaiah thought of Coffin, Bellamy, Fallon, Briggs, appearing to him in visions and nightmares alike. Even Essex, scarred by whatever he had suffered in a previous life, if his word was to be trusted.

All resurrected.

"There's others that are getting sick," Isaiah said, and he could tell his voice was pitched toward desperation. "Please, you *have* to know something of what she's been doing, Calder. Anything that can help us."

Isaiah grabbed his shoulder. Even through the bandages, he could feel bone jutting through what had been layers of skin and muscle, now pitted and pocked with lumps, obstructions beneath the fabric. The stained fabric bandages felt like seaweed laid over gravel. Out of sight, but knotting up his shoulder from beneath. Calder twitched, and Isaiah dropped his hand immediately.

"*Nothing.* There's nothing," Calder said. He fell against the back of the chair in which he'd been propped, like a disused rag doll. His eyes fluttered shut, and his breath came raspy and labored, as if he could do no more than focus on continuing the squeezebox pumping of his of his lungs.

Isaiah drew back. "I'm sorry . . . "

He could feel how weak and insufficient his apology sounded, hanging in the rotten air in Monteiro's quarters, surrounded and penned in by pieces of Jerry Calder lining the walls in jars, and he couldn't help but let the helplessness seep in under his skin, surrounding him from all angles.

That evening, Isaiah stayed up topside on the *Merciful*, putting off what seemed to be an inevitable return to tell Hendricks what Calder had said to him. No part of him relished the thought.

As he sat, a shadowy blur of motion appeared, and resolved into a figure, dropping a pail to water level. They brought it back up to drink deeply from it, disappearing before he could move any closer or call out. He wasn't certain he would have been able to stop them even if he had.

Hendricks was by no means the only one with a lust for salt. If Sharpe wouldn't allow them to take up seawater to drink, some of the sick had started cajoling the still-healthy to bring them salt. A few of their number were caught spiriting away small packets of the stuff from the kitchens, and the cook was seen ladling in spoonfuls to rations of ale in exchange for debtors marks. In their regular rations, in the packed meat that they were given, they were flooding themselves with more and more salt.

Isaiah couldn't help but think that it was just making it easier for the ocean to reclaim their bodies when death finally came for them.

He was pulled from this line of thought by the creeping feeling of being watched. Essex was crouched on top of a crate, peering down at him silently. Isaiah jumped.

"Hello." Essex was grinning cheekily at him.

"Gods below. Don't scare me like that."

He looked him over, curious, and hopped down from his perch

on the crate to tug him into a kiss. Isaiah could only enjoy the sensation for so long before he pulled away. The echoes of the Calder's barely-there voice still rattled about inside his skull, and something inside his gut felt jittery. Shaken up.

Essex simply looked him over, tracking his expression intently. "What's wrong?"

"Nothing."

"You look . . . " he said, trailing off for a moment to search Isaiah's eyes. " . . . unsettled."

Isaiah sighed, but kept Essex close. "I spoke to Calder, about what Monteiro means to do to him."

"Whatever for?"

Isaiah's mouth was suddenly dry. "No . . . no reason." Telling Essex that he'd risked being caught by Monteiro for Hendricks's benefit felt like admitting weakness.

"You once asked me to be honest with you." Essex said carefully, not blinking once. " . . . Now it's your turn."

He was right, of course. But Isaiah couldn't shake the sense that something in his expression had sharp edges. He had seemed so . . . human the night before. Essex had been warm and gentle under his hands regardless, in a way that nearly let him forget where the two of them were, *who* they were.

Speaking with Calder made Isaiah remember the terrifying, polyphonous voice that had emitted from Essex's mouth the night before Coffin had died, that had sounded alien yet familiar all at once. It had sparked up something in his brain just shy of sheer terror. The decay that had followed him had brought pale dread along with it, and the whole of the ship was threaded through with it. The thread was wound around Essex, as much as he had tried to ignore it.

"I just thought he might know something, what with his being around Monteiro day in and day out," he said, standing firm. "Hendricks is sick, and getting worse. I don't want to see her picked apart under her knife."

Essex looked at him with something like pity. "And you think that will be what saves her?"

"No, I—" Isaiah started, feeling outfoxed. "Calder is still alive when others have died. There must be a reason for it, even if he doesn't realize it himself." He gripped Essex's forearm. "There has to be something."

"Does there?" He said, cold-voiced. "Or is the surgeon just prolonging his fate for her own sake?"

Isaiah dropped his hand, edging out of his arms. "I don't *know* anymore, Essex."

Essex let him go, and he stalked belowdecks, the anxious, fearful pit in his stomach sinking heavier and heavier. Isaiah couldn't bring himself to look back to where he left him on the main deck.

As the ill steadily grew in number, the cabins adjacent to the surgeon's quarters had been transformed into additional sick bays for those too weak to get in and out of bunks by themselves. It was the day that the mates' cabins began to be swapped over from serviceably hewn tables and chairs to plain flat-lay bunks that Isaiah was charged with cleaning linens for the newly sick. He was transporting a heavy basket of sheets when Monteiro pushed past him on her way up to the main deck. Dropping off the linens in an empty corner, he stole after her, careful to keep well enough away and to step quietly.

" . . . And how do you propose we do that?" Isaiah caught the tail end of Sharpe's reply.

"No, absolutely not. There's no precedent for . . . " Lice said, half talking-over him.

"For what? Advanced illness?" Monteiro said, cutting her off. "For this, whatever this is?"

"I understand that you're just trying to do your job, Doctor—" Sharpe said, conciliatory.

"No, no, she's fucking not. She's trying to get us into a bloody mountain of debt with the shipping company," Lice amended sourly.

"I take no small issue to the implication that I don't know what's at stake for all those—"

"These experiments must *end*, Doctor," Lice replied, clearing her throat. Her voice had grown scratchy and strained.

"I realize that you have your concerns Miss Stowe, and I have my own."

"You may *realize*, but I don't think you damn well understand our situation," Lice said, venomous. "You've been able to skip over to whatever vessel you like well enough in your time with Pyle, Coffin, and Thacket, but for this ship? All aboard stand to be in months, *years* worth of debt to the company if we don't. Meet. Quota." Isaiah couldn't see Lice's expression, but the thud of her boot on the boards advanced further, punctuating each word as it grew more and more hoarse. He could hear her belabored breathing even from where he stood.

" . . . How long have you been experiencing symptoms?"

Their backs were mostly to him, but from Isaiah's vantage point he could see Lice's face contort. "I'm not experiencing—"

"How long, Miss Stowe?" It was not a question so much as a command.

"Nothing is *wrong*," she said, trying to project her voice.

"I see," she replied, after a beat of heavy silence. "As I mentioned to Captain Sharpe, the financial promise of a disease of this nature cannot be underestimated."

"*Financial promise*—Do you fucking hear yourself?!" Lice snarled.

The outline of Sharpe seemed shrunken, shriveled in comparison. He shook his head, and turned to her. " . . . What's our remaining numbers?"

"Reduced by a third."

" . . . And the stores?"

"Reduced by half."

His voice was thin and wavering, barely carrying in the air. " . . . Well . . . what should we do?"

"Anything but this." She pointed her chin toward Monteiro. Lice barked a dry, humorless laugh. " . . . At least Coffin knew how to take action."

Isaiah jumped. He whipped around at top speed; Yesayan had walked up behind him and hit him square on the middle of his back.

"Oh.," He started, but his look gave him pause. He looked exhausted, with dark bruise-like circles around his eyes. "What is it?"

"You're wanted above again. They're running low on—" He paused to hack out a chest-rattling cough. "Low on hands by the topsail."

"Aye."

Isaiah turned to catch one last glance toward Sharpe, Monteiro, and Lice, stood in a tripartite face-off. Lice's stare was fixed on Sharpe with nothing short of contempt.

"And stop . . . stop your eavesdropping." Yesayan said, voice running congested and rough in between the words. He spat over his shoulder, and caught his breath.

" . . . Aye." He bolted up above decks, heart jumping fast.

In the days to come, there was no indication that Sharpe, or Lice for that matter, had even remotely considered the possibility of turning back. The crew was worked as hard as would be borne, with more and more work piled onto those who hadn't yet fallen. Even when three more of their number grew hot with fever, with a fourth developing bloody sores along their gums and at the creases of their skin, they were all charged with appearing in watch shifts. Sometimes they saw whales spouting in the distance in pods, or vast schools of fish sparkling below the surface of the waves, just within eyesight. They were never actually there.

Isaiah didn't seek Essex out for that time. He had left their prior conversation anxious and frustrated, and the likelihood of repeating the argument again seemed high. He spotted him in passing, doing small tasks as charged by Sharpe or Lice, but in no great rush to complete them. The rest of the crew treated him as a sort of passing oddity, and he did not try to speak with Isaiah again.

For the remainder of the week, duties were maintained, and a few more whales appeared, and then disappeared again like smoke on the wind.

They could not catch a single one, and a low hum of panic steadily rose onboard the *Merciful* as the living hungered and the ranks of the dead grew in number.

It wasn't long after that Demir passed into the next realm. It wasn't Isaiah's job to wrap him up, but he was charged with the task of helping haul him—the body—out and onto the deck of the ship. The sight of the canvas wrappings that they'd laid so tightly over Coffin's and Bellamy's body wrinkled and loose over Demir's pulled at his conscience, and with his face wrapped against the smell of the newly dead, he adjusted the canvas, tucking the old man's chin against his breastbone, tucking the folds smooth. Hearing his father's voice in his ear, reminding him to never leave a job undone, Isaiah fished out his largest needle and heaviest waxed thread and sewed up the edges tight until the top of Demir's grey-fuzzed head disappeared beneath dun-colored wrappings.

He was moving the body up to the main deck when he saw that Álvarez was already there, standing watch. He wore the look of someone lying in wait for something. His shoulders were slumped and he didn't look up as Isaiah wrestled the dolly holding the body up from the bowels of the ship.

"I heard that nobody was there when the light went out of his eyes," he said quietly, keeping his head bent, staring a hole in the planks below him. Isaiah could see the raw outline of the bones beneath his skin, jutting outwards. He'd been strong, easily muscle-bound, before. Now, he seemed to need to concentrate hard on each shallow exhale.

"No. I don't think anyone was," Isaiah replied. "I'm sorry for him."

When he finally looked up, he realized that Álvarez wasn't so much crossing his arms, as holding them down in place over his upper stomach. A kind of odd pallor cast his skin sallow, and Isaiah couldn't tell if it was hunger or the infection eating him hollow.

"Sorry?" he said. "For what?" He laughed, but it was all teeth, no gums. Even if Álvarez's laugh drew a few stray glances, nobody thought to look up at the body joining the rest of the dead in the realm below. They were consumed with their work.

"I'm sorry that we're here at all," Álvarez said. "Sharpe should have never been allowed to take an inch on this brig." He bit out the last words sourly.

"Did Lice put you up to spreading this idea? Or did you come up with it yourself?" Isaiah said, keeping his voice low.

Álvarez just stared at Isaiah over the dead man's body between them "The sick are dropping like fleas off a dog." His normally black-brown eyes had a kind of haze over them. "And the *Captain* still doesn't take us to port to re-provision, doesn't turn us back neither. Can't find whales despite the fact that we should have arrived in the best hunting grounds available weeks ago. Do you even know if we're back on course?" His fingers grew tight on his braced arms, still staring hard. " . . . Where we are, exactly?"

Isaiah felt his face grow warm. "Then do something about it. For as much good as it'll do us now," he said, letting the handle of the dolly fall to the deck with a heavy thud. He sensed heads turning. "What's stopping you?"

There was a brief, dense silence between them. Álvarez stared, and Isaiah stared back.

"Nothing. Nothing at all." Álvarez said, expression turning frigid as he turned away, leaving both him and the cloth-wrapped body grim and unmoving on the deck. "Least of all you, Chase."

The most exhausting part of the rapid shortening of the *Merciful*'s crew roster was that double, and even triple work shifts had become standard for all who were well enough to keep on two legs. So when Isaiah had finished one set of duties for the evening, and was promptly charged with going back on night watch up on the main deck, he was awake to hear a rolling swell of motion below his feet.

A shuffling rumble of bodies moving below echoed upwards through the very timbers of the ship. As if it was the morning, and the early alarm bell had roused them. But it was the dead of night, and the sounds were unmistakable. It was the crew, rising up from their bunks, from their work stations.

Isaiah sat frozen at his post. He heard a clattering, raised voices, and the vague thuds of doors being thrown open, and realized he had absolutely no idea where Essex was. He was on his feet and moving before was conscious of it. Immediately, a man's scream tore up from the bowels of the *Merciful*, punctuated sharply by a series of muffled gunshots. He froze in his tracks.

After, there was a thick, dense sort of quiet. It was punctuated only by the distant sound of Lice's voice giving some series of commands.

Isaiah caught a flutter of motion out of the corner of his eye, and, to his relief, he realized Essex was perched high up in the mainsail, immobile, face curtained by shadow against the moonlight. From his position nearer to the prow, standing at the watch post, Isaiah couldn't tell if he was looking at him or down at the deck, and what was happening below.

Before long, a band of crewmen carried two bodies up onto the deck, one thin and none too tall, and one wholly withered, covered by discolored linen bandaging and the scraps of what had been his clothing, still stained from the day he'd last worn them to work. Calder wriggled and gasped as they set him flat on the planks. Sharpe was already dead.

"Put him down." Lice said. "He's suffered enough."

At her word, two of the crowd set down the still-living Calder. Isaiah's mind revolted as Calder writhed limply, and the feeling of sick burned at the back of his throat. He clapped a hand over his mouth before he could say anything or make any kind of sound.

"He has *value,* Miss Stowe," Monteiro said, scrambling up behind them from belowdecks, desperation writ large across her features. "He won't recover, but when we reach Shaliston Port the company will *want* to take the opportunity. Think of the utility of such a condition to the company, if the army could use—"

"*Captain.*" Lice said, voice ragged. "It's Captain Stowe."

"Yes. Captain, of course."

Lice took her hand and slotted the gun into it. "I said, put him down."

Monteiro's expression curdled, and dropped.

"Do it." Someone called from the crowd. Isaiah couldn't tell whose voice it was.

"Let this be a lesson," Lice said. "On the priorities we hold to on this ship."

Isaiah cringed and turned away, as the brutal crack of a gunshot echoed out over the water beneath them.

That morning, the trio of bodies were fed into the sea. It was less an honored custom, and more of a grim chore to be completed along with scraping the hull and coiling the line. Lice had presided over the speedy wrapping-up of Sharpe's body with only perfunctory ceremony and dry eyes, and nobody would say who, exactly, had killed him the night before.

Isaiah didn't dare intervene to fix the wrappings around either of the two men, to fold them more neatly instead of letting them stay rumpled and messy around his slender body. It seemed too daring an act, especially as Álvarez's final warning to him rang in his head, as clear as as if he had been speaking it aloud in that very moment.

Least of all you, Chase. He hadn't even been able to watch Calder die. It had simply had happened.

Meanwhile, Monteiro watched them silently as they put the corpses overboard and made no comment. The word mutiny was never uttered by any of them, not once.

CHAPTER TWENTY-TWO

THAT NIGHT, Isaiah laid amongst the half-empty bunks and tried to ignore the sounds and smells of death as they came. Exhaustion eventually betrayed him. One moment, he was awake, hearing the muffled coughing noises of someone a few beds down the row from him, the next, he had fallen into a dream.

He didn't realize it at first, but the whole ship was soaked through with salt water. The deck was sodden, the planks of timber soft underfoot and well on their way to rot. He rolled out of his bed in what felt like slow motion and, as clear as anything, knew that they were below the surface of the water. His vision warped and rippled slightly, and walking was hard. The straw padded mattresses and once well-reinforced bunks were falling down around him. What had been Bellamy's bed was sporting a massive hole in the center; a heavy growth of seaweed poked up through the boards, and a heavy crust of barnacles and sand lined the floor. Rocks jutted up, angular and covered with underwater moss, and splintered up the ship's decking and the look of it wasn't quite so different from his last scried vision, of the boat being pulled apart by invisible hands.

Some part of his mind realized that the *Merciful* was dead and rotting. Past, present, and future.

Slowly, he made his way up the shattered steps up to the main deck, crawling up over the sandy wreck of what was once the main deck. The crew was there. Bent double, frozen in time, coralized and punctured with gaps in stomachs, necks, limbs missing. They were like carved statues melded to the ship itself, encased bodies turned to raw mineral material. Hardened. Inhuman.

What would have been a deep sense of mourning felt dulled, muted, and he moved to the nearest one, in the shape of someone he thought he recognized. He reached out through the water and, as his fingertip made contact with the hard exoskeleton of the calcified crewmember, it shrunk away from his hand in an instant, crinkling in on itself with one multiarticular motion, like a living thing would. Isaiah gasped, choking in on the sudden intake of water, his lungs suddenly burning, and he remembered that he couldn't breathe underwater—

The person had curled in on himself, like an insect in its death throes. Contorted, they fell on their side, mouth open, as a swarm of tiny ink-colored crabs scuttled out from between their hardened lips in one horrid, glimmering cloud.

As Isaiah sprung back from the crumpled animal that was the calcified body, a pair of hands grabbed hold of him by the shoulders, pulled him backwards.

"Careful," Essex said, voice low and sounding like the muffled clatter of rocks swept over one another by an incoming tide. He held him tightly, and Essex's hair was far longer than it had been in the waking world, and lank with clumps of salt and flakes of bluish seaweed. His pupils had expanded far beyond the reaches of his irises, almost entirely blacking out the whites of his eyes. The veins which had only lightly latticed about his temples in waking hours extended, and ran purple-blue beneath his skin. Bloodlines snaked away from his temples, down his cheek and along the column of his neck, wending their way deep below the surface.

"Why let them do this?" He asked, frozen in front of Essex. "Stop them from killing each other, killing themselves?"

Essex didn't blink, instead moving to push Isaiah's hair back from his eyes.

"Because they need to be reminded of the way of the world."

"Reminded of what, exactly?! They lay in charms and tokens, they pray as they get sick—" He was cut off when Essex moved his hands to hold the sides of Isaiah's face, void-like eyes sucking in light hungrily. He'd pressed his thumbs to the highest point of Isaiah's cheekbones, while his fingertips carded through the hair behind his ears.

" . . . They bathe in blood at the charge of those that stay on shore, who would like to think their hands clean. It can't be allowed to happen without recompense." Essex's face didn't shift, didn't alter even an inch from the impassive expression which occupied it.

Isaiah scrambled in his wake. "But the crew . . . they have lives, homes, families . . . "

"People, humans—they're eager to forget that they came from the depths, once. They call on minor gods to calm a fear of what they once held close. To guard against those who grow comfortable seeing the other side." He pressed his palm against Isaiah's face in a motion which, in other circumstances, might have been comforting. "Those of them kept safe on land, safe in their minor devotions, will only listen to a loss of profit."

Essex leaned in next to his ear, speaking quietly, as if they'd be overheard by someone, by something. His breath was ice cold on his cheek. "They must begin to value blood once more."

Isaiah awoke the next morning in a frigid sweat. Sitting up, he reoriented himself and gave the bunk a once over; the space below him was empty as it had been since Bellamy had died, the wood of the inner hull of the ship next to him was still nut brown and solid to the touch. He still had to reach out a hand to press hard against the inner hull, to be absolutely certain. The wood didn't give way beneath his fingers. He gulped down a lungful of musty mid-morning air, letting it fill his chest to the brim.

A crewmember was passing by, shaking those who were still in their beds awake, checking pulses, making sure the crew still breathed. They stopped short, and down the line, and he could tell that someone had stopped moving.

Hendricks was absent from her bed that morning—when Isaiah asked around, frantic, he was told that she'd been escorted to the surgeon's quarters sometime late last night, that she hadn't been able to swallow. Lump in her throat, she'd said. Isaiah shook himself, and skirted around the people still left in the bunks, not wanting look any of them in the eye after the events of the mutiny.

He found Hendricks propped up on a bed pushed up to the back wall of one of one of the makeshift sick rooms. Three beds in all, squeezed tightly together, with barely space for one person to move between them without brushing up against the next. The one furthest away held someone who was covered by a sheet. Monteiro was nowhere to be found.

"Isaiah," she croaked.

"Hey now—" He said weakly, feeling dissipated and inadequate. "You're awake."

". . . Aye. Where did you run off too, the other day?" The words strained and grew thin as they came up from her throat.

"I tried to talk to Calder. See if there was anything he could tell me of what Monteiro's been doing to keep him alive. If he knew anything to help you."

". . . Oh." Her brow tightened. She looked whittled away, as if the sickness had been feeding off of her muscle, her bone. "Not so much of a use now, is it."

Isaiah didn't know what to say to it. She was right. "Have you been able to get any food down?"

She looked at him askance. "Don't think there's much left to give me." She blinked suspiciously in his direction. "No rations to spare. Y'look awful."

"That's rich coming from you right now. It's been a strange day and night. " He hadn't accounted for the fact that he was likely still damp with sweat from the nightmare. "Just bad dreams."

". . . Did you see it happen?"

Isaiah briefly considered bringing up how terrifying it was to see Monteiro put Calder down like an animal. Considering she was technically within her care now, it seemed ill-advised.

"I kept well out of the way." It wasn't exactly untrue.

"Bellamy always said you couldn't lie," She scoffed lightly until it turned into a dry cough. "Beginning to see what he meant."

"I didn't know it was a matter of record."

"Well, now you know." She said. "He used to say quite a bit about your tossing and turning in your sleep. Talking too, sometimes, speaking of bad dreams."

A chill pulsed through him. He tried to recall what his last dream had been before Bellamy died, but came up blank. There had been too many to keep track of ever since Essex had been brought on board.

"Be a friend and distract me. What'd you dream about."

"I . . . I said it was a *bad* dream."

"A story, then."

"If I'm a bad liar, I'm a worse storyteller."

"Just humor me, Chase." she said. "I don't wanna think about this for a minute."

Essex's words from the dream rung in his ears. *They call on the gods to calm a fear of what they once held close.* He couldn't be bothered to try and distinguish what was said in the dream from reality, not anymore. The odds of it coming to pass were too high. Hendrick's whittled-away form seemed too close to the coral-form crew in his dream to seem possible.

" . . . Chase?"

"Oh, sorry, I was just trying to . . . remember." He replied, not quite able to look at her.

"Why do you look so panicked?"

"I'm not—"

"*Fine.*" she said, struggling to settle comfortably. She ended up achingly propping herself up by her elbows. "Go on then."

She would understand. She had to.

Still, he recalled, almost too easily, the sight of his father being led away from the house by men dressed in black judge's uniforms, with dour expressions clouding their faces. His mother had pushed at the backs of one of the men, screaming something fierce. Her screams of rage had turned to long, wracking sobs soon enough, no matter how long Isaiah had tried to hold her and calm her.

There were no men in black coats here. No judge, no jury, and nobody to tell him that direct communion with the gods, even through dreams, was blasphemous. There was no council, only the superstitious living and the once-superstitious dead who could tell no tales of what they saw on the other side.

A thin, snaking voice in the back of his head whispered that Hendricks might be dead soon, anyway. And then who would she tell?

"I saw the *Merciful.* Drowned and rotting." It felt painfully understated to say it like that, so directly. Hendricks raised an eyebrow.

"That's it?"

" . . . No." He still couldn't look her in the eye. "Es—the man. The man from the belly of the whale was there." Hendricks groaned and laid back on the cot.

"I said give me a distraction, not tip-toe around it," she said. "Alright. *Don't* tell me."

He scrambled to salvage the moment. "Let me finish, then." He righted himself and continued.

209

"The ship had been . . . sunk. And I woke up on the floor of the ocean, but not breathing didn't bother me. The crew had been . . . I dunno. Taken over, I guess. By coral and barnacles, and the like. As soon as I went to touch one—" He tried to find the words for it, and decided not to lean into the gory details. "They were just . . . wrong. Not alive, not dead."

She squinted up from her pillow. "Taken over, like the sickness here?"

"They'd become part of it. The ocean, I mean," he said haltingly. "It felt . . . weighty. Like a fell portent."

"Huh?"

"Look, can I tell you something? In confidence?" She let out a series of wracking coughs, trying to muffle the sound behind a hand riddled by protrusions under the skin. It didn't do much.

" . . . Aye."

He clenched his fingers, one by one, feeling the minute points of tension in every muscle closing in and out. His fingertips brushed the scar on his palm that Essex had kissed so delicately, and it steadied him.

"I sometimes have dreams that . . . tell of what's yet to come."

Isaiah could feel the words hanging taut in the air between them. Her eyes widened.

"Chase." He could see her jaw tighten. "If you're telling me what I think you are . . . "

"I don't speak with the gods directly. Not on purpose."

" . . . Are you serious? Or are you just insane?"

"I'm serious, and I'm *not* insane."

"Then you're *trying* to curse us all—"

His stomach dropped anchor-heavy. "*No*, of course I'm not!"

She reached up and grabbed him by the front of his shirt, still capable of a burst of strength even in her sickness and exhaustion. "You . . . you've called the gods from the other realms to this ship," she said, through a tight jaw. "That man showed up here because of it, hasn't he?"

"I haven't! I swear to you."

She dropped his shirt and let her hand fall, seemingly unable to hold it any longer. He stood quickly, skirting away from the side of her makeshift sickbed.

"I knew I heard you going somewhere. To see him." She looked him over, eyes still wide and horrified.

Isaiah froze.

"He witched you somehow, then? Or you've witched him." Her voice grew tinged with fear. "Is that it?!"

"That's not true, I promise—"

"Don't promise me." Hendricks' head fell back to the pillow, all the strength gone from her. "Not when I don't know what you've done to us."

"I wouldn't do anything to purposefully call down any fell luck to the crew!"

"But you would stand by and watch it happen? To the captain?" She stared up at him, and something in her had hardened to stone. "To the crew?"

All he could do was shake his head. Any words he would have tried to say dried up in his mouth. " . . . No." He croaked. "You're . . . I haven't—"

He could barely finish the sentence. A roil of sheer panic burbled in his gut. Not daring to look back, he fled up to the main deck.

Lice, who had been the hardiest of them, now wheezed shallowly when she walked or got up from sitting. Monteiro was summoned to take a look at her and there was a brutal argument, with Lice chewing out the mate that had brought the surgeon in.

Eventually, she gave in. Monteiro spirited her away to gods-knew-where and by the time the sun had gone down, she had returned, looking ashen but able to walk and talk. She stood to address them at the fore of the mess hall slowly. Painfully.

"Alright, attention." She gripped the back of Coffin's, then Sharpe's, then her chair with white knuckles.

"I understand that you've been worked hard. I know full well that the . . . the losses suffered have been difficult." There was a low, muttering grumble in response. The dozen or so faces that looked up in her direction were hardened, either with anger or sorrow or some combination of the two. She tilted his chin up, straining to be heard, struggling to get breath into lungs. It should not have been a difficult task, given the predominant quiet that had fallen over the remains of the *Merciful's* crew.

"We will be continuing on to the hunting grounds, as soon as we can find some port at which to restock." Isaiah, who had been keeping his head down for the entirety of the day, nearly choked on a scant mouthful of bread. The crew's grumble increased in pitch around him. "However, until then, we will carry on as chartered. Duties will be distributed for each shift according to ability. I don't want to," She paused to suck in a labored breath. " ... To see a single person shirking. We must ... carry on and mark down this debt if we're to ever return to Shaliston Port."

She didn't wait for the collected crew to acknowledge her words, and sat back heavily in the Captain's chair, with Monteiro tracking her movements carefully.

A slender chorus of ayes rang out, and then fell to silence. The mutiny had put no more rations in anyone's mouths than before, and all the salt in the world wouldn't help them survive the long journey back home, let alone bring in more catch.

Although he could barely taste the food in his mouth, Isaiah finished the scant amount of watery gruel on his plate, and skirted out of the mess hall as quickly as he could hall, trying not to be noticed by anyone. Hendricks had not shown up for dinner.

The rest of the evening passed, both tiresome and frantic, with duties upon duties piling up for the night shift and for the following day, with the less sick growing worse and the somewhat-well pulling more than what they could carry. With Calder gone and Monteiro cowed by Lice once more, Hendricks and some of the other afflicted crew were returned to the regular bunks that night. It was an effort to save space and to restore order, Lice had said, and so the beds were fuller than they had been for days.

From a distance, Isaiah watched Hendricks lay still and listless. He hadn't truly accounted for how small she was until that day. He had well over a head of height on her, and her already slim frame sunk into the paltry sackcloth mattress. Standard issue, and nothing more.

The crew began their nightly laying in of tokens as soon as their paltry supper was done. The stink of boiling iron ore and squid ink began again, and the earthen, metallic odor coiled through the bunks. Isaiah sat curled up, knees to his chest, as the crew gathered in Morrow's old spot to begin. Yesayan's low voice carried steadily over the assembled group as he chanted.

"This young man, that died fain soon-
Left shore in sail, under cold and bloody moon"
"Ah, shit—"

Isaiah could tell the sound of Hendricks' voice, even weak and far down at the end of the bunks. He started up from his bed, darting to the end of the cabin where the circle had gathered around the dull glow of their stove. Her body was lain flat on the ground inside the circle, limp.

"Stop, she doesn't—" Isaiah started.

Yesayan, Phelan, and the silent, grim faces of the other crew around them stared up at him. The end of the needle was poised over Hendricks' wrist, part of a line already laid into the inner part of her arm. The sleeve had been rolled well back, to reveal a dotted map of uneven lumps, straining against the surface of her skin. Dots of blood pin-pricked along them. Her eyes were open, and she stared blankly up at him.

"Doesn't what?" Yesayan asked, eyes stony.

She had thought it all nonsense, before. Had mocked Morrow with him.

"Get out, Isaiah," Hendricks said. Her voice was hoarse and she barely moved but her expression was as hardened as the rest of them. Isaiah bolted.

Isaiah tried to sit up near the prow, knees pulled up to his chest, but the steady hum of fear that had blossomed after his accidental confession to Hendricks was now a red-hot, blistering roar of panic that wailed against the back of his sternum.

After the mutiny, Essex had taken to lingering about the crew and watching them intently, no longer disappearing for long periods at a time. And so it was easy to find him at the far end of the top deck, observing a few whalers as they stood watch.

Wordlessly, Isaiah pulled him to an inconspicuous spot near the hunting boats, and Essex followed without argument.

"Look, I'm sorry," Isaiah started.

"Oh?" Essex replied, fixing him with a look.

"I'm sorry for . . . arguing with you. Earlier," he said. "I didn't know that they were going to do what they did to Calder, to Sharpe—"

"So you admit that there was no reason for trying to help them?"

"She was planning on selling parts of him back to the company! Lice put a stop to it."

"She put a stop to Sharpe, too."

"I didn't know that would happen."

"You're the one who can see the future, and you didn't know that was how it would end?" He asked, brows raised.

Isaiah could feel himself nearing the very end of his rope. "Gods, that's *not funny,* and it *doesn't work like that.*"

Essex sighed, laying a hand on his collar. "What is it, then? You seem—"

"I made a mistake," he blurted. "I told someone about my dreams."

"Who did you tell this to?"

"The who isn't important . . . "

"Isaiah," he said quietly. "Please tell me."

"*No.*"

"I want to protect you."

"No, I—" That was exactly the problem. Isaiah did not know what Essex would do if he heard that Hendricks had immediately tied Essex to the *Merciful*'s downward spiral, had accused him of cursing the ship and the crew. "After what's happened . . . I just can't tell what they'll do. They're getting desperate, and scared."

"What happened?"

"They didn't . . . they didn't take it well." Isaiah shuddered. He had avoided dwelling on the days that had led up to his father's death, but the memory had come to knock back at his door again, louder than ever.

"You once told me of what happened. To your father." Essex pressed a kiss to his forehead, and the swelling, all-consuming tide of panic in Isaiah didn't abate. "That will not happen to you."

With that, the man from the belly disappeared from Isaiah's side, leaving him standing, useless, beside the empty hunting boats.

CHAPTER TWENTY-THREE

SAIAH DID NOT sleep that night. Dreaming would have been too much to bear. The thought of seeing his father again, neck wrapped in a scarf of rope, would have driven him over the edge and into an entirely different kind of madness than he was used to. Instead, he tucked himself into a corner of the ship and shivered and waited for day to come.

It was only when the sun just began to rise, beading up light over the horizon, that he went below and saw that Hendricks had died.

She lay flat on her bunk, chin jutting upward, and riddled with barnacles that had finally sprouted through the skin. Her mouth and eyes were open wide.

He sunk to his knees next to the bunk and shook.

I want to protect you.

There was a reason Essex hadn't pressed him for the name of the person he had told his secret to. Hendricks had been last person that Isaiah had expressed concern about, the last person alive that would be left to tell about his dreams, and Essex had known that. He had all but told Essex who he would have trusted enough to speak about such matters to. Besides him.

Isaiah had also implied that, as much as he had trusted her, that she'd feared him anyway.

They wrapped her up in canvas, and her body slipped into the water that morning with a smaller splash than seemed possible. Essex looked on with the rest of the crew, still and silent. His mind circled around the thought that he did not know to what extent Essex was happy to see the crew grow weak and die, to see them infected and put back to the sea.

As they meandered further south, it only grew colder.

After committing Hendricks to the waves, they'd all been given a fresh set of duties to keep occupied, and Essex was no exception. As always, he felt no need to operate under any kind of urgency, and was simply staring beyond the ship, eyes tracking the horizon. Looking out for something.

"Stop your gawking," Álvarez barked, and pushed Essex forward a few steps. He rolled his shoulders a little, as if limbering them up for something.

"Aye, sir," he answered.

The watch changed out with nary a word from Lice, and Isaiah didn't spot where he had gone after that.

He scaled the mizzen-mast to fix a tangle of line, and caught a glimpse of Álvarez, leaning out over the rail toward the aft. He followed his line of sight but there was nothing to be seen; just a blank expanse of blue-green ocean dotted with waves. Isaiah was at a loss as to his fascination, and he flicked out a spyglass to more closely inspect the empty air. Apprehension fizzled in his chest.

"SPOUT SIGHTED OFF PORT SIDE," Álvarez bellowed as loud as his lungs would allow. He had clambered halfway up a stack of boxes, and was staring out to the horizon, spyglass in hand. "A whale—finally . . . *finally* . . . "

Isaiah, squinting hard, leaned out from his perch and scanned the faded blue border where sky met sea. Below him, there was a straggling burst of commotion in response, as the crew nearest to his post startled into motion. Someone cut over to the helm, rattling Lice's shoulder, spinning her westward and gesticulating frantically. There was a rush of shouts and voices, cutting up into the air between Isaiah and the *Merciful*'s main deck, all down below straining to see the creature.

He hadn't noticed it before, but Essex was up in the rigging one mast over from him, staring over at the scene, scrub brush sitting idly in his hand, expression utterly blank. Isaiah saw him blink, just once, and suddenly there was, indeed, a whale. Roaring up from the depths at an incomprehensible pace, the massive creature breached the surface a few hundred yards away from them, massive and cleaving the spray in two with its fleshy grey-black spine.

"What are you *doing*?!" Isaiah hissed. When Essex turned his attention to him, his irises were gone.

"Giving them a chance," he replied, and he smiled right at him, with inhuman eyes and gleaming teeth. Isaiah's skin prickled all over at the waves of power emanating from him.

"Well, get after it then!" Lice shouted and in that moment of euphoric purpose a command from her was as good as the word of the gods themselves and the lot of them ran, stumbled, half-crawled to take up harpoons and knives and instruments of butchery. Hands shaking, Isaiah unlashed the ropes he'd just got done fixing in place, scrambling down to the deck. "First to draw blood gets full rations tonight!" There was a feral cry from the crew in response, of words mixed together with shouting.

They're going to die on this water. They are going to be killed here and I'm the only one who knows—

"Whoever's strong enough to assemble, to the hunting boats!" Yesayan called from his place near the wheel. Those who could run moved as quickly as they could to stations for a full-fledged hunt, and a chorus of ragged coughs and labored breathing trailed behind them. The *Merciful* cut jaggedly through the waves, skirting and pitching through the surf toward the creature.

His dread mounted higher as the crew around him pushed and clawed to make it to the boat. A few had open sores, wounds that had rubbed away lesions on their limbs to reveal shingled plating of oyster shells coating their bones, others had growths that looked like nubs of scale pushing out from the skin and splitting the inky tokens they'd so carefully laid in for days and weeks.

He spied a dark spit of rock-dotted land rose up in the near distance, jutting out like a wooden spear into the water. Just past the jagged rocks sticking up from the water, Isaiah could see that it merged into a proper shoreline, with wide boulders dotting the course toward land. The rocks fused together and joined at odd angles, and there was a spot of bedraggled white, and if Isaiah was seeing things right, it looked like some kind of signpost, or banner marking the land itself.

It was a white flag of surrender.

The chance to *choose*. He was giving them the chance to choose land and the possibility of safe harbor, and not a soul noticed its presence when set against the massive whale taunting them just near the horizon.

"Easy on that there, we need our heading!" He heard Yesayan

shout from the other side of the deck. "CHASE, over on the port-side line!"

Lice was still half-mesmerized by the sight of the whale, staring over the side and into the far distance, her eyes darting back and forth as it cut through the water, tracing its rippling form, fat with oil. Fat with coin.

He realized too late that Álvarez had been directly across from him, trying to do up the next line tight.

"That . . . that spit of rocks is just there," Isaiah said, scrambling for small talk. "We could divert and see if there's supplies, we could—" He trailed off when he saw that Álvarez was silent and fixed him with a look of raw, unfiltered suspicion. He'd seen that look before, on the faces of villagers and on the people who'd come to take his father away.

He glanced between Isaiah and where Essex had been moments ago, and before he could open his mouth to speak Isaiah made himself scarce. Álvarez shouted something after him, but his ragged words were lost beneath the sound of the waves and the creaks of a ship pushed to the breaking point.

The waves curled and chopped at the side of the ship, and the wind that carried them beat against full sail.

"Miss—"

Lice's eyes burned, coal-like, in a face that was ashen and hollow, despite the confidence in her gaze.

"—*please*, I need to speak with you."

The bones protruded from behind the skin sharply, as if she'd been whittled out of wood. "It's *Captain,* Chase. You should be getting ready to cast off for the hunt." She shook her head, seeming to gather herself. "Spit it out,"

"There's a spit of land just over there, to the East."

"That's a line of rocks leading to nothing," she said, voice rasping and dry.

"It could be some old merchant's supply stop," he pleaded. Lice's expression shifted from confusion to a degree of suspicion not far from what Álvarez had shown. "We should be sending volunteers to go ashore, if another ship has stopped here before, there might be—"

"If it's anything, it will still be there when that whale is done being tried out."

Isaiah gaped. "That's just what I'm saying, we have less than half a crew still standing, and next to no stores left, and if something were to go wrong." He could feel his tone growing desperate. "We should be taking the opportunity to *resupply*—"

"CHASE." She flicked her coat aside. The handle of Johanna Briggs' pistol gleamed in the light, as polished as when Coffin had first brandished it as a prize. "For that, you've earned yourself a spot in the hunting party." Her lip curled, cracked and dry and dusted with salt. "Get out of my sight."

He obeyed. Beyond the length of the *Merciful*, the rocky outcropping was padded by a layer of mist where the warm mass of land met the cool water, and it was impossible to see what ran beyond the ridge of land. Isaiah could feel himself losing control of his breathing, and Essex had descended from the mast.

"Able bodied crew to the FORE, I said!" Lice called, and there was no escaping it. He had positioned himself just back and to the east of her. Not close enough to be obvious, but separate enough that the majority of the crew had gathered away from him in their rush to prepare the boats. Isaiah was panicking, heart thudding in his throat, and *there had to be something to do.* Anything to divert them.

He palmed a sizable harpoon head from the open trunk of hunter's tools, tucking it in his waistband, next to his sheathed work knife.

"Phelan, Yesayan, Álvarez, Chase," Lice called, staring him dead in the eye. "Get after the damned thing. Don't think of coming back without a body."

Throat tight, he made his way over to where Phelan and Yesayan had already begun jerkily hauling down the skiff, as if every motion the two took was painful.

He hopped in after the others, with the barbed and honed iron of the harpoon tip cold against his opposite arm. He could feel it cutting into the skin; the sting of it sliced through the panic and sharpened him.

The last thing he spotted before they began to row was Essex, perched on the far end of the ship, shoulders curled in and head bent, animal-like, in the direction of the whale.

At their backs, the *Merciful* grew small. His arms were screaming, he could *hear* the wheeze of the other three men, with Álvarez and Yesayan in front, and Phelan beside him. In any other hunt, it would have been a miracle that the current was with them. Instead, the curved chops of waves hurried them along faster than they should have gone with three sick and four starving rowers. Despite the motion, the whale just hung in the water. Moving slowly to and fro, spouting occasionally. The animal was an island of flesh, ripe for the taking.

Essex is holding it there. Making it simple for them. Just like for Bellamy.

"Listen. We have to go to shore," Isaiah said. Pretending to hold a cramp in his side, he slipped the harpoon from his belt. "There was a sign there, and it looked like a banner of some kind—"

"Just shut *up,* Chase," Phelan replied.

"Will you listen to me!"

Quickly, he hooked an arm around Álvarez's neck, he pressed the blade to his windpipe. He unhooked his work blade at once, pressing the tip of it straight to the fleshy part of Yesayan's back right next to his spine. "We are *going to that outpost.* If there is a flag, *someone has been there and escaped."*

None of them moved.

Phelan stared. *"Bleeding gods* Chase, the whale—"

"I *said,* we are going to that outpost," he repeated, pressing slightly deeper. He felt a thin trickle of something warm and wet dripping from Álvarez's neck, and he could hear the high whistle of the other man's labored breathing. "We *will die* if we go after that whale."

Yesayan stared back at him, bloodshot eyes wide with panic. Phelan was clutching his chest, still trying to catch his breath from rowing with the current. They had the look of starving dogs, one missed scrap away from withering away.

Isaiah's hands trembled.

" . . . Do it." Álvarez said.

He held the blades to the backs of their necks as the hunting boat approached the outcropping, and Isaiah soon realized that the jagged rocks weren't rocks at all. The shattered hull of an ancient caravel jutted its nose up out of the water. A piece of mast leaned against it, coated with some slick black substance that could have been decaying seaweed or tar or who knew what else. A half-collapsed rack of decking supported it, dashed against the massive boulders themselves, which were encrusted with barnacles and mussel shells that popped shut as they got closer. He shivered.

"Gods above protect us and guide our hands . . . " Phelan murmured, shaky.

"Careful," said Yesayan. "Look at those rocks. It's a good thing we stopped where we did."

"All-gods damn you, Chase." Álvarez said.

"Just . . . keep moving," Isaiah replied. "This has to lead somewhere."

There were odd shapes moving underneath the water as they maneuvered themselves beyond the partially-submerged wreckage. Things that sent ripples up against the wall of the skiff.

"Don't look down," he said.

"What? Why?" Phelan said.

Yesayan, at the prow, startled back, sending them all rocking. "BLEEDING mother above—"

Bellamy's rotting body was floating just below the surface.

"Who is that?!" Álvarez shouted.

"It's—" Isaiah started.

"*Sharpe*," Phelan breathed. He stared unmoving, down at the body, shocked into stillness. Isaiah scrunched his eyes shut, opened them again. There was no body in the water, just slight ripples leading down to pitch dark below.

"Phelan, *stop staring*." Yesayan called back to the aft.

He was bent almost double, leaning into the surface.

"Stop it!" Isaiah grabbed his vest and gave it a strong tug. He blinked heavily, eyes distant.

"Hands . . . hands off me, Chase."

Isaiah let go and took up the oar to paddle not daring to look down, in case the face in the water changed shape again.

The land warped as they drew nearer. Past the wreckage, the boulders didn't just disappear into a bluff, but instead seemed to meld into a series of rocky hills, dotted with nooks and crannies. The flag he'd spotted from the *Merciful*, what could have marked a merchant outpost, was in fact a battered, aged cotton shirt. It was bleached bone-white and threadbare, caught between two boulders, standing stark and pale against the dark grey-green of the rocks.

Just beyond, the rocks seemed to be sucked inward, almost as if pulled back into the heart of the earth itself. They formed a cave that would normally be hidden, unless one approached it directly. It shouldn't have been possible, and the steady whine of panic that had been silenced by his brief, desperate redirection of the hunting boat kicked back up, a notch higher than before.

The entrance was slick with moss and seaweed, and it made landing the boat tricky. The four of them scrambled out and tried not to slip, as Phelan tied up the boat as quickly as he could manage. There were dregs of mostly shredded rope stuck in between the rocks and old, mildewed plant life.

"Let's make this quick," Álvarez said.

"Aye . . . "

"Aye."

Walking on dry land took some adjusting to, especially while picking over rocks and shipwreck debris. Phelan and Álvarez both walked bow-legged up ahead of Isaiah as Yesayan stumbled his way behind. The entry to the cave itself was dry, and the lack of wind blowing made it feel nearly warm, by comparison. The quiet was all encompassing.

A rough crunch abruptly broke the silence.

"Shit." Álvarez cursed.

"All well?" Phelan called.

" . . . Just stepped on something." There was a hollow skittering sound across the stone of the cave floor. Isaiah bent down a hand in the womb-like dim until he touched ground.

Shells. The floor of the cave was scattered thoroughly with dozens upon dozens of pearlescent white shells. His hand flew to the inner pocket of his vest. The shells that Essex had produced for him were still sitting soundly within. Heart hammering, he slowly retracted his hand from its hiding place. Hundreds upon thousands of peachy white cockle shells of all different sizes lined the floor, scattered in piles here and there, rolling under their feet. Isaiah's heart thudded.

"We . . . we need to leave here." He started. "We shouldn't be wandering around."

"You're the one who bloody well wanted to come," Yesayan called back. He kicked a foot at one of the piles, sending the round shells scattering and rolling like a child's jacks. The crackling tinkle of them echoes around the cave walls. "It's nothing. You brought us here for *nothing.*"

As their eyes adjusted to the dim light coming from the entrance behind them, the walls of the cave were thrown into clearer relief.

"What's all this?" Álvarez said.

Simple outlines of dozens upon dozens of whales were scratched into the walls, lined up in rows and squished on top of one another. Distinct sizes, shapes, scar-lines on each marked each one. Isaiah knew immediately.

"A count," Isaiah said, voice strangled. He reached out a hand, hovering over the etching, but not daring to make contact.

The abrupt and distant crack of a gunshot echoed in from off the water, and Isaiah felt his stomach sink like a dropped anchor. "We need to leave. *Now.*"

The hunting boat had barely bumped the edge of the *Merciful* before Isaiah was grabbing hold of the ladder that dangled over the side, and scrambling up.

The deck was still. A gun hung limp in Monteiro's hand, and there was a wide streak of blood painting the deck. Her eyes were wild.

Essex was gone.

"What in the gods' names—" Yesayan said, and the sea below them began to churn.

With a vast sucking noise, a shelf of water pulled down at one side of the ship and the *Merciful* rolled at a brutal pitch. Isaiah stumbled and the rest of the crew went with him, as the sudden slope of the deck sent tack and ropes flying to the starboard side.

"Down, DOWN, hit the deck—" Álvarez shouted, and as soon as he did the waves began to lash back, rocking to and fro and gaining momentum, sending sharp bits of spray climbing further and further overboard and soaking them. Isaiah dove down, taking Álvarez with him as the wind began to whip the ship hard.

"What did you do?"

Monteiro's eyes were wide and feral.

"*He's not human!*"

"I said, what did you *do*?!" Isaiah shouted, over the gale-force wind.

A grappling crunching noise echoed to the starboard, sending the boat shuddering and listing heavy over to one side. Calder crawled up over the edge of the railing hand over hand, half-bone fingers dug deep into the wood, his forehead weeping old, blackened bile from a gunshot wound, and the bodies of the dead crawled up behind him.

Essex was suddenly standing before them, an utterly humorless grin stretching from ear to ear, the back of a crewmember's bloodied neck held tight in his palm. He dropped the body to the deck and it hit the planks with a wet, thick, thud.

Screaming, Monteiro scuttled back, boots scrambling for purchase on the rolling, bloodstained deck, gun no longer in hand. Essex crossed the gap between them in a few easy, long strides, reaching for her head. Prying open her mouth with one hand, he pulled a long, charcoal-black rope of seaweed up from her insides with the other, and what remained of Calder descended on her.

From behind Essex, Briggs' intricately engraved pistol clicked impotently in Lice's hands as she struggled to reload it with bullets. With a ragged yell, Álvarez lunged to plunge a boat axe into Essex's arm.

"STOP—" Isaiah screamed.

"*You never, ever learn, do you?*" Essex shrugged out the axe blade and it hit the deck with a slick, metal clatter, and Álvarez collapsed, tremors rocking through him as he spewed a seemingly unending stream of jagged-edged bits of shell from his mouth. His voice rang impossibly loud, and the wave that had sent the *Merciful* rolling crashed over the deck.

Whipping around, he grabbed hold of Lice by the throat, sea anemone spines piercing through the skin where he touched her neck. She gargled and choked in place, spewing blood and bile as the spines emerged out the other side.

"*ESSEX!*"

Another wave pounded them, and he dropped Lice, who slumped lifeless to the deck.

"Please—spare them—*please*," Isaiah shouted, the spray of salt in the air emitting from the man's very skin stinging his eyes and drenching him.

"*I can't and I won't.*" When he spoke, it was the same many-voiced utterance that had echoed through Isaiah's head before, when he'd desperately been seeking any other conclusion other than this one. When he had hoped to look for any end other than tragedy and terror. The sound of some god, maybe all of them, emitted from Essex's mouth, screaming and crying and whispering through him. "*I have had enough of these humans and their lies. Their cruelty.*"

"Why can't you just *leave* them!" Isaiah said, drawing closer to him. "I want to be away from here! I want *you* to be away from here!" He could feel tears mingling with the salt water in his mouth.

Essex's eyes were wide, staring pools of black, netted by olive-green veins. The wound in his arm bled unimpeded. "*They will chew the world out. They will leave only bones behind.*" The voices shrieked, howled in pain, rattled the deck, with the whirlwind gale around them sending the once-repaired mast snapping and splintering into nothing. The crew screamed.

The gun slid out of Lice's lifeless hands and skittered across the deck.

Isaiah picked it up. He pulled the trigger.

Suddenly, Essex's chest wept purple-red blood. His face fell, shocked and sad and mournful all at once and Isaiah felt as if it was his own chest that had caved in.

"You've killed me, my love."

He reached out to Isaiah. Isaiah flinched, and the gun clattered to the deck, useless.

Essex simply reached out to brush his jaw. He spoke in his own voice. "You deserve so much better than this ship. A better life for your soft heart," he said, his bloodstained hand gentle on Isaiah's cheek. "I'm sorry."

He stepped away from Isaiah, and the *Merciful*'s deck ripped in two.

The infernal slam of the waves against the ship grew louder and louder, and vicious spouts of water pierced through the stomach of the ship and overwhelmed the sounds of the crew dying. Skin sliced and burst into mangled pieces. Mouths opened and choking, pure seawater flowed up. Crabs and sea eels made their way up from gullets where they had been growing for days upon weeks upon who knew how long, peeling apart flesh and organs as they crawled toward the light.

The seaweed that had been nursing all around them, that they'd tried to ignore for so long, grew brilliant emerald green, and finger-like tendrils clawed up from inside the deck, peeling up the rectangular, regimented boards. Popping up iron nails and sending dense coils of rope and sail flying wide, pieces of the ship snapped toward the water as if they belonged there, as if the *Merciful* had always wanted to be a wreck. As if it had always craved the tearing apart.

Isaiah was running across the splintering deck, then diving, falling past bodies and wave caps stained with foaming blood, his limbs burning with the strain of it, and suddenly there was water all around him, filling up his mouth and nostrils and this was how he would die, *this* is how he would die, drowning in the all-devouring water.

He closed his eyes tight as he fell below the crushing waves.

CHAPTER NULL

WHEN HE FINALLY came up for air, gasping, lungs aching, he was farther away from what was left of the ship than should have been possible. The sea was like ice on his skin. It would have been so easy to just stop kicking.

A low brown and green hill was barely visible between the waves.

Out on the water, the place where the *Merciful* had sunk still churned. Pieces of wooden decking, distant strands of rope and shredded canvas floated out beyond the waves like muddy curls of hair and flaps of pale skin, twisting and sinking downwards to the sea floor. If he strained, he could still see the roiling froth where the ship had been dragged down. He wondered if you could still dream, once you were dead.

His legs were screaming from exertion, and his shoulders ached fiercely, but Isaiah managed to keep his head from slipping below the surface of the water.

Bits of seaweed mixed with grime stuck to Isaiah's face and hair, and he finally felt the barest drag of sand below his feet. As he clambered up onto land, his arms wobbled, like the limbs of a newborn calf fresh from the womb. He spat out blood, unsure if it was his own or someone else's, and the sickly iron taste coated his tongue.

Hauling himself past the reach of the waves with the last of his strength, he pressed the whole of his body against the dry, pebble-studded sand beneath him. The salt water drained from his skin, his hair. He let the rocks below press hard and bruising into his body, let the solid ground stay put beneath him as he inhaled the smell of sand and dirt mixed with rock. The gale that Essex had summoned had disappeared as quickly as it came, and the sound of the relentless waves echoed into the still air.

Isaiah finally sat upright. He caught a glimpse of his own hands, and blood was dried on them, crusted in rusty half-moons under the fingernails.

He watched the horizon until the waves returned to their natural, rhythmic beat. Essex did not surface, and neither did any of the bodies.

The ship, and the crew onboard, had been swallowed up.

His fingers felt the place where Essex had last touched him, hand ghosting over the skin as if over a bruise. The clouds turned back, and a light breeze blew over the shore where he sat, brushing through his hair. Everything ached. But he breathed in and out, lungs still straining behind his ribs, and he tried to steady the uneven hammering in his chest.

The whaleship *Merciful* was taken back down by the mouth of the hungry sea, as if it had never been there at all.

ACKNOWLEDGEMENTS

I owe approximately five years worth of thanks to my agent, Tamara Kawar. Her constant enthusiasm, steadying hand, and her patience in guiding me through my multifarious early ventures has been invaluable.

To Alex Woodroe, Matt Blairstone, and everyone else who touches Tenebrous Press, for understanding not only what this book *should* be, but what it *could* be. I can imagine no better hands to help shepherd it out into the world. It's an honor for *From the Belly* to be Tenebrous's first novel, although I'm not quite sure how or why it's earned the privilege. Regardless, your dedication and pure love for the genre shows through in everything you do. Hail the Tenebrous Cult.

Thank you to all the friends who read early, horribly underwritten, semi-incoherent drafts of this novel, and were excited about it anyway. You didn't have to be so kind, but you were, and that's what matters so much to me.

More specifically, to Charlie, Ashia, Shazleen, Jas, Ronnie, Sam, Kouji, Dri, and Ann for helping to keep my sanity during the many years it takes to survive a global pandemic and publish a book. Your feedback, excitement, and constant cheerleading means the most. To Son, for being a goofy, inspiringly relentless sibling in ventures both criminal and creative. Here's to fighting for many, many, more. To Morgan, for being a constant source of calm and love, and for being the very first person to hold a printed copy of this book, even if you had to make it yourself. I'll never forget it.

Thank you to the New Bedford Whaling Museum, the Peabody Essex Museum, and the coffee houses of Marblehead and Salem for providing the inspiration and raw fuel needed to create the world of the Whaleship Merciful. Many thanks to Herman Melville and Eric Jay Dolin. You really should pick up both *Leviathan* and *Moby Dick*, if you'd like to learn more about whales and whalers, both fictional and historical. Hand to god, they're much more exciting than you'd think they are.

Horror is a community as much as it is a modality, and so a hearty thank you is owed to all the writers, reviewers, and genre enthusiasts who inspired, blurbed, or spread the word about this book on its long journey. No writer is an island, no matter how much we might want to be, and your intellect and gusto makes me what I am.

To my family, for all being relentlessly themselves, letting me go as fast as I could in the direction of my, admittedly, kinda batshit spooky dreams. I couldn't do anything in this life without your support, sense of humor, and love.

And last, but certainly not least, to you, dear reader. Thanks for sitting with me while I told you a story. I hope that it took you someplace new, even for just a little while.

CONTENT WARNINGS

Being a work of mature Horror, a degree of violence, gore, sex and/or death is to be expected.

In addition, *From the Belly* contains:

Alcoholism/alcohol abuse;

Suicide;

Explorations of PTSD;

Animal death.

Please be advised.

More information at
www.tenebrouspress.com

ABOUT THE CONTRIBUTORS

Hailing from a haunted seaside town in northern Massachusetts, **Emmett Nahil** is the author of *Let Me Out* (Oni Press, October 2023), and a writer of horror and speculative fiction centering marginalized perspectives. Favoring the historic, the strange, and the gory, in his other life Emmett makes video games as the Narrative Director and co-founder of Perfect Garbage Studios.

Chris Shehan is an American comic book artist living in Austin, Texas, best known for his work in the American comic book market with multiple publishers, working on interior art, cover art and concept art.

Megan Llewellyn is a medical illustrator and comics creator in Chapel Hill, North Carolina.

TENEBROUS PRESS

aims to drag the malleable Horror genre into newer, Weirder territory with stories that are incisive, provocative, intelligent and terrifying; delivered by voices diverse and unsung.

NEW WEIRD HORROR

FIND OUT MORE:

www.tenebrouspress.com
Social Media @TenebrousPress

Printed in the USA
CPSIA information can be obtained
at www.ICGtesting.com
LVHW091240030524
779175LV00008B/99